Sugar and Skulls

Sugar and Skulls

LM Terry

Sugar and Skulls

Dedication

This book is dedicated to anyone who has had to show their mean side. Don't ever feel guilty for protecting what is yours.

"Sometimes, being too nice is dangerous. You have to show your mean side once in a while to avoid getting hurt." ~ *unknown*

Table of Contents

Chapter One

Jesse ~ 10 years old

The other girls are waiting on the curb for their turn on Rick's bike. I'm sitting on the ground, doodling with sidewalk chalk. Every day, their mama shoos us outside to play. Sometimes, we roller skate but today they are taking turns on their brother's bike. Rick is the only one with a bike. It's a big family, so there's a lot of sharing that takes place here. I'd never ask for a ride, and he's never offered to give me one. Not that I would want to ride with him. I'm content sitting here in the sun, creating my pictures.

My stomach growls and I think about going in to see if I can sneak a piece of bread or something. They feed me here, but it isn't like grandma's food. I think Janet puts a full saltshaker of salt in everything she makes. Luckily, their dog, Mop, likes salty food because I wait until everyone leaves the table and then I give him mine. I try to eat it, but I just can't.

I don't know how long I'll be here. The lady in the suit told me I had to stay until they found my Aunt Renee, but I don't know how long that will take. I've never met her. My mama died when I was little. Grandma said mama took too much medicine and it killed her. I don't know how that happens. I looked at grandma and grandpa's medicine bottles and it says right on them how much to take, clear as day.

Grandpa said my mama was a bad egg. I don't know what that means but he told me I was a good egg. I don't know how he could tell one way or another. You can't tell if an egg is bad unless you crack it clean open.

Anyhow, I don't really mind it here. There is always something to do. The Ditsworth's have eight kids. Four boys and four girls. The girls are around my age, and they are nice. I like them. They let me follow them around all day and did I mention they have roller skates?

I do miss grandma and grandpa though. Like a lot. So much that I cry myself to sleep almost every night. I'd give anything to go back to living with them. I'd even give up the roller skates to go back home.

I take my whole hand and smear over my drawing. Perfect, now it looks like a real sunset. A shadow darkens the sidewalk in front of me. I squint, shielding my eyes from the sun to find Rick hovering over me.

"Want a ride on my bike?" he asks, his forearms draped across the handlebars.

"Um, I don't know," I say quietly, dropping my eyes back to my sunset.

"It's real fun," Cindy tells me. "Go on."

"Okay." I stand up and dust my chalky hands on the front of my t-shirt.

Rick motions for me to sit on the banana seat in front of him, so I do. He tells me to put my feet up on the middle of the handlebars with my hands beside them. I don't know about this. It doesn't feel very safe, but Rick is bigger than me. He's a teenager so he knows what he's doing. The other girls ride with him all the time and they've never crashed.

We take off and ride a few blocks till we get to the school parking lot. I'm worried I'm going to fall off, but Rick is nice and puts his hand on my hip so that I don't slide off the seat. We ride for a few minutes in circles when I notice that Rick's hand is not on my hip anymore. He must not know where he is touching me. With my legs like this my shorts are riding up. He doesn't know. My cheeks heat and I wonder if I should tell him. He would probably be embarrassed if he knew cause I sure am.

Rick continues to circle us around the parking lot and I'm starting to feel more uncomfortable. I hope he takes me home soon. I don't like this. The longer he digs around the more it hurts. He must know what he's doing.

In school they taught us that people shouldn't touch your private spots. But Rick is. He's touching my private spot. Panic bubbles inside me. My eyes dart around the empty lot, looking for help.

Does he do this to his sisters too? Or just me?

"Isn't this fun?" he whispers in my ear. I shake my head no and he laughs. It hurts and I want to go home. Tears are threating to spill down my cheeks. I try to sniff them back. I don't want Rick to think I'm a cry baby. I'm not a cry baby.

Suddenly, he stops, and both our feet drop to the ground. I look up at what made Rick stop abruptly. A man is standing in front of us. A scary man with pictures all over his skin. "What's going on here?" he asks as he lights up a cigarette, blocking our way.

"Just giving my sister a ride on my bike," Rick answers.

I drop my eyes to the hand Rick just had in my shorts. Blood is caked along the nail of his finger. My eyes slowly rise up to the man standing in front of us. His eyes are where mine had been... on Rick's hand. His gaze rises to meet mine. "Is that so?" he asks. Smoke rolls out of his nose like an angry bull.

"I'm... I'm not his sister," I sniff, pushing Rick's arm off the handlebar so I can get out from between his arms. I stumble a few feet away from the bike and cross my arms over my chest. The man crouches down in front of me.

3

"What's your name, sweetheart?" he asks.

"You're not supposed to talk to strangers," Rick grumbles beside me. The man gives him a look that shuts him up real fast.

He looks at me again. His eyes are so pretty. They don't match the rest of him. His eyes are blue green. When he turns his head, they change color. Just like my mood ring. It was mamas. It's the only thing I have of hers, well had. I'm not sure what happened to it after grandma and grandpa died. It's usually blue when I wear it but one time I got angry at the paper boy for throwing grandpa's paper in the mud and it turned black. That's what this guy's eyes look like, like he's caught between angry black and calm blue.

"My name is Jesse," I tell him. I don't know why I tell him. Usually, I don't talk to adults much. But this guy made Rick stop his bike so that's something.

"Jesse, just the girl I was looking for. Your daddy sent me to give you a message. He wants you to know that he's real sorry for what happened to your grandparents, and he'll be coming for you soon."

"I don't have a dad." I chew on my bottom lip, sad that this guy has the wrong Jesse. If I had a dad then I could live with him, and I wouldn't have to eat Janet's salty food every day.

"You do and he'll be coming for you as soon as he can." He takes my chin in his hand. His hand is black with a skull inked over the entire thing. His skin peeks out where the eyes, nose and mouth are. "Now, one more thing. Don't let this little prick touch you ever again. I see you're a nice girl, Jesse, but sometimes, you have to be mean. Especially, if you are protecting what's yours. Got it?" He tips his head, and his eyes catch the sun making my heart all gooey.

I glance at Rick nervously, nodding my head slightly.

"Go on, head back to the house. Prick will be along shortly." I want to giggle at how he keeps saying Rick's name wrong, but I don't.

Instead of running home like the scary man told me to, I hide behind a tree on the corner of the lot and watch them. The scary man stands in front of Rick, and it looks like he's really scolding him.

He takes Rick's hand and holds it up in front of his face and bends his fingers. It looks like it hurts. And. Then. They. Snap. Rick screams and I cover my mouth so that I don't do the same. The man looks up and his eyes meet mine. I take off running and don't stop until I get back to the house.

I take two steps at a time until I get to the bedroom I share with the other girls. Watching out the window, I see Rick walking his bike home with one hand. His other is cradled against his chest. Snot and tears are running down his face. I've never seen him look like this. He's always Mr. Cool.

I think Mr. Scary knocked him down a few pegs.

Janet rushes towards him. I push the window up a crack so I can hear them. "Rickie, what happened? Oh my god!"

"I fell off my bike," he grumbles.

He didn't tell on the scary man with the pictures.

Grandpa had pictures too. He told me he got them when he was in the Navy on a big boat. He said they were his secrets and that he had them tattooed onto his skin so he could take them to the grave. I don't know what that means but I guess he got his wish.

Janet gathers all the kids into her van and off they go. I'm sure she just forgot me in the rush to get Rick to the doctor. It's okay. I like being alone. It gives me a chance to sneak into the pantry for bread.

After I have my fill, I head to the tiny bathroom we all share and pull down my pants. There's some blood in my underwear. I think he scratched me. I still don't know if he knew what he was doing or if it was an accident, but it hurt, so I don't think I'll be riding on Rick's bike anymore.

Rick has to wear a cast for a long time after that day. He doesn't talk to me, and he doesn't ride his bike. Which is good because if he asks me again, I'll have to be mean like that guy told to and tell him no. I don't like being mean.

Unfortunately, once his cast is off he goes back to giving rides again and I have to be mean and tell him no thank you. I always add the thank you so that it doesn't sound so mean.

One night, at dinner, Rick decides to sit next to me at the table. I'm patiently waiting for him to finish so I can give Mop the rest of my too salty pasta, but he's taking forever. The other kids have all left the table and it's just the two of us. Janet has her back to us as she busily washes dishes and cleans up the kitchen.

"How come you never want a ride on my bike anymore?" he asks.

Maybe he didn't know he was touching me there. Maybe that man broke his fingers for no reason. I start to feel bad. I shrug my shoulders and continue to push pasta around with my fork.

Rick puts his hand on my leg, and I freeze. Slowly, he moves it up, up, up. My eyes dart to Janet, silently pleading to her. *Please turn around, please turn around.*

She doesn't.

The good news is I don't have to eat salty food anymore.

The bad news is I won't get to use the roller skates ever again.

Chapter Two

Dirk

"What the fuck do you mean you don't know where she's at?" I can hear Bill grind his teeth over the receiver.

"They moved her. She stuck a fork in the kid's leg," I reply, lazily leaning against my Harley.

"Goddammit!" he roars.

"I'll find her, dude. Chill."

"Why would my daughter stick a fucking fork in some poor teenage boy's leg? Huh? Explain that to me, Dirk?"

"Well, she's a lot like her old man, evidently."

He huffs at this, not a subject he can argue since he's currently sitting in prison for offing a rival club member in broad fucking daylight, in front of the courthouse I might add.

"Why? Don't fuck with me. My baby girl wouldn't do that for no reason."

"You don't even know her. She might be an evil little bitch like her mother."

"So help me god, Dirk," he warns.

"Okay, okay. He was messing with your girl. I caught him with his hand in her pants on his bicycle and before you freak, she wasn't letting him. I could tell by her fucking tears. I broke the little fucks fingers. Assumed he would have learned his lesson, but I guess he has bigger balls than I thought. I may have told her she might have to get a little mean to protect herself, you know?"

Dead silence.

"And why didn't you kill him?"

I sigh. Should have known broken fingers wouldn't be enough for Bill. "She was watching."

He grumbles and I hear him inform someone he has two minutes left and to fuck off. I wait for his orders.

"Have Raffe put the charm on that social worker and find out where she is."

"Got it," I toss my cigarette to the ground and fire up the bike. "What about the kid?"

"Leave him. Hopefully, he remembers he fucked with the wrong girl every time he picks up a fork."

I laugh. Yeah, bet he didn't see that one coming.

It takes pretty boy, Raffe, a bit of time but eventually, he charms the pants off the social worker (literally, I saw the woman's bare ass pressed against the window of her office). Anyhow, he gets Jesse's location. Bill is definitely not going to be happy. They stuck her in some Catholic boarding school for troubled teens. She's ten for fucks sake.

Chapter Three

Jesse ~ Twelve years old

My grandma always said bad things come in threes. Now I don't know if that's true but if it is, this should be my last bad thing. One was grandma and grandpa dying, two was Rick and his icky fingers and three, well, let me tell you about three...

After sticking that fork in Rick's leg, the lady in the suit told me I couldn't stay at the Ditsworth's no more. So, she took me to St. Mary's home for troubled girls. She said they haven't found Aunt Renee yet, but that's okay. Grandpa always said she was a bad egg, just like my mama. But let me tell you, the name of this place fits. These girls are trouble.

I stay out of the way though and keep quiet. For the last two years, I've shared a room with a girl named Sandra, she's boy crazy. She sneaks out every night and when she comes back, she has these purple marks all over her neck. She stares at them in the mirror like grandpa did his medals from the Navy. She sure is proud of them. I think they look like she was attacked by a vacuum cleaner, but I don't tell her that. That would be mean, and I don't like being mean.

It's not bad here. It's all girls and I like that. No boys mean no Ricks. Or pricks. Sandra told me what a prick was and now it makes sense why that scary man was calling him that.

I've been worried that the scary man did have the right Jesse and my dad might be looking for me. How would he find me here? I'm sure he was wrong though. Grandma and grandpa told me I didn't have a dad, but everyone has a dad right? I mean, I know how babies get into this world and it's not like my mom was the Virgin Mary or anything like that. Not a bad egg, a bad egg couldn't get pregnant by divine intervention. That's something I learned here at St. Mary's.

The learning is the best thing about being here. The girls are all older than me, but I haven't had any problems keeping up. In fact, I help the other girls with their homework and in return they sneak me candy. I keep my stash hidden under a loose floorboard cause Sister Catherine would smack my knuckles if she found them. The food here is good though, so there's that.

Everything was going well until Sister Catherine told me I was to be an alter server at church on Sunday mornings. Not something I wanted to do. Not now. Not ever. I don't like having everyone look at me and I'm not sure I even believe everything these folks are telling me. Grandma and grandpa didn't go to church and I'm fairly certain mama didn't either. But I had no choice. So, I did.

It didn't take awfully long to become Father Gabriel's favorite server. Probably, cause I'm quiet and do what I'm told. After every service, he always thanks me and tells me what a good girl I am. He's nice, but he smells funny, like that smokey stuff they use in church.

But two Sundays ago, it changed, which brings me to the start of bad thing number three. Father Gabriel gave me a ride back to St. Mary's instead of Sister Catherine. She didn't seem surprised, so I guess it's normal. But it made those little hairs, you know the ones you have on the back of your neck? Well, it made mine stand clean up. Nothing happened, he dropped me off at the front door and drove away.

Last Sunday, I decided not to wear a dress or shorts or nothing like that. I wore my long pants. I don't know why I was nervous, but I was. I wish I had someone to talk to about it, but I don't. The other girls would probably laugh at me. Since they're older, Sister Catherine doesn't make them do this alter duty stuff.

After church, he didn't take me straight home, he took me out for ice cream. I love ice cream. Strawberry is my favorite. Part of me wondered if Father Gabriel was going to want something from me since he paid for my treat. Evidently, he didn't because we just ate our cones and then he dropped me off in front of the doors just like last time.

"Jesse, Father Gabriele is here. Get your shoes on, he is waiting for you downstairs," Sister Catherine calls from the other side of the door. Sandra gives me a funny look. It's Tuesday. Why is he here on a Tuesday? I shrug my shoulders and do as I'm told.

"Jesse," Father Gabriele greets me as I head down the stairs. "Do you like pizza? I'm having a few servers over as a way of saying thank you for all of your hard work." He places his hand on my shoulder, not even waiting for my answer and quickly ushers me out of the house.

As we are walking to his car, I see a boy a few years older than me sitting in the front seat. I usually sit in the front, but I don't mind. "Jesse, this is William."

The boy nods to me and I do the same. He looks as nervous as I feel. "Do you live here?" he asks as Father Gabriel makes his way around the car.

I nod at him with big, terrified eyes. Something feels really really wrong. He smiles at me kindly, and it helps calm my nerves a little bit. His eyes are brown like chocolate bars, and they match his hair. "I live at the boy's campus on the other side of town," he tells me. He smiles again, and I notice his dimples. He's cute and he seems like a nice boy. At least I'm not alone with Father Gabriel, so there's that.

When we get to Father Gabriel's house, I smell the pizza. It smells so good it makes my mouth water. I thought there would be more people here but it's just the three of us. William and I dig in, filling our plates full.

"You two are my favorite," Father says as he sets two glasses in front of us. "How about we celebrate. Do you know how adults celebrate?"

We both shake our heads no, unable to answer with our mouths full.

He laughs. "Why with a little wine, of course." He fills our glasses, watching us out the corner of his eye. "But you won't tell the Sisters will you? They wouldn't be happy with me for treating you both like adults."

I've never had wine, but it does smell good. William gives me a funny look, but he picks his up and gulps the entire thing down. Father fills his glass again. Hesitantly, I pick up mine and take a sip. Wow, it's... I don't know, it's strong like grape juice, but I guess it isn't terrible. Father places his finger on the bottom of my cup, encouraging me to finish the rest. I don't want to look like a wimp, so I do.

He pours me another glass and then excuses himself, telling us he is going to change into something more comfortable. William finishes his second glass of wine while I watch. He looks at me. "Drink your wine, Jesse. It will help," he tells me.

"Help what?" I ask. My head feels funny, and I start to giggle.

He looks sad. "Just do it, okay?"

I nod and swallow down the rest of my wine.

"I'm sorry if he makes me touch you."

I blink at him. What does he mean? I'm full, dizzy and I want to go home. I try to stand but fall back into my chair. William holds my hand in his. "Promise me you won't hate me after this?" he whispers, right before Father Gabriel comes back into the room.

12

I didn't have time to answer him. I wish I would have had time to promise him that I would never hate him. He was the first boy I ever kissed, and he kissed me like I was the prettiest girl in the world. I could never be mean to him, but I don't think the scary man would want me to be mean to William for touching what was mine.

No. Not to William. I could never be mean to him.

The following Sunday, William and I are both serving. He looks at me nervously but when I offer him a smile, he appears relieved. He smiles back. Father Gabriel even smiles when he sees us both smiling at each other. We were all so busy smiling that he didn't even notice when I dropped my candle right at his feet until it caught his perfectly white robe on fire.

One thing I learned that day, is that Father Gabriel screams like a little girl, just like Rick. Maybe it's a prick thing.

The good news is that William and I will be friends forever.

The bad news is I had to leave behind all the candy I had stashed under the floorboards at Saint Mary's home for troubled girls.

Chapter Four

Jesse ~ Fourteen years old

I've been saving all the money I have so that I can go and get all my secrets tattooed onto my skin just like grandpa. That way I can take them to my grave. There's a tattoo shop nine blocks from Aunt Renee's. I wanted to go inside the first day I found it, but I didn't want to go empty handed.

Aunt Renee lives in Trap County. There isn't really a town here, it's just Trap County. A place where folks come to get away from the law. Don't get me wrong, there's law here but with a little green, said law looks away. It's a dusty, dirty place smack dab between Reno and Vegas.

Anyhow, I've been here two years and I like it. Everyone pretty much minds their own business. Everyone but me. I pay attention to everything. I'm going to rule this place someday. I'm tired of the suit lady moving me around. I haven't seen her since I set Gabriel on fire, but I know she'll move me again if I'm mean. I try not to be mean, but I have to protect what's mine.

Things are good here... so far. I know good things don't last but maybe this time will be different. Aunt Renee pretty much ignores me. I don't mind. I have plenty of things to do here. I spend most of my time painting pictures on anything I can get away with. Mostly nice pictures, except one time I painted a troll on the side of Tina DeAngelo's house because she was mean to Ian Cain. Ian is in a wheelchair and Tina was downright rude to him, calling him names I would rather not repeat.

I push the door open to Big Dan's Tattoo, a little bell dings as it opens, and a big guy looks up from the back of the room. He had been leaning over another man who is lying on his stomach. The big guy shuts his buzzing machine off. "What can I do for you, little lady?" he asks, not moving from his chair.

I walk up to the counter that separates the back from the front and dump my entire can of money right in the middle of it. "I want a tattoo."

He stares at me blankly for a few seconds and then tips his head back and laughs loudly. "Did Dirk send you down here to prank me?"

"I don't know any Dirk." I tap my fingers on the counter.

"Don't tell me you're being serious here?" he asks. The man lying down turns so that he can see me, he winks and flashes me a nice smile but not in a skeevy way, no, more of a friendly way.

"I am serious."

He laughs again. "Honey, you have to be eighteen, or at least sixteen with a parent's consent to get a tattoo here."

I'm sad for a few seconds but then I shrug my shoulders, ready to move on. I guess I'll just have to wait until I'm eighteen because I don't have any parents. I shove all my money back in the can and then climb up on the stool at the counter to look at this big book he has filled with drawings.

"Sweetheart, this isn't a place for a little girl to be hanging around. Why don't you go on home?"

"Did you draw all these?" I ask him.

He sighs but fires up his little buzzy machine and goes back to work on the guy in front of him. "Not all of them but most," he answers while he works.

I continue to look through the book. There are lots of pictures like the ones my grandpa and the scary man had tattooed on them. "So, do people pick tattoos out of this book then?"

"Some people do. Some folks have their own ideas and then I draw up what they describe to me."

How wonderful to have someone let you put your drawing on their skin. I put mine on paper and sometimes, buildings, sidewalks, or trains. The paint cost me money, so I don't get to do it as often as I want. Thinking about someone wearing my drawing on their skin, sounds amazing.

"I like your drawings. Can you draw one on me, like with an ink pen?"

His buzzy machine shuts off and I look up. He's staring at me. "Girl…"

The other guy interrupts him. "Hey, man, this is about all I can take for today anyway. Just give the girl what she wants. No harm in drawing on her, is there?" The guy sits up before walking over to a mirror on the wall to check out the artwork on his back.

"Uh, yeah, there is. I don't need any angry parents down here screaming at me for drawing on their kid," the big guy says gruffly.

"I don't have any parent's," I tell him quickly. "Just an aunt and she won't care. She's never home anyway. She works at Bell's House of Tail, so she sleeps all day and works all night."

"Come on, man. I know your big, dumb ass can be nice once in a while."

16

Big Dan runs his fingers through his beard, looking at me. I bounce on the stool and give him my best *please I'll love you forever if you do this* smile. He rolls his eyes. "Fine, what do you want me to draw and I'm not drawing anything inappropriate so choose wisely."

I jump off the seat, tugging my drawing out of my back pocket and hurry over to him before he changes his mind.

"I thought you wanted one of my drawings." He chuckles but takes the paper from my hand. I like his laugh. It's loud and when he does it, you can tell he really means it.

He stares at my drawing. The other guy glances at it over his shoulder. They both look up at the same time. "Who did this?" Big Dan asks.

"I did. It's my grandma and grandpa. I don't have any pictures of them, so I draw them all the time. I don't want to forget what they look like. My grandpa had pictures on him from when he was on the boat. He had one of a pretty girl, that's how I know you can tattoo pictures of people on me. I, not today but when I'm eighteen," I rattle off quickly. I probably shouldn't have drunk all the coffee Renee left in the pot this morning, but too late now. I pull up my sleeve and offer him my scrawny little arm.

The other guy shakes his head and pats Big Dan on the back. "Looks like you might have some competition, Big Dan. See you next week, same time," he says and then he grabs his black leather jacket and heads out the door.

"Let me clean up real quick and find some goddamned pens and then we'll get started. Are you sure your aunt won't get pissed?" He wipes down the chair the other guy was in and then pats it for me to sit.

"Nope, she won't care," I say, smacking my gum between my teeth.

It tickles when Big Dan gives me my ink pen tattoo, but I sit perfectly still because I don't want him to mess it up. I ask a zillion questions about

17

tattooing while he works. He stops every now and then to answer and show me what he's talking about. By the time he's finished I've decided that I'm going to be Big Dan's partner. He has two chairs, so it only makes sense.

When he finishes, I go over to the mirror to take a look. Wow, it looks just like my drawing, maybe even a little better than mine. I smile so big I think my face is going to break. "Like it?" he asks.

"I more than like it. I love it!" I squeal and rush to my can so I can pay him.

"No, no, this ones on the house," he says.

"Are you sure? Cause I got money. I work real hard for it. On Monday's I go to Bell's and take the trash out of all the rooms. She pays me ten dollars for doing it and then on Wednesdays, I go to old man Tom's house and take his dog for a walk. He looks real mean but he's a nice dog. To me anyway. Sometimes, he growls at people, but I think it's just because he's old. Old man Tom growls too, so maybe it's just their thing. But anyway, I get two dollars each time I take him on walk. And then on…."

Big Dan laughs. "Okay, okay, I get it, girl, you work hard for your money. How about you just pay me with a drawing."

I nod enthusiastically at him. Trading is good. Sometimes, I trade for things I want. Like one time I traded with Samuel at the hardware store. He gave me two cans of spray paint and all I had to give him was Renee's phone number. She wasn't too happy about it, but I got the paint, so there's that.

"I'll draw something real special and bring it to you tomorrow," I tell him as I'm making my way to the door. It's easy to talk to this guy, he's nice, even if he looks like he could take his fist and pound you right down into the dirt.

"Sure thing, kid." Before I step outside, he stops me. "Hey, you got a name?"

I turn and smile big. "It's Jesse but you can call me Jess if you want. All my friends call me Jess."

"Okay then, Jess, my name is Big Dan. See you tomorrow."

I nod at him and then run all the way to the store. I'm going to need some paper and pens because I got lots of ideas for Big Dan. After I get what I need, I head over to William's, pausing under the window of the trailer to listen for his foster dad. He yells a lot, but we both agree it's better than being around Father Gabriel.

The lady with the suit moved both of us here after the fire. William didn't do anything mean but I think the lady in the suit saw that Father Gabriel was a bad egg and that William and I were best friends, so she found him a home near me so we would at least have each other.

I knock on the window. It only takes a few minutes and William comes outside. "Hey, Jess." He takes the steps in one big jump. I pull my sleeve up to show him my arm. "Aw, that's real cool." He ruffles my hair like I'm a little kid, but I don't mind. Ever since we came here, he treats me like a little sister. Not how Rick treated me but like a real sister. I like it. He makes me feel safe.

We walk to the garage together. I rattle on about my day and he listens. He rolls the door open, and we circle the rat rod he's working on. He's sixteen now and hoping he can get it running so we don't have to walk to school anymore. It's not far but still, who wants to walk when you can ride. Especially, in something cool like this. I've been working on some dope designs to paint on the side once he gets it finished.

He slides under the rod, and I sit down beside him on the cool cement. I pull out my new sketch book and get busy on the designs for Big Dan while William continues to tinker under Sylvia. That's what we named her. William told me that you have to name your ride. I don't know where we came up with Sylvia but whatever, it works. "Hand me that wrench by your knee, will you?" he asks, holding out his hand.

I place it in his hand and peek under to see what he's doing. He is smart when it comes to mechanics. He told me his real dad was a mechanic and that's where he learned most of what he knows. His foster dad helps him work on the rod, but only when he's not drinking. When he drinks he's good for nothing.

"I've been thinking, Jess, I don't think it's safe for you to be walking around after dark like you do."

"I'm not stupid you know? I pay attention to what's going on around me."

He slides out from underneath the car. "I didn't say you were stupid, did I?"

"No. I'm sorry," I drop my eyes to the drawing in front of me.

He sits up and puts his hand on my knee. "You're a pretty girl, Jess, and... well, you're getting older and that's making you even prettier. I just don't want to see you get hurt. Okay?"

"Monsters don't only come out in the dark, William." I knock his hand off my knee and start to gather my artwork.

"Jesse. Don't be mad," he says, following me out of the garage.

"I'm not mad." And I'm not. I know he's worried I'll put myself in a bad situation, but the thing is bad situations find me, no matter how hard I try to avoid them.

He grabs my arm and spins me around to face him. He tucks a strand of my wild, dark hair behind my ear. "I just don't want you to have to set fire to someone else. They'll take you away from me and who knows where you'll end up."

I drop my forehead to his chest and whisper, "I know." He hugs me for a few minutes before letting me go. "I'll try not to walk around at night."

"You're lying," he smirks.

"You know I can't graffiti in the daylight, right?" I laugh and run away from him.

He yells behind me. "You're something else, Jesse Miller."

"One of a kind," I yell back.

Chapter Five

Jesse

When I get home, I hurry through my chores. Once I get the dishes done, laundry started, and floors vacuumed, I start supper. Aunt Renee doesn't like to clean or cook. It took me a whole month to get this place cleaned up when I got here. The suit lady had told Renee it better be done before she returned, or I wouldn't get to stay. Renee didn't care one way or the other, but I wasn't about to let that happen, so I cleaned the place up real good.

"Whatcha making, girly?" Aunt Renee asks as she plops down at the kitchen table to put her makeup on.

"Grilled cheese, want one?"

"Sure, hun."

I butter a few more slices of bread, happy that Renee is in a good mood today. It only takes me a few minutes to finish and then I sit down beside her with our plates. I watch as she puts the last layer of mascara on her eyelashes. She's so pretty. Sometimes, I wish I were pretty like her. William says I am, but I don't think so.

She smiles at me. "Someday, I'll teach you how to do this." She puts her lipstick on and then smacks her lips together for a finishing touch. "I'll have to beat the boys off you."

"I don't like boys."

"You like that boy you hang out with all the time. What's his name?"

"William."

"You like William, don't you? He's a cutie." She pushes her mirror off to the side and studies my face.

"Yeah, I like him."

"Well, maybe you should wear a little makeup for him."

"I don't think William likes makeup or girls. He likes cars," I tell her, scrunching up my face.

She bops the end of my nose with her finger. "Okay, well if you change your mind, you come find me and I'll teach you all my beauty secrets."

I smile and nod. Renee is super happy today. I like this Renee. A knock on the door interrupts our meal. "Answer that will you, sweetie? Tell Jimmy I'll be out in a minute." She hops up and rushes to the bathroom.

I don't know who Jimmy is but whatever. When I open the door, Jimmy is leaning against the railing. He doesn't move. He just looks me up and down in disgust. He looks past me and hollers inside, "Hey, you didn't tell me you had a fucking kid."

Placing my hands on my hips and standing as tall as I can, I inform him that I'm not Renee's kid. He smirks and pushes past me, making himself at home on the sofa. He stretches his arms out along the back of the couch and crosses an ankle over a knee like he owns the place.

23

We stare at each other for a few minutes, and I know somewhere deep down in my gut that bad things don't only happen in threes. I sigh, grab my sandwich off the table and head to my room. I hear Renee and Jimmy leave a few minutes later. I thought she was going to work but she must be going on a date. She does that sometimes. This feels different. She was too happy and he was too comfortable sitting on the sofa.

I pull my new sketch book out and get to work on my drawing for Big Dan. I draw for hours before Renee comes back, assumingly with Jimmy. She is giggling and he is grunting. Yuck with a side of puke. I dig around under my pillow and pull out my headphones, popping them into my ears.

The next day, I wake up to Renee cooking breakfast.

What. In. The. Trap County. Is going on?

"Hey, sweetie, want some breakfast?" She places a giant stack of pancakes in the center of the table."

"Yeah, sure. Thanks," I say, giving her the side eye as I pour myself a glass of milk.

We sit down at the table together. The toilet flushes and Jimmy comes strolling out of the bathroom. He pats me on top of my head as he walks past. I watch as he kisses Renee on the cheek and then sits down next to her. She is smiling like an idiot and pilling up a plate full of food that she slides in front of him. "Thank you, baby," he purrs in her in ear, making her blush. They continue to talk to each other throughout breakfast like I'm not even there until I stand up to leave.

"You didn't ask for permission to leave the table," Jimmy interrupts their conversation to scold me.

I just stand there with my plate in hand, staring at him like he has two heads. I look at Renee, but she avoids my gaze instead looking down at her plate. "I've never needed permission before," I state, unblinking.

"That was before I became your new daddy," he tells me.

The good news is Renee now cooks our meals every day.

The bad news is I'm positive bad things don't only come in threes.

Dirk

"Yeah, man, everything's quiet for now. Word on the street is the Desert Devil's VP hitched up with some bitch in Trap County and he's pushing their shit there. It's junk." I'm giving Bill his monthly run down. This shit is getting old, but the fucker is hopefully getting paroled soon. His hearing is in a month. We've had Raffe fucking a few of the board members, so we're fairly confident it will happen this time around.

"Yeah, that shit needs shut down. Trap is in our jurisdiction. The Desert Devils might need reminded of that. Isn't your cousin's shop set up in Trap?" Bill asks.

"Yep, Raffe's been going to him once a week. Dan has been doing a sick piece on his back. Maybe I'll tag along next time and see if I can find anything out." The chick sleeping next to me wakes up and grabs my dick. I shove her hand away, pushing her off my bed onto her ass. I motion with the snap of my fingers to get the fuck out of my room. I'm in the middle of business, she knows better.

"Eh, just have Raffe ask him about it. You need to be working on finding Jess."

I roll my eyes and light up a cigarette as the bitch slams my bedroom door. That was the final strike, that will be the last time she gets my dick. "The fucking worker closed up shop on her coochie. No one's getting in, not even Raffe. She told him Jess is set up good and she isn't having a bunch of bikers ruining it for her."

"That fucking bitch. Do you think she knows I'm Jesse's dad and that's why she won't spill?"

"I don't know, man. She says the girl has had enough shit for a lifetime and doesn't need anything else bad happening to her. Not sure what that means, but I don't know what else you want me to do, Bill."

"I'll be out soon enough and then I'll find her." He hesitates and sighs loudly over the phone. "Maybe the worker is right, and I should just leave her the fuck alone."

"Every girl needs a father," I tell him.

"Yeah, maybe. I'll see where she's at. If it's better than with me, I'll leave it be."

"You want my honest opinion?"

"You're my right-hand man, Dirk, of course I want your opinion."

"You find her, and you never let her go."

He grunts and hangs up the phone. Wish I could help a brother out but I'm not sure what we can do until he gets out and puts the squeeze on the worker himself.

Chapter Six

Jesse

I tap my fingers on the counter while Big Dan looks through my drawings. "These are good, Jess, but I only asked for one."

"I know but once I started I couldn't stop. It keeps me busy. You can have them all."

He pops open his cash register and hands me a crisp hundred-dollar bill. "Don't cheapen yourself, doll. You're a good artist. I'll buy these from you."

"Are you going to tattoo them on someone?" I bounce on the stool excited that one, he likes my drawings and two, the thought of them being put on someone for the rest of their life is super cool.

"I'll add them to my book. If someone picks one of yours, I'll make sure to take a picture and show you."

I nod my head like crazy. "I want to learn how to tattoo."

"You've got to be eighteen to apprentice but if you want to come around and watch, I won't stop you. You just keep working on your art, okay?"

"I can do other stuff, like clean or whatever you need. I'm your girl," I tell him with great enthusiasm. He just gave me another place to hang my hat and now that Jimmy is staying at Renee's, I plan on avoiding home like the plague.

"Let's just play it by ear. Okay?"

"Deal." I place my hand out to shake on it. He chuckles and engulfs my tiny hand in his big bear paw one.

Becoming friends with Big Dan is one of the best things to ever happen to me. This is where I feel the most at home. Here and with William.

I spend the next few weeks watching Big Dan work his magic with the tattoo gun. He is an amazing artist. He may be built like a tank, but he's as smooth as butter when it comes to his art.

I'm sitting up at the counter drawing when Raffe comes in for his weekly appointment with Dan. I like Raffe, he makes my heart flutter like there's a little butterfly in it every time he comes in. He's beautiful. I don't know how to describe him. He's a cross between a Disney movie and a grunge film. He gives me a peck on the cheek as he passes by, causing me to almost fall off the stool.

Pretending to work on my drawing, I watch him take off his shirt out the corner of my eye. I slide off the stool and grab a chair so I can get a closer look at Dan's work. Really. I'm focused on the tattooing and not on the man. Honest.

"So, what's new in the world of the Rebel Skulls?" Big Dan asks Raffe.

"Bill got paroled, should be out in a couple weeks."

28

"Cool, cool, bet my cousin is happy."

"Yeah, we all are. Dirk's been busting his ass, trying to keep everything together for the last fourteen years. We're having a big bash. You should come."

"Shoot me the date and time and I'll be there." Big Dan snaps his gloves on and gets to work. I watch as he glides over Raffe's back, leaving a trail of ink as he goes. It's fascinating to watch.

"Only took me fucking two female board members and one dude to get it done."

Big Dan looks up at me, meeting my eyes. "Mouth, Raffe."

"Oh, shit yeah. I forgot the kid was here. Sorry." He turns and flashes me a brilliant smile.

"I know what fucking is. I'm not a flower. I won't wilt at the sound of a few curse words, Dan." I tell him, scowling. He tips his head back and laughs.

He goes back to work and Raffe continues running his mouth. "Hey, Dirk asked me to see if you've heard anything about Jimmy shacking up here in Trap. Guess he's selling some bad shit. We can't have that."

My ears prick up. Jimmy? Like Renee's Jimmy? Asshole Jimmy who thinks he's my new daddy and tells me when to go to bed Jimmy? I want to ask, but I keep my mouth shut. I've learned to be a listener, an observer.

"Haven't heard," Big Dan says as he pauses to wipe the excess ink off Raffe's back.

"Keep your ears open, yeah?"

"Sure thing, man."

I sit, chewing on my nail as I ponder over what Raffe said about Jimmy selling shit. What kind of shit is he selling? When he moved in, all he had was his clothes, a guitar, and a box of who knows what.

When Dan is finished with Raffe, I tell Dan I'll see him the next day and follow Raffe outside. He throws his leg over his bike and then notices I'm hovering nearby. "What's up, kid?"

"I know a Jimmy. Maybe it's the same one you were talking to Big Dan about," I tell him shyly.

"You do? Does he wear a Desert Devils jacket?" he asks.

I shake my head yes. He narrows his eyes at me as he lights up a cigarette.

"Well, Jess, my advice is to stay away from him. Okay?" He blows smoke out of his mouth and points a finger at me.

"Um, he lives with me, so yeah, that will be hard to do."

His eyebrows shoot up and I see a look of concern flash over his face. "Really?" He tilts his head and studies me a little closer.

"Yeah, my aunt fucks him," I say, trying to sound as bad ass as he looks sitting on his bike.

He laughs and all his dazzling teeth sparkle white in the bright desert sun.

"Is there something you want to know about him? I mean, I could maybe find out what you're wanting to know."

"Naw, honey. You just try to stay clear of him. He's a bad dude." He starts his bike, the rumble waking up every happy cell in my body.

I watch as he heads down the road, then I turn and slowly walk towards William's house. I know Jimmy is a bad dude. I've known he was

30

a bad egg since seeing him on Renee's porch a few weeks ago. When I get to William's, he's in the garage tinkering with Sylvia.

He looks up and smiles at me. "She's going to be ready for the first day of school," he says, tapping a wrench to his chin, leaving a streak of grease behind. I laugh and walk over, running my thumb over his chin to wipe it away. He stares down at me.

"Good, I can't wait to get back to school."

His head is still tilted down, his gaze boring into me. "Is Jimmy bothering you?" he asks, a crease forming between his eyebrows. He's searching deep in my head for any secrets I might be keeping from him.

"Naw, just being his normal asshole, I'm the boss of this trailer, self. It's cool. Don't worry about me, William." I turn away from him and run my hand down Sylvia. She's a bad looking rat rod.

We make plans to hang out over the weekend and I head home. When I get there, I'm greeted to at least twenty bikes parked around the trailer and men hanging out, drinking beer everywhere. Renee is getting in her car, headed to work. "I saved you some supper," she hollers and then shuts her door and backs out of the driveway. I look around, unsure of what to do. I push past all the bikers and head inside. No one is in the trailer, so there's that. I reach out to grab the plate of food Renee left on the table for me, but Jimmy reaches around and latches onto my wrist before I do.

"Where the fuck have you been?" he asks.

"Hanging with my friends. Looks like you've been doing the same," I taunt. I know it's stupid, but I hate him so much. He's not my dad and I don't like that he acts like he is.

He squeezes my wrist painfully, making me wince despite my best effort to not show him how much it hurts. "You need to have your ass home by eight, every night."

31

I scoff but he tightens his grip even tighter. "Fine. You're hurting me." I try to pull my hand away but it's no use, it only makes it hurt worse, so I try my best to relax in his hold. It's then I notice his pupils are fucking blown out. You could drive one of those small foreign cars right through them.

He lets go and takes my plate from me, walking over and dumping it in the trash. "Good girls, who get their ass home, get supper. Bad girls get sent to bed." He points to my room. I stomp off and am about to slam the door, but he follows and rips it out of my hands. I start to back up. He matches me step for step, backing me into the wall.

My heart is going to beat right out of my chest. I stare at a stain on his shirt as vodka breath rains down between us. "Maybe you need a good spanking," he says in a voice I've only heard him use with Renee.

I don't say anything. *Statue. I am a statue. He cannot hurt me. He cannot hurt me.*

He laughs and backs away, keeping his eyes trained on me. "Someday, little girl. Someday." And then he turns and closes my door behind him. I slump to the floor, wishing my bedroom door locked.

That night, I lie in bed, listening to the music and laughter coming from outside. I decide right then and there that I'm going to listen to everything that comes out of Jimmy's mouth and I'm going to report it all to Raffe. He doesn't like Jimmy. I don't like Jimmy. Maybe the group Raffe belongs to can get rid of him. If not, I'll have to find a way to do it myself.

A few weeks later, I go to the hardware store to buy a lock for my door. The only problem is I need a drill to install it and Aunt Renee doesn't have anything like that. I would buy one, but man are they expensive. I could get one from William but then he would ask too many questions.

The door dings as I walk into the tattoo shop. A scent lingers in the air. Something that smells awfully familiar. I can't quite place it. Big Dan is wiping down his chair. He looks up at me. "You just missed my cousin," he tells me.

"Bummer. Is he as pretty as Raffe?" I tease.

He laughs. "No, you'd probably run out of the room crying if you saw him," he dishes back.

I roll my eyes. "Whatever, Big Dan. Nothing scares this girl."

"Everyone's scared of something, doll." He finishes cleaning up while I stand by the door nervously. I hate asking for favors and I need a favor from Big Dan.

"I'm getting ready to head out. I'm going to see an old friend of mine who just got out of prison," he says, shutting the back lights off.

"Sounds fun. Hey, do you happen to have a drill, like you know, so I can install a lock like this?" I point to the chain lock on his front door.

He stares at me for a long time. "What are you locking?"

"Oh, Aunt Renee's lock is broken on her front door, so I thought I would help her out and put a new one on. To be safe, you know?" I look at the floor as I say this.

He goes to the back and then comes out with a drill in a bright orange case. Before he hands it to me, he tips my chin so he can see my eyes. "If you ever need anything, you can come to me. You know that, right?"

I nod and blink quickly. Something about the way Big Dan said that makes me get a funny feeling in my chest. Just like it does when William talks to me. He hands me the drill.

Setting it on the floor, I wrap my arms around him and give him a quick hug before picking it back up and running out the door.

Chapter Seven

Jesse ~ Sixteen years old

"Practice on the grapefruit and then maybe, a big maybe, I'll let you try your stuff out on me," Big Dan says as he tosses me a grapefruit. I catch it in one hand and smirk.

"Don't trust me? I thought we were friends," I pout.

"We are. I trust your art. I just want to see how bad you mutilate the fruit with the needle first." He laughs.

I get to work on the fruit. He hovers over me and nudges my hand when he thinks I'm going a little too deep. "Pretty good for your first time. Practice a few weeks and then we will go from there. I can't let you do any work on the customers, but I might... might... let you do a small piece on me."

Jumping up from my chair, I give him a big hug and then head out to meet William. We're supposed to take the rod out to get ice cream.

When I get to the corner near William's house, I see him standing on the porch with someone. I slow my steps to watch as he smiles, then leans down and kisses the person. A girl. He just kissed a girl. A girl who is not me. I stop dead in my tracks. My heart sinks like the titanic. The iceberg skates along my body, the sound of impending doom clear as day in my ears.

The girl shifts and I see that it is Penny Larson. Penny just kissed William. *My William.*

He looks up, smiling until he sees me. He tells her something and then jumps the steps, heading towards me.

What do I do? Well, I run. He yells my name, but I don't stop.

He doesn't follow me. Was I expecting him to? I don't really know. I don't have time to think about it though because when I get home, I see something more horrific than William kissing Penny. My bedroom door is gone. Gone as in MIA. What the hell?

Jimmy clears his throat from behind me. I turn to see him sitting on the couch with a smug look on his face.

"Two years I've let you lock yourself away in that room. No more. I don't know what you're hiding but it stops now."

My eyes scan the trailer for any sign of Renee but evidently she's at work. Well fuck.

"I'm not hiding anything, Jimmy. I just like my privacy."

"Hmm." He shrugs his shoulder and flips on the TV. "Your aunt is gone for the weekend, so why don't you get started on supper?"

Bad thing number four, which is Jimmy, continues to plague me. I go to the kitchen as my mind runs rampant, trying to figure out what I should do. The man from my childhood enters my thoughts. *Sometimes, you have to be mean, Jesse.*

I start supper, putting the sauce on to simmer. My eyes dart to my bedroom, my insides shake. This is bad. Real bad. I head to the bathroom and dig through the medicine cabinet, finding the narcotics that are prescribed to Renee for her migraines. I grab a few and crush them up with a bottle of perfume and brush the powder into my hand. When I get back out to the kitchen, I crack open a beer and dump all of it inside. I finish cooking and set the beer down beside Jimmy's plate.

"This is good. I think you're a better cook than your aunt," he compliments.

He eats everything on his plate, then drinks the entire beer before asking me to be a sweetheart and grab him another. Soon, he is staggering out and plopping himself on the couch. I swallow another bite, praying to Father Gabriel's god that the pills knock Jimmy out. They do.

I sigh. I saved myself today. *What the hell am I going to do tomorrow?*

As I'm packing a bag, someone knocks on the door. I quietly shut my light off and hide in the closet. If it's William, I don't want to see him and if it's one of Jimmy's friends, I don't want to see them either. The knocking continues and then the door opens.

"Jimmy, Jimmy, wake up, you fuck. I got the shit."

"Yeah, yeah," Jimmy mumbles, still half asleep.

"Fuck, dude. I'll leave it right here. Clean yourself up, man." Then the door opens and closes and it's quiet again.

I quickly finish packing a bag, then tiptoe out to the living room. And then I do something stupid. I open the case that's sitting by Jimmy. It's filled with little baggies full of white powder. Fuck. I bet there are hundreds of them in here. Hundreds. So, what does this bitch do? I take them with me, of course.

When I get outside, its dark, so as fast as I can, I make my way to old man Tom's house. He's gone for the month, visiting his daughter in Phoenix. He gave me the key to take care of his dog while he's gone. I unlock the door, feed, and water the dog, then crash on the couch, exhausted.

The next day, I head to Big Dan's, hoping Raffe is there for his weekly appointment. He is. They are working on a leg piece now. I patiently watch while Dan works and when Raffe leaves, I follow him out. "Hey, remember when you were looking into Jimmy a few years ago?"

He eyes me warily. "Yeah."

"I have something of his I think your group might be interested in."

He laughs and shakes his head. "Jimmy is the least of our worries right now, Jesse. We got a shit storm going on that little girls like you wouldn't understand."

It's like a knife to my heart. Everyone pushes me off. Well, maybe not Dan but everyone else. Renee, William, my Dad and now Raffe. He isn't going to help me. I don't know what to do. I need to get rid of Jimmy or he's going to hurt me. This I know for a fact. I see the looks he gives me. It's the same look Rick gave me. The same one I saw on Gabriel's face.

Sometimes, you have to be mean, Jesse.

"Fuck you!" I yell at Raffe as Big Dan comes out from the shop.

"What the hell, Jess? What's going on?" Dan asks, stunned that I cursed at poor Raffe.

"Nothing." I turn and storm off.

I head home. Jimmy is ripping the trailer apart. "What are you looking for?" I ask him. Dumb to poke at the monster, I know but I never said I was smart.

"A suitcase," he answers angrily.

"I think Aunt Renee has one in her closet. Are you going somewhere?"

He stops and stares at me. "Fuck no."

I shrug my shoulders. "What do you want for supper?"

He doesn't answer and storms out of the trailer. I laugh and go into my aunt's room, taking all of her makeup, some of her clothes and then I head over to stay at Tom's. I'm not staying at the trailer with no locked barrier between Jimmy and me. I have to protect what's mine.

Of course, William spots me. "Jesse, Jess. Wait up, will you?" William yells. I keep walking. "What's wrong? Why won't you talk to me?" he asks after he catches up to me.

"I'm busy," I tell him with no emotion in my voice.

"Okay. Hey." He steps in front of me, blocking my way. I try to go around him, but he holds me by the shoulders. "I know what you saw. We need to talk."

I blink at him.

"Come on, Jess," he pleads.

"There's nothing to talk about. Now, if you'll excuse me, I have things to do." I try to shake myself out of his grip.

"I was going to tell you about Penny. It just happened. I didn't mean to hurt you," he says. I see the honesty in his eyes.

But he hurt my heart and guess what? It's mine and I protect what's mine. *Sometimes, you have to be mean, Jesse.*

"Just because you put your lips on mine and your hand between my legs doesn't mean you owe me anything. I don't care who you're banging." He winces. It was a low blow. I know. He didn't want to hurt me back then. Gabriel made him.

"Jess..." he lets his words trail off as he releases his grip on my shoulders.

Sugar and Skulls

My shoulder bumps into his as I brush past him. "It's fine, William." My heart breaks into a thousand pieces as I walk away from him, they fall all over the sidewalk. I don't stop to pick them up. Who needs them anyway? They were the pieces I reserved for William. I don't need them anymore. *Don't look back. Don't look back.*

When I get to Tom's, I shower and get dressed in my aunt's black leather pants and black tank top. I brush my hair until it's a shiny, blue-black temptation. Today, I take what's mine. Trap County doesn't belong to the Desert Devils and it sure as fuck doesn't belong to the Rebel Skulls. It belongs to me. I'm one of a kind. One. The only one I can depend on.

There isn't one thing that goes on in this town that I don't know about. Well, I didn't see the Penny and William thing coming but what did I expect? I knew William and I were never going to be a thing. Too much happened to us back when we first met. Secrets both of us will take to our grave. It's okay. I'm glad he found someone. I hope he's happy. One of us should get a happy ever after and between the two of us, he is the one who deserves it most.

It only takes me two days to sell all of the shit in the suitcase. I know what you're thinking. I'm contributing to the shit show that is Trap County, but these people will get their drugs one way or another. Besides, I'm like Robin Hood, except I take from the users and give to the poor. Nobody recognized me with my skull makeup and the few who bothered to ask for my name, I told them to call me Sugar. My grandmother used to tell me I was made of sugar and spice and everything nice, so it seemed appropriate.

Anyhow, I know who needs money in this town. I've quietly infiltrated myself into this place over the years. So, last night I dressed in my skull outfit and in true Robin Hood fashion delivered the cash to those in need. All except for the portion that I will re-invest into buying more product. Like I said, these people will get their drugs one way or another and this way I can make sure they're getting quality product. This time around, it was probably junk because the Devils are strictly out to put green in their pockets. But I've met the right people and I've been assured I'll be getting some grade A shit from here on out. I'm going to push the Desert Devils clear out of here. No one will buy from them again.

Monday morning rolls around and I head to the shop. Big Dan looks up from the counter when I walk in. He points to the stool across from him. "Do you want to talk?" he asks.

"What do you want to talk about?" I snap my gum between my teeth.

"What was going on the other day between you and Raffe?"

I mindlessly flip through his book of designs. He reaches over and closes it. "Look at me, Jess."

I do with an exaggerated, wide-eyed stare. He crosses his big arms across his chest and leans back in his chair, rubbing his hand through his beard with an expectant look on his face.

Sighing, I stare up at the ceiling. "Remember when he was asking you about Jimmy from the Desert Devils?"

"Yeah."

"Well, he lives with me. Well, not me. My aunt. I'm an unfortunate by-stander in the arrangement."

He leans forward, placing his arms on the counter. "You're shitting me."

"No, and I've been trying to help Raffe, but he doesn't want it. He thinks I'm too young. So, it's whatever. I don't care anymore. If he won't help me, I'll help myself."

"What do you need help with?" he asks, a frown and a bunch of wrinkles form on his forehead.

Shit. I said too much.

"Nothing. I don't need anyone's help. It's good. Life is good."

"A young man came around looking for you this weekend. Said you hadn't been home, and he was worried about you."

I roll my eyes. "I was staying with a friend."

"Goddammit, Jess. I sense something going on with you and I want to know what the fuck it is." He grabs my chin and forces me to look at him.

"I'm. Fine," I state dryly.

And for the following year, I am fine. I continue my weekend life as Sugar, selling drugs and giving all the money to those who need it. Renee and Jimmy don't even notice I'm not living with them anymore. Old man Tom is letting me squat in the trailer out back of his property, letting me shower and stuff in his house. I pay him a little in rent and help him take care of the dog, so it's a win win.

That is until the suit lady starts butting her damn nose in my business again.

The good news is she doesn't send me somewhere else.

The bad news is the good news I give you never lasts.

Dirk

"What's Big Dan doing for you now?" I ask Raffe.

He pulls up his pant leg and shows me this sick piece with skulls and roses. "He's got this girl that's working for him, it's her design. Pretty rad, huh?"

"Big Dan has a woman working with him? Why do I not believe a word of this?" I laugh.

"Not a woman. I said girl, fuck face. She is sweet and undeniably talented. He's been letting her do a few designs on him and damn, bro, she is a natural. Jess has even been doing designs on herself. How she does it I have no idea. She's a tough little cookie."

"Hmm. How old is she?" I swallow back half my beer and give Bill a one finger salute as he pulls up on his bike.

"Turned seventeen a few months ago. That asshole Jimmy is fucking her aunt. I warned her straight up, he's bad news."

"I need to get over there to see Dan. Maybe I'll head over there this weekend."

"Yeah, you'll miss the girl though, she doesn't do weekends. Dan says she goes MIA every weekend. Big fucker worries about the little thing all the time. She's a fucking knock-out. Don't say that to his face though. I learned the hard way and now I keep all my wicked thoughts to myself."

I laugh hard as Bill walks up. He pats Raffe on the back and throws his cigarettes on the table, taking a seat with us. "Howdie boys," he drawls.

"So, good news, the Desert Dipshits haven't been able to sell shit in Trap. Some bitch that calls herself Sugar has the market locked down tight."

"Who is she?" Bill asks, with lazy interest. "You know we're going to have to shut her down. It's our county, you know?"

"Yeah, if you can figure out who she is, let me know. Nobody is talking. She dresses in leather and paints her face like a goddammed skeleton."

I roll my lip ring between my teeth. "Raffe, are you losing your pretty boy touch?"

"Fuck, man. My dick works fine, nobody is spilling. They love this bitch. I guess she takes care of the less fortunate and we all know there's plenty of that in Trap. So, yeah, they don't want to see us shove her out. She keeps shit rolling and the drugs are clean. Doc tells me overdoses are almost non-existent since she started selling."

"I want to meet this Sugar. Get me a fucking meeting with her, Raffe," Bill says, leaving no room for arguments.

Raffe sighs. "May as well ask me to get you an interview with the fucking Queen of England," he grumbles and walks away, kicking rocks.

Bill laughs and then runs his hands through his dark hair.

"How did your meeting go with the worker?" I ask.

"The bitch is still trying to find Jesse to bring her in for the damn DNA test. Says she took off from her aunts, wherever the fuck that is. Right now, she's listed as a runaway. So, I'm just fucked, man."

"Well, shit. Wait…" my mind is moving pieces of a fucked-up puzzle around. Bill is studying my face as I try to put the edge pieces together and then slide the middle ones in place. *No fucking way.*

"Bill, I think I might know where to find her. Plan on riding with me this weekend and we'll see if I'm right."

"I've got nothing better to do. If you help me find her, I'll give you whatever your filthy, non-existent heart wants.

I grin and toss the rest of my beer back. How many seventeen-year-old girls named Jess are there in the world? And if my cousin is taken with this one then it might just be because she's one of us. Skulls have a way of recognizing their own.

Chapter Eight

Jesse ~ Seventeen years old

I'm watching William rub Penny's swollen belly from behind a tree. They stopped in front of the grocery store. He still tries to talk to me. Sometimes, he follows me around like a lost puppy, but I kick him to the curb each time. I shouldn't be jealous. Shouldn't be. But a small, tiny, barely noticeable part is.

It's not like I'm girlfriend material anyway. I'm jaded as fuck and overall, just not a nice person to be around anymore. I've taken mean to the next level. Well, that's not entirely true cause everyone here loves me. Most people have figured out I'm her... Sugar. Yeah, tattooing myself wasn't the greatest idea cause those things are hard to fucking hide. But whatever, nobody is going to talk. I know because the last time someone had the balls to utter my real name while I was dressed as her, got a fucking bullet in their foot.

I protect what's mine.

Anyhow, I'm trying to decide if I want to blow this popsicle stand and head to Cali. I'm tired of the desert. I long to see some fucking color. Like Jesus, this is the blandest place on the earth. I try to brighten it up with my murals, but you can only do so much.

I rip my eyes from William and his pregnant girlfriend and head to the shop. Raffe's bike is parked out front. I'm excited to see what Dan's got done. He's getting one of my best designs tattooed on his leg. It's dark and sexy and I absolutely love that it is going on Raffe's beautiful body. Even if he is an asshole and thinks I'm nothing but a kid.

When I walk in, they both look up and smile. I love it here. I'll always love it here. Yeah, I'll never make it to Cali since the thought of leaving this place makes my heart ache. I lean over to study Dan's work. "It needs more shading there." I point to the spot on the skull I'm talking about.

Raffe laughs. "I always knew she was going to steal your business someday. As soon as she's legit, I'm switching to her."

Dan smacks him in the head. "No way is she touching you. She can only work on the ladies."

I laugh so hard I snort. "Whatever, big guy."

I head to the back to gather a few supplies. I'm working on a sugar skull piece on my arm. Dan's been helping me. He gave up a long time ago on sticking to his, *I have to be eighteen before he works on me,* rule. I'm good at doing them on myself but sometimes, it's simply logistics and I just can't reach or get the right angle.

The door dings, so I head out front to see if I can help since Dan is busy with Raffe.

Fuck me. It's suit lady.

"Do you know you are listed as a runaway, Jesse?" she asks, not even bothering to say hello.

Dan and Raffe both look up and Raffe audibly gasps. I hear him whisper a *fuck* under his breath.

Her eyes roam behind me and when she sees him, her face turns bright pink, her eyebrows shooting to her hairline. I'm going to go out on a limb and say Raffe has fucked suit lady.

"As you can clearly see I'm not on the run. I'm here in Trap County, right where you left me," I tell her while yawning at the same time.

Suit lady recovers and tugs on the hem of her jacket, composing herself. "While that may be, your aunt has informed me that she has not seen you in some time."

I laugh and take a seat on the stool. It's been a year since my aunt's seen me.

"I need you to come with me, Jesse. I need to talk to you about a few things and you have to go back to your aunt's. I'll have to place you somewhere else if you don't agree to stay with her. We both know that with your previous behavior issues and your age, no foster family will take you. You'll end up in a juvenile detention center until you turn eighteen. Neither of us want that, so let's grab your things and get you moved back in with Renee."

I turn around, realizing that Dan and Raffe are now privy to my private business. Raffe is white like he's seen a ghost. I suppose seeing a past fuck will do that to a guy and Dan looks like he wants to turn me over his knee, ground me or some shit.

"Fine. But you have to tell Renee I want my goddamn bedroom door put back on."

She shakes her head and looks confused.

"Yeah, no door, no go."

"Of course, of course, come on," she says impatiently. I'm sure she's in a hurry to go ruin more kid's lives today.

I grab my bag, stopping by Dan to squeeze his arm. "I'm fine. Stop looking like someone kicked your dog. I'll see you tomorrow." He nods but doesn't say anything as I follow the suit out.

When I get to suit's car, she says we have to make a stop at the local doctor's office before we do anything else. "Why the doctor?" I ask, smacking my gum loudly to annoy her.

"Someone has come forward; he says he's your dad. We have to run a DNA test and then we will go from there."

What!

"I don't have a dad."

"Don't be silly. Everyone human on the planet has a dad. It's biology, Jesse. You're a smart girl, come on now."

I shake my head. *Your daddy is coming for you.* I hear the scary man with tattoos say in my head.

Well, it certainly took him long enough. So long in fact that I don't need him anymore.

Maybe he should have come before mama overdosed.

Before grandma and grandpa died.

Before Rick.

Before Father Gabriel.

Before Trap County.

Before I became a mean girl who doesn't need a daddy.

I don't need anyone.

No. Fucking. One.

We get my blood drawn, pick up my shit from old man Tom's camper and then head to Renee's. She is sitting at the table smoking a cigarette and Jimmy is watching a stupid game show. He chuckles when we walk in, making my skin crawl.

Suit lady looks at him. "Put her door back up." She points to my old room. He shrugs, shoots me a smirk and heads out to the shed to get the door.

"Next time she goes missing, call me," she tells my aunt who looks about as enthused as a dead rat.

"Sure thing," Aunt Renee says. She puts out her smoke and gets up to hold the door open for Jimmy who is now bringing the door inside.

"You call me if you need anything and I'll call as soon as I get those results," suit lady tells me.

"What results?" Jimmy asks, stopping in the middle of the living room, peeking around my bedroom door.

"I'm sorry, but confidentiality," suit lady answers with a smug look on her face. "Keep in mind, Renee, you receive monthly payments to take care of Jesse. I expect that is what they are being used for."

I walk suit lady out and she pauses by her car. "You have less than a year, Jesse. I know this isn't an ideal situation. Just stick it out a bit longer. Okay?"

Nodding, I wave and turn back towards the trailer, steeling myself for what is to come. I notice William lurking a few trailers down. If I weren't so damn stubborn, I would break down and talk to him. I want to but it hurts too much to see him. He's always watching me though. Still the big brother. Too bad I'm busy being a snotty little sister.

Renee is getting dressed in her slutty work clothes when I get back inside. She tells me she is working the entire weekend. My eyes slide to Jimmy. He's pretending to watch the game show still blaring on the television. He isn't really watching though. I feel the interest rolling off him in waves and I want to puke. As soon as Renee leaves, I'm out of here, no way am I staying. Even if I have the door back to my room.

My room looks exactly the same. I run my finger over the dusty dresser and plop down on my old bed, waiting for Renee to leave so I can make my escape. I lie back, staring at the ceiling. My eyes close and I think about the blood test. The one that might link me to someone in this world other than Renee. It doesn't matter. I don't need him. I don't need anyone.

Unfortunately, I'm as stupid as they come, and I fall asleep. When I wake up, the room is dark except for the light of the moon pouring in through the window. I grab my bags and tiptoe through the living room, praying to Gabriel's god that Jimmy is either gone or passed out.

"Going somewhere, Sugar?" Jimmy drawls.

"Just let me go and when the fucking suit lady comes back, you can ring me. I'll leave my number."

"You've sure grown up, Sugar," he says, standing from the couch.

It's then I realize he's been calling me by my street name. I'm almost one hundred percent certain that he's not using it as an endearment. He knows. He knows I'm Sugar. I pull my bag up higher on my shoulder, wishing I had my gun. I begin to inch towards the door. "You know, Jimmy, this is a win win. You guys get to keep the money you get from the state for taking care of me and I get to be by myself, no offense to your parenting skills or anything."

He lunges for me, knocking us both to the ground. "You know how much trouble you've caused me, *Sugar*," he spits my street name in my face as he hovers over me. He pins my arms over my head with one hand, the other tightly wraps around my neck.

49

LM Terry

Jimmy takes the entire weekend to show me just how much trouble I caused him. I fought for a long time. The carpet was rough on my cheek as it rubbed back and forth over the course material, my tears soaking into it. All I could think about was how I had let the tattooed man down. I didn't protect what was mine. I tried but Jimmy is so much stronger than me.

After a few hours, I stopped fighting. Since the trouble I caused not only took money out of his pocket but his clubs, several of them were invited over to join in the fun. Minutes of terror, turned into hours of pain and humiliation, turned into days of leaving me nothing but a broken shell.

At first, I thought of a million ways to be mean to Jimmy. Each idea meaner than the previous but I've given up on that. There's not one mean thing I could do to him that would be worse than what he's done to me.

I'm in my bed now, lying on my stomach, eyes focused on the wall by my bed. I heard Jimmy cleaning the place up and then the roar of his bike as he drove away. I'm not sure what day it is but surely Renee will return home at some point.

Jimmy informed me that this was just the beginning. My debt to them won't be paid in full for the foreseeable future. Sugar is now their bitch. She is going to pay by selling their drugs and sucking their cocks. Since I'm Sugar, I guess that means I'm their bitch too.

The pain in my body is the only thing that signals to my brain that I'm still alive. I feel dead inside. Dead, just like the skull I paint on my face when I become her. Empty, hollow, nothing but bones and an occasional beat of heart.

I've got money hidden under some tires in old man Tom's back yard. I knew no one would steal it there. No one can get close to that dog but Tom and me. Maybe I should go get it and try to catch the bus somewhere.

50

Yeah, I'll get the money. I'll lie low at Tom's until I feel good enough to get on that bus and then I'll never look back. I've learned a lot from Big Dan. Enough that maybe I can open my own shop somewhere. Somewhere far away from here.

What if I go somewhere new and the same thing happens? This seems to be a pattern in my life. I must have something tattooed across my forehead that only pricks can see. Like a neon flashing sign that flashes all pricks welcome.

Doesn't matter I guess. I couldn't protect what was mine, so they took it. I'm tired of being mean. Tired of being me. Tired of…

Someone is knocking again. They've been knocking off and on for hours. I wish they would stop.

I just need to get the money and lie low in Tom's camper for a while.

Don't think about it. *Don't you fucking think about it.* It's fine. I need to get out of here before Renee comes home or worse, Jimmy comes back. I shift my head a tiny bit to see what time of day it is. It's dark. Perfect. No one can see me. Not like this.

I drag myself up, grab my shorts and t-shirt from the floor, throw them on and walk out. I don't take anything with me, not even my shoes. Tom's house is only a few minutes away. Something trickles down my leg, but I have to keep going. I have to get away from Renee's.

Someone pulls up beside me. I ignore them and continue to limp along, cutting through the empty lot so they can't follow me with their car. *Please go away. Please go away.*

I stop when I hear William's voice. "I found her. She's in the lot to the north of Emerson trailer park. Yeah, come quick." Heavy boots stomp behind me. I try to hurry away but I trip and fall onto the hard, dusty ground. I'm crawling behind a bush to hide when he catches up to me.

"Jess." He drops to the ground in front of me. I curl up in a ball, hiding my face from him.

Someone else kneels beside me. It's Penny. She puts her arm around me, and I lean into her, rubbing my hand over her swollen belly like I saw William do the other day. His baby is in there, all protected and shit. I should give my money to them so they can get the fuck out of here and raise this sweet little thing somewhere else. Yeah, that's what I'll do. I don't have a chance anymore. I didn't protect what was mine. These two have a future. I know William will make a great daddy. He will. And even though I hate to admit it, Penny will make a great mother.

William stands and yells to someone. "Over here, hurry." Then he drops back beside me. "Jesse, look at me, Jess," he pleads. I don't. He will see what they took from me. "Jesus Christ," he whispers.

Penny runs her hand over mine and holds me tight to her. Yeah, she will make a fantastic mother. This little peanut is a lucky little guy or girl. William and Penny will protect them from the pricks. For the first time my heart aches to belong to someone.

I hear more boots stomping towards us, so I push myself up off the ground quickly. I need to get to Tom's, I haven't fed and watered the dog in I don't know how many days. He's probably starving.

"Jess, where are you going?" William doesn't touch me. He just follows beside me while I limp my way along. I keep my head down and focus on moving my bare feet, one in front of the other. That is until large boots enter my vision, halting me in my tracks.

My entire body is shaking now. I'm suddenly cold, so cold. Big Dan doesn't move. I can feel the heat radiating off him, so I take a tiny step closer. He doesn't move a muscle, and nobody says anything. My teeth are chattering now, so I take another tiny step.

Then another.

And another.

Another.

His arms wrap around me, and I burrow myself deep into his chest.

The good news is Dan is warm just like I would imagine a big grizzly bear would be.

The bad news, well, you already know the bad news. I've lost something and I'll never be able to get it back.

Chapter Nine

Big Dan

I don't know who I want to kill more at the moment. The last three years Jesse has become like a daughter to me and now I know why. She's Bill's kid. She doesn't even know this yet. When the social worker came and took her a few days ago, I was dumfounded. Jesse had been living on her own for the past year and no one even knew. Not until Bill came forward to claim her did social services go looking for her and when the aunt didn't know where she was, they listed her as a runaway.

An entire fucking year.

I've known Jesse has had it rough. Everyone in this god forsaken county has it rough one way or another. When Jess left with the worker, Raffe literally stood up and then collapsed to the ground. She has managed to find the soft spot of two grown ass, burly men. Well, I wouldn't call Raffe burly, but you know what I mean.

Her young friend William has been worried sick about her. He's been keeping an eye on her trailer for us, said she hadn't left for several days. It's a giant shit show. My cousin Dirk and Bill showed up Saturday morning in the midst of this cluster fuck. Raffe apologized profusely to Bill for not figuring out sooner that our Jess was his long-lost daughter.

And now here she is, falling apart in my arms. I want to run with her. Take her away from all of this. Bill and Dirk stayed at my place, we didn't know what was going on and we didn't want to overwhelm her. My gaze catches Raffe's, all I see is horror in his moonlit eyes.

"Hey, William, why don't you take your girlfriend on home, and we will take care of Jess," I tell the kid.

He looks at his girlfriend who is silently crying. "I can't leave Jesse," he whispers. "You don't know what she's been through."

Jesse pulls away from me. "William, follow me," she says quietly. "You all wait here for a minute, please."

She doesn't look at anyone. William takes her hand and I watch as they open the fence and slip into Tom Winslow's back yard. The beast of a dog starts barking but Jesse walks right up to him. He licks her face as she kneels in front of him. She points to a pile of tires and William lifts a few of them and pulls out something covered in what looks like a trash bag.

He walks back to the gate and waits for her. She pats the dog's head before joining William along the fence line. She takes the item from William and unwraps it. She takes what looks like cash out, then wraps it back up and pushes it against the young man's chest. He shakes his head. I glance at his girlfriend. She's watching the exchange with sadness in her eyes. She whispers, "I think you should know this isn't the first time she's been hurt."

Raffe's gaze shoots to hers. "What do you mean?"

"I don't want to tell her story. It's hers to tell, but William and Jesse have history. Not a pleasant one. They are both lucky to have each other." She tears her eyes away from William and Jess to stare at the ground. "I didn't mean to come between them. I wish she would let him back into her life."

William's scream draws all of our attention back to them. He is holding Jesse's limp body in his arms. I run over to them. "She just passed out," he says, looking into her face helplessly.

"Maybe we should take her to the hospital," William's girlfriend frets.

All three of us say no in unison.

Raffe takes Jesse from William's arms. I grip his shoulders and look him in the eye. "Take your girlfriend home and get some sleep. Come by my place in the morning. I'll take good care of her. I promise." I shake his shoulders slightly and he nods.

"Call me if she needs me. Please call, no matter the time." He wraps his arm around his girl, and they head back to his rod.

"I'll get the car. Wait here," I tell Raffe.

He's looking down at Jesse with tears in his eyes. "This is all my fault," he says.

"Stop, she doesn't need you feeling sorry about this shit. She needs you with your balls intact. She needs you to be ready for war."

He nods once and lifts her up higher in his arms. I run to the car and pull in front of Tom's, watching as Raffe comes around from the side of the house with her. He carefully climbs in the back seat, and I close the door behind them. "We've got to call Dirk and give them a heads up or some shit," I say as I pull away from the curb.

"Oh fuck, man. Stop the car a minute," he says in a grave voice.

I pull the car over and turn to peer into the backseat. He flips the flashlight on his phone and runs it over her from head to toe. I dive for my door, getting it open just in time to be sick. Fuck. Fuck. Fuck.

56

"What do we do, man?" Raffe asks.

I don't say anything, wiping my mouth off on my jacket. Starring out at the open road in front of us, I realize the gates to hell have been unlocked and there will be no going back. "Someone's going to die for this."

"Yeah," Raffe agrees.

"She needs a doctor. We have to tell him. He'll kill us both if we don't take her to him right the fuck now."

"Yeah," he says again, stunned into one-word responses.

I dial Dirk. He answers in one ring. "Find her?" he asks.

"Prepare Bill for the worst possible thing he can imagine. We're on the way now."

"Is she dead?"

"No, but I'm sure she wishes she was."

Dead air.

"Call a doctor, Dirk," I say before hanging up.

We've all had a hand in this, me included.

I fucking came here to get away from the club. Shit, I didn't want any part of it. I wanted to do my art in peace, and I had that until I met the little pack of dynamite who is currently in my backseat. I would do anything for her, anything. Including going back to that life.

Jesse mumbles from the backseat. "I... wait, hey, I need to go back to Tom's," she says, her voice cracking. I look in the mirror and see her trying to sit up, pushing herself off Raffe.

"You're not going anywhere but to my house," I tell her.

When she doesn't respond with her normal smart-ass remark, I look in the review mirror. Her head is leaning against the window and her eyes are tilted towards the moon. "I let him down," she says, her eyes dropping to mine in the mirror.

"Who?" I ask, breaking eye contact for a moment to glance at the road.

"The scary man with the tattoos. I let him down. I didn't protect what was mine," she says with so much sadness and despair it wedges a thorn into my heart. I can feel the blood slowly trickling out around it.

Raffe pulls her into his arms. "Shh, baby. You didn't let anyone down. Just rest, sweetheart."

The scary man with the tattoos. Dirk. She's talking about Dirk. Jesus, what the fuck is going on here?

When we get to my place, the house is dark. Dirk and Bill must be getting the doc. I carry her in and take her straight to my room, laying her down on the bed. She immediately rolls away from me. "Raffe, wait for Dirk and Bill. Explain what we know. Send the doctor in when he gets here. Everyone else stays the fuck out till I them different, that includes Bill. Got it?"

"Yeah, got it," his voice cracks. He closes the door quietly behind him.

"I don't need a doctor," Jesse groans after a few minutes of silence.

"That's not up for argument, Jess." I sit on the edge of the bed and drop my head into my hands. I don't even know where to go from here.

"No one is touching me, big guy. Point me in the direction of your shower." I turn to look at her. She's sitting up, hugging her knees.

"Jesse, you are letting the doctor check you out."

She looks me in the eye. "No. Just let me shower and I'll be on my way. I need to get out of here."

"Jesse, there is a lot going on here you don't know about."

"No," she points a tiny finger in my face. "There's a lot you don't know. You can't keep me here."

I laugh. Even as beat up as she is, she's still a goddamn ball of fire. She throws all her weight at me. She kicks and scratches. I don't want to hurt her, so I get up, leaving her flailing about on the bed. "I'll be back in with the doctor," I say before closing the door behind me.

Something crashes against the door just as the latch catches. I look up to find Raffe with a red-faced Bill in a headlock. "Hey, man. Look. Bill made it back," he smirks, tightening his arm around Bill's neck.

Jesus Christ. Like father like daughter.

Dirk

When Raffe told me that Jess thinks she disappointed me, it made me stop breathing. I don't know why. He said he didn't know if she was talking about me but as he was relaying her exact words I knew it was. The scary man with tattoos. That's me. Anyway, I had to get out of there. This shit is just all too goddamned heavy.

A noise draws my attention to the back of Dan's house. I watch as Jesse crawls out the window and then falls a few feet to the ground with a thud. I should help her up. Should.

Before we go any further in this, whatever this is, you should know that I'm an asshole. Straight up. I'm the kind of man that makes other men's balls shrivel up. The kind that makes women clutch their children tight to their thighs when I pass them on the street while at the same time, making their cunts soak clear through their fucking mommy yoga pants.

59

Priests drop to their knees to pray when they see me, certain I'm a sign of the beginning of the end. The kind that makes cops keep their hand poised on their weapons. The kind that makes old women clutch their pearls, lick their lips, and then slip their grey-haired old men blue pills in their morning coffee.

You either love me or hate me. No in-between exists when it comes to me. Very few are on the end of the love spectrum and if they are, it's because they're hoping my vibe rubs off on them. They are of the dark variety.

Jesse pops up on the other side of the hedge and slowly turns as if she senses I'm behind her. Our eyes lock.

Jesse isn't a little girl anymore.

"Going somewhere?" I ask, lighting up a cigarette.

"You got a shower?" She doesn't move, just stares at me. She's like an angel that fell from the sky. A dark, little nymph of an angel. Lovely.

"Sure do, but I don't think Big Dan is going to be happy with your little escape attempt."

I take her in as she stands there. She has dried blood streaks down both legs and what looks like rug burns along one side of her face. Her lips are cracked and bleeding. Big Dan was right, she needs a doctor, but I'm a firm believer in women's rights and all that bullshit. Her body, her choice. "Don't you think you need a doctor?"

"No. I need a fucking shower," she grits through clenched teeth. She takes off down the sidewalk.

"Dan isn't the only one who's going to be unhappy about you taking off." I'm sure she knows that my presence is a good indicator that her father is near.

"Yeah?" she yells back, not even pausing. "Tell him I'll be back real soon."

She is tossing my words from years ago right in my face... his too. *He's coming for you real soon.*

Why do I feel like she is a sacrifice in this whole crazy mess? A sacrifice who was tossed into an active volcano. Only she didn't burn, she didn't even need anyone to rescue her. No, she pulled herself up from the molten, hot lava and clawed her way out.

"Goddammit," I follow hot on her heals while pulling my phone from my pocket.

Suddenly, she spins around, making me bump right into her. I reach out to grab her so that she doesn't fall backwards.

"Don't you dare fucking call them," she warns.

"You're awfully big for your britches aren't you? I don't take orders from little girls."

She shoves me in the chest so hard that I release her. "Good thing I'm not a little girl. You can call them *after* I shower. Jesus Christ, what does it take to get you thick headed men to understand a girl needs a fucking shower!"

She stomps away and I put my phone back in my pocket. This is a first for me. The first time I've ever let a woman change my mind. Bill is going to fucking kill me.

After a few minutes of walking, she cuts behind a tall wooden fence and then hops over a shorter chain link fence into a backyard. I jump in right behind her but regret it the minute I do. I come face to face with a dog that looks so mean, so nasty I think I might piss myself.

She kneels beside him to calm his growl. "He's with me," she tells the dog. He growls and bares his teeth, showing me who's boss. She laughs. "Yeah, yeah boy. He looks tough but pft, he just let me walk all over his tattooed ass." She pats the dog on the head, and he backs away, letting me slide past him.

I'm offended. Truly offended. Did she just put me down? I follow her into the house. She heads right for the bathroom.

"Hey, you know I'm only being nice to you cause your hurt right? I am tough. Remember, I broke every finger on that punk teenager's hand for you."

She sets a towel on the counter, then leans in to crank the shower on. "Yeah, so tough. I had to finish him off."

"You stuck a fork in his leg that's hardly finishing him off," I say, leaning against the doorframe, watching her.

She stares at me as she lifts her shirt over her head and my heart stops. Christ, she's definitely not a little girl anymore and holy fuck is Bill going to kill me if he finds out I saw her in a bra. I turn quickly, noting the bruises on her ribs before closing the door behind me.

I can hear her laughing hysterically on the other side. Goddammit, this girl is something else.

I've got to call Bill. I pull my phone out and make the call.

"She ran away. Where the fuck are you at?" he growls as soon as the call connects.

"Chill, dude, you're going to give yourself a fucking heart attack."

"The doctor is here, and she isn't. So, yes, I'm having a fucking heart attack," he grits through the receiver.

"She climbed out the window. Don't worry, I followed her to a house about twelve blocks from Dan's. She's fine. She just wanted a damn shower."

"Get her ass back here," he yells.

Dan takes the phone from him. "Dirk, what the fuck, man?"

"Jesus, she just wanted a shower. We're at some house with a dog that looks like a demon from hell."

"She's sneaky, dude. Keep an eye on her and get back here as soon as you can."

"Yeah, yeah." I hang up and take a look around the place. Doesn't look like she lives here. No sign of a woman living here at all.

The shower is still running but it's been twenty minutes. I knock on the door. "Everything okay in there?"

No answer.

"Did you fucking drown or what?"

Still no answer. Fuck. I push open the door. "Jesse?"

When she still doesn't answer, I reluctantly (and I mean reluctantly for the sake of my nuts) push the shower curtain aside.

She is clawing at herself. I reach in to stop her, but the water is scalding hot. "Jesse, fuck, stop!"

I turn the water temp down and step in, clothes and all. She falls to the ground and crouches in the corner of the shower still trying to tear at her skin. I kneel down beside her and grip her hands in mine tightly.

"I'm sorry," she says frantically.

"Sorry for what?"

She looks up at me. "For not protecting what was mine," she says, so tortured it feels like a lash to my soul.

I pull her to stand by her hair, making her eyes go wide. I tug her into my chest. "You did, you protected what was yours," I tell her.

She shakes her head. "I didn't. I didn't."

"Hey, listen to me. I can see that you protected yourself. It doesn't matter what they did. You fought. You fought hard but sometimes, you have to stop to live to fight another day. You did what you had to do."

She blinks at me a few times as my words begin to sink in.

"You're not giving up are you?" I ask, still gripping her hair tightly in my fist.

"No." She pauses, and I see a fire ignite in her eyes. "I'm going to kill them."

I give her a wicked smile. "No, *we* are going to kill them."

I release my grip on her hair and she drops her forehead to my chest. I hold her until her trembling subsides. "You want to tell me who *they* are?" She rolls her head back and forth.

She pulls away from me and tries to cover herself with her arms. "I'm... I'm good," she stutters.

Quickly, I take a step back. "Yeah, shit. I'll wait for you out there. We should be getting back to Dan's."

She nods in agreement, not taking her eyes off the shower floor.

Chapter Ten

Jesse

What the hell am I thinking, breaking down in front of this man. When the door closes behind him, I quickly get out of the shower and dress. Fuck, what have I done? Now that my head has cleared a little, I realize I've gotten myself into yet another sticky situation. Dan is friends with scary tattoo man and my dad. Great, simply great.

I take a deep breath and head out to face things head on... well, sort of. He turns when he hears me. He is dripping wet. "There's a clothes dryer in the kitchen." He looks down at his wet apparel. His t-shirt is sticking to his muscular chest. A dark wet dream if I ever did see one. Damn.

"Yeah, maybe I should dry them, otherwise your dad is going to ask questions." He laughs awkwardly.

For some reason, I think awkward is new to him. Good. I toss him a towel and point to the kitchen. When he leaves the room, I go over my options. I could go with tattoo man to see Dan, Raffe and my dad. Um, I think I'll take a hard pass on that. I plop my aching body down on the couch.

My original plan was to hop on a bus, but I've never run from anything in my life. No, I've either set it on fire or stabbed it. However, now I find myself caught between two dangerous clubs.

Just as a plan formulates in my head, a dark shadow moves past me, drawing my eyes upward. Jesus.

Jesuuuus.

I can't help myself. I rise from the couch and stand in front of him. I've only seen his face and hands. But with only a towel, I see the whole canvas and it's almost completely covered. My eyes devour his naked torso. He should be listed as one of the great pieces of dark art. He's an exquisite blend of black ink and man. I reach out and let a finger trail over the sugar skull that is etched into his skin over his rib cage. It's done so well it appears as if she's caged inside of him. Peering out between the bones, she speaks to me. My eyes roam up the ink, climbing up his neck until landing on his mood ring eyes.

The electric current that hums between us gives me new life. A renewed sense of strength washes over me. My hand roams back down to the edge of the towel, sitting ever so delightfully at his hips. In one swift motion, I rip it off and take a step back, keeping the towel in my grip. My eyes run down his dark thighs. My mind is already filling in the blank spots on his body.

Yeah, those are mine now. I'll be etching myself there soon.

"What are you doing?" he asks with a mildly interested smirk on his face.

"Leveling the playing field."

"I guess now that we have seen each other in our birthday suits, perhaps we should properly introduce ourselves." He reaches out for the towel, but I pull it back just out of reach.

"You already know who I am."

"True, Jesse, I do know who you are and who your dad is, so can you please give me that towel before he barges in and so kindly removes my favorite body part."

"Hmm, I thought he was waiting for me at Dan's?"

He huffs and I see his muscles tense. He wants to make a dodge for the towel but is worried he will scare me after what I've just been through. What he doesn't know, is that I don't scare easily. Fear does nothing but warn you danger is near. He is dangerous no doubt, but not to me. "Well, are you going to tell me your name?" I ask.

"I thought I was scary tattoo man." He smirks, still holding his hand out for the towel.

Fucking Dan. I take a few steps back, but he remains frozen in his spot. "Well, scary tattoo man, until we meet again." I salute him before taking off full speed out the door. Let's see if he's willing to take off after me in his stark ass naked condition, just as the sun is rising I might add.

When I get home, Jimmy and Renee are sitting at the table having breakfast. Renee looks up from her plate of scrambled eggs. "Where have you been?"

"Oh, you know, I got up early for a morning jog."

Jimmy narrows his eyes at me over the edge of his coffee mug. He calmly sets it down. "Running from something?"

"Nope. Just thinking I should take better care of myself. Hey, why don't you guys join me in the morning?"

Renee laughs. "Honey, I ain't running unless a zombie or some other monster is chasing me."

I grab a plate and help myself to the rest of the eggs in the pan and then sit down at the table right beside Jimmy. "Well, good thing there are no monsters here, huh Jimmy?" He scowls in my direction.

"Girl, what happened to your face?" Renee asks, not really caring. Some days, I wonder how it's possible she is the daughter of my grandmother. My grandma would have rushed to grab the first aid kit. She would have fixed me up with kisses to boot. But not Renee. No, not her.

"Well, turns out I'm a bit clumsy. My feet got tangled up and I took a skid in the gravel."

I'm not sure if Renee was even listening. She gets up from the table and heads to the bathroom, leaving Jimmy and I alone.

"I thought maybe you took off." He cocks an eyebrow at me in question.

"Nope. Just went for a jog like I said."

"Good. Cause you know I'll find you if you take off, right?"

"I got a deal for you," I tell him, pushing my plate to the side. I give him my full attention even though I want nothing more than to run for the door.

He smirks and leans back in his chair, putting his arms behind his head. "Let's hear it."

"I'll sell your drugs but as for getting you or your buddies off, well that's off the table."

He snorts, pulling his head back. His arms drop in front of him before he leans in close to me. I force myself not to back away. "You don't get decide what's on the table, little girl."

"I guess we could leave it on the table but then I would have to tell my brand-new daddy about it." I don't want to use my father, but the best

68

weapon is the deadliest one and right now the president of Jimmy's rival club is just that. I've listened to Big Dan and Raffe enough to have put the pieces of the puzzle together. I know who my father is, he's the president of the most feared MC club in the states.

He laughs. "Oh, so you found a daddy. A sugar daddy for Sugar?"

"I'll give you that one, Jimmy. That was funny but no. I found my real-life daddy. You know the kind of daddy who would put his fist through his daughter's bully's face."

He runs his tongue across his teeth and sits back a little. "If this new dad of yours is someone to be so scared of, why wouldn't you tell him all of it? Why wouldn't you tell him about the drugs too?"

"See, I have this one little problem. You know my secret identity. I'd like to keep that between the two of us."

His fingers work their way through his beard as he ponders over what I said. "So, you really did find your dad." He nods to himself like he's a genius for putting all this together. "You don't want new daddy finding out his little girl paints herself up at night to do the devil's work. I get it but I don't give a shit about the new guy. You still live under my roof."

I shrug my shoulders. "Okay, whatever dude. I'm sure he'll be here real soon so... the offer stands until he comes a knocking." I walk away, leaving him sitting at the table.

My mind frets over meeting my father as I pack my shit. I'm a little angry, knowing that I'll have little choice in the matter soon. I've been able to stay ahead of them so far but men like Dan, Raffe and tattoo man won't be had for long. They'll find me soon enough. Eventually, they'll subdue me by sheer brutal force. Just like Jimmy but I know they're not like him. No matter how mad I am at them for trying to boss me around, there is a part of me that likes it. A small part.

This is not how I envisioned meeting him. Not at all. I didn't have that white horse storybook shit going on in my head, so you can quit feeling sorry for me right now. No, I'm not high on all that Disney magic shit.

I sit back against the headboard and pull my legs up to my chest, thinking about it. How did I picture this going down? I guess I thought he would show up, smelling of some piney aftershave with a gift in hand. A white box with a big black bow, yes, black, like I said I didn't drink the Disney Kool-Aid. Inside that box would be a pair of roller skates. Just like the ones the Ditsworth sisters had. I would be so happy because he had known what I had always wanted. Like we had some invisible connection or shit.

A quiet rumble pulls me from my thoughts, the sound steadily getting closer.

Ah, the cavalry is on the way.

Jimmy slams my door open. "Just who is daddy dearest?" he asks quickly, going to my window and peering out the side of the curtain.

"Oh, I don't know what his name is."

"What the fuck do you mean you don't know his name?" He looks away from the window to stare at me.

"I didn't ask. But I did find out that he's the president of the Rebel Skulls. Know him?"

His face blanches as the bikes roar into our dinky trailer court. He drills me with an expression I hope to see again real soon. Patience. I will see it again. The day he realizes it was not the old biker president that was a threat. It was the little girl he should have been worried about. "Deal," he simply states and walks out of my room.

I pick at the polish on my nails, waiting a few more minutes. The roar of bikes rattle the glass panes, waking up the warrior inside me. Glancing at my reflection in the mirror over my dresser, I envision the skull that hides beneath my flesh. How fitting, maybe I've always belonged to the Rebel Skulls.

Renee and Jimmy are both anxiously peeking out the curtains when I leave my room for the last time. They both turn to look at me. I shift my bag up higher on my shoulder and hold out a small piece of paper with my number on it to Jimmy. "If you ever want to invest in some good ink give me a call." I shove it in his hand. Renee looks from Jimmy to me. Before I walk out, I pause, saying quietly, "Take care of yourself, Renee." Her only response is to drop her eyes shamefully.

With one last look around, I turn and open the door. On the other side, I find Big Dan, his hand paused in mid-air, moments from knocking or I should say beating on the door. I push him back and step out, closing the door behind me. "Nothing to see here. Let's go," I say.

"We know he's here, Jess. Have him come out," a big man, not as big as Dan but still rather large, says in a calm though growly voice.

I stop on the top step and stare him down. He has the same black hair, although peppered with white and the same intense green eyes I see in the mirror each morning. I tip my head to the side. "Who?"

Dan touches my back gently. "Jess, you need to tread lightly here."

I take another two steps and hop down the last few until I'm standing directly in front of my father.

"Tell Jimmy to get his ass out here. I'll kill him and then we can move on from there." The man cracks the knuckles of one of his hands in the palm of the other.

"Kill Jimmy? Wow, what did he do to you?" I ask, laughing lightly.

His eyes narrow and he looks over my head at Dan. I glance over to Raffe and wink at him. My dad catches it. He glares at Raffe, making him shift nervously on his bike. I laugh again, then I notice tattoo man, I've dropped the scary... like really, I left him with his mouth hanging open and bare butt naked. I pretend to shoot him with my finger. "I knew you'd eventually catch up," I tease. He glares at me like I just called his mom a whore or something. Perfect.

Let's be honest here. I know they have all the real power. Sort of. My attitude, my actions, my perception is all I have. It's all I've ever had. If you don't like the way the situation looks then change the way you look at it. I shift my focus back to Dear. Old. Dad.

His face is turning a slight shade of purple. "Jesse, I'm not messing around. Was Jimmy the one who hurt you?"

"No."

He grits his teeth. "Who did?"

I shift my bag to my other shoulder. "No one. I fell off a ladder while painting a mural."

"Jesse," he says on a sigh. His eyes plead with me, his sad, sad eyes.

"I know you're not letting me stay, so let's just go. You're scaring the shit out of the neighbors." I tip my head to the other shitty trailers surrounding us. Curtains are pulled back, beady eyes peeking out.

He takes the extra helmet off his bike and hands it to me. I take it but walk past his bike and head for Big Dan's. When I look back, I register the hurt on his face. That's fine. He's hurt me more than anyone. He knew about me and for some reason he chose not to come find me. Not until now. Not until every last piece of my soul had been broken.

Dan pats him on the back while they talk quietly to themselves. My dad offers him a nod and then hops on his bike and fires it up. Everyone follows along behind him. One by one the bikes roar down the dusty road.

Big Dan doesn't say anything to me as I climb on the seat behind him. When I wrap my arms around him, he pats my hand. The bike vibrates beneath me, reminding me that I'm alive.

The good news is my dad finally came for me.

The bad news is I'm not sure if I should be happy about it.

Bill

She is beautiful. My baby girl is everything I imagined. She's nothing like her mother and believe me when I say that is indeed a blessing. Goddammit, I loved her mother, but the bitch was weak. I wanted her to be my queen. She wanted to be the queen of smack. I literally had to lock the whore up to keep her clean while she was pregnant with Jesse. Honestly though, I don't blame her. I blame the Desert Dipshits who sold her the shit. Fucking white powder pussies.

And now I find out their VP hurt my baby. Jesse isn't talking but she will. She's simply scared. Beneath the bad girl act is my little girl. She is there. I'm here now and no one will touch her ever again. The Desert Devils will pay. They will pay for taking her mom away from her and they will pay for what they did to her. Oh, how they will pay.

I don't know what the fuck that social worker was thinking leaving her with her aunt. She's no better than her sister. And then there's the fact that Jimmy was living there. Jesse would be better off on her own. But all that's over. She's with me now. Well, not with me with me. That girl is as stubborn as I am. When she refused to ride on my bike, it crushed me. That hurt worse than any punch or bullet I've ever taken.

This was not how I envisioned our reunion. I imagined picking her up and taking her out to dinner at a nice restaurant and showing her how a man should treat her. Not threating to murder a man right before her eyes.

What hurts the most is that I missed the first seventeen years of her life. I should have been there to protect her, and I wasn't. I have no one to blame but myself. Anyhow, I'm not going to let regret hold me back from making things right with her.

That's the only reason I agreed when Dan suggested she stay at his place for tonight. He promised to not let her out of his sight. I'm not sure if anyone can keep her from running off. She's a slippery one. Hell, she even slipped past Dirk. Speaking of Dirk, that fucker is acting strange. And just what in the fuck was up with the wink she threw Raffe?

The first thing I'm doing when we get back to the warehouse is warning all those motherfuckers no funny business with my daughter. I'll flat out kill anyone who touches her. Period. End of Story.

I slam the door open to the warehouse and raise my hands above my head. "All right all you dick wads. Let's get one thing straight..." Every. Damn. One of them. Looks at the ground. Jesus, do they all feel guilty for looking at my girl?

What the hell am I going to do? She's too damn pretty. Just like her mama. I've got one thing going for me though... Jesse also has a brain.

Chapter Eleven

Jesse

Relief washes over me when Dan turns off before the freeway, all the other bikes continuing towards it. He's taking me to his house. Thank god. I need a fat minute before I face my dad again. He is one intense motherfucker.

However, once we're inside and it's just the two of us, I realize it might have been better to hang with the crowd. He points to the couch, heads into the kitchen before coming back out with two sodas. He cracks one open and hands it to me.

"Start from when the social worker picked you up from the shop." He sits down beside me and kicks his booted feet up on the coffee table.

I take a drink as my eyes drift around his place. I was here last night but I was a little out of it. It's nice. Clean and simple. Eventually, my eyes land on him. "Let's just say I've been busy."

He runs his hand through his beard. "I saw the state you were in."

"I'm good. Really. Nothing a little soap and water couldn't wash away," I tell him.

His phone rings. Saved by the bell. He points to me as he gets up to leave the room. "Don't you fucking dare move," he orders.

Nice try, big boy. I need to meet up with my guys. Get everyone on the same page. I'm not selling Jimmy's crap in my county.

What will I do with the stuff he gives me? Well, I have a plan for that. I can do this. I can. I pull my phone out of my pocket as I head out the door. I'll send a message to the guys. A voice stalls my finger over the send button.

"You just don't give up do you?"

Strong arms wrap around me, hauling me off my feet. I juggle to keep my phone from falling to the ground as he tosses me over his shoulder. He unceremoniously dumps me on the floor in the middle of Dan's living room.

Big Dan comes out due to all the commotion. "Jesse," he bellows.

My eyes go the white paper bag in tattoo man's hand. He notices me eyeing it and hides it behind his back.

"Where the fuck do you think you're going?" Dan asks.

"Um, to get some fresh air. I didn't realize I was a prisoner here." I jump to my feet.

"Where did you find her, Dirk?"

"Just stepping off the porch," Dirk answers nervously.

Dirk. Alright I can work with that. Dirk the jerk. Dirk the....

"Jesse. Sit down." Dan gently grabs hold of my arm and guides me back to the couch. "We are not finished."

"Well, I got what you needed." Dirk shoves the white paper bag in Dan's chest and rushes out the door.

Dan sits down beside me, rips the bag open and sets the contents on the coffee table in front of me. "Do you know what that is?" he asks.

I stare at the box. Why hadn't I thought of that? Why? Because I've done everything in my power to forget, that's why. I nod my head yes, a knot slowly creeping up my throat.

"We are not saying you have to take it. It's your choice, Jesse. Your Dad wanted to make sure you had the option."

My dad. My dad made sure I had the plan B pill. I've looked after myself for so long that I don't know what to think about all this. Him, Dan, all of them. My mind flits to Penny and her swollen belly. Penny and William will make wonderful parents. I hope he's using the money I gave him to get out of here. They have a chance.

What chance do I have? None. I'm trapped here in Trap County. It literally has me by the proverbial balls. I can't do that to someone else. I... I just can't.

My bottom lip begins to tremble. What would my grandmother tell me to do? Oh god, I need her. I haven't cried in so long. It used to be something I did every night after my grandparents died and then life just kept coming for me. I guess I shut my emotions off. But this could be a life....

Dan leans over and gently rubs tiny circles over my back. I shift on the couch so that I can see him. He doesn't look away. "Whatever you choose. We all stand behind you."

I glance back at the box. If I take that pill, I'm admitting to them what happened to me. They will know for certain someone hurt me. If I don't take this one though, who knows if I will be able to secret away to buy myself another one.

"Jesse, we know what happened to you. It's not something you have to hide or be ashamed of. Whoever hurt you is the one who holds the shame." He sits forward on the couch and wraps his arm around me, hugging me close to him.

I grab the box, rip it open, take the pill and vow that Jimmy will pay for this. Jimmy will fucking pay for everything. This should not have been a decision I was forced to make.

I set my soda can on the table and wipe my mouth on my wrist. Hot tears come hard, and they come fast. Big Dan wraps me up in his big arms and settles us back into the couch. He lets me cry, holding me tight the entire time.

The good news is… there is no good news. No, there is always something good. The good news is my Dad thought of my future when I couldn't see beyond my nose.

The bad news is I'm not sure I made the right decision and fact is, I will never know.

Dirk

"I'm going to hang outside Dan's place tonight," I tell Bill over the phone.

"How is she?" he asks, his voice cracking.

"Feisty as all get out."

He chuckles lightly.

"Give her some time. Once she realizes you aren't going anywhere she will open up to you."

"Yeah, I suppose you're right." He pauses, sucking in a breath before continuing. "Did she take it?"

"I don't know, man. I gave Dan the bag and split. She's comfortable with him, so I thought it best I step out while they sort it out."

"I'm going to kill him, Dirk. I know Jimmy hurt her."

"We've got to be smart about this, Bill. She needs you. I don't think you ending up back in the slammer is going to do her any favors. If it was him…" I pause to light up a smoke. "If it was him or whoever the fuck it was, let me do it."

"I can't ask that of you, brother."

"You didn't. Let me have this one."

Bill doesn't say anything for a long time. "You still there, man?" I ask.

"It needs to be long and painful," he says with a deadly calm to his voice.

"Oh, it will be." I hang up and lean against my bike, thinking of all the ways I am going to torture that bastard.

A few hours later, Dan steps out. "You may as well head home, Dirk. She's sound asleep."

I push myself off my bike and take a seat by him on the steps. "Good. I don't think she's slept for several days."

He grips his hair and breaks down. I've known my cousin… well, shit, I've known him my whole life. I've never seen him like this. "This is shit, Dirk. She didn't deserve this."

"No girl does."

He lifts his head, looking at me with tears in his eyes. "I should have done more. Jesus, Dirk, I knew something hadn't been right." He stands up and starts pacing in his yard. "How did I not know she was Bill's kid?"

"There's nothing we can do about what's already happened. We've got to focus on the here and now."

He stops and stares at me. "I want her to stay here with me."

I shake my head. "I don't know, Dan. Bill is ready to have his baby girl by his side. He's waited a long time for this."

"She has school and friends here." He leans against a tree and stares up and the sky. "And she's got me and the shop. You can't take that away from her. Not now."

A pang of something unfamiliar hits me in the gut. He's right, he has a relationship already in place with her. I'm nothing but a stranger. For some reason this bothers me. Really bothers me. Is it *jealousy*? No, can't be. I've never envied anyone. Ever.

"I'm going to talk to Bill about it tomorrow. He's living at the warehouse, that's no place for her."

"I live at the warehouse, Dan. There will be other women there. It's not like she'll be the only one."

"Women. Dirk… she's just a girl."

I stand up, drop my cigarette to the ground and grind it into the sidewalk with my boot. "She looks like a woman to me."

Next thing I know, I'm flat on my back, looking up at the stars. What in the fuck?

"Shit, I'm sorry, man." Dan offers a hand to help me up. I accept, hesitantly. My cousin has never hit me. He jerks me to my feet. "Dammit. I'm so fucking sorry. This has me messed up."

Dusting the dirt off my backside, I try to get my bearings. Fuck, he has a mean punch. "It's cool."

He tries to wipe the blood off my lip, but I push his hand away. "I'm going to assume she took the pill?"

The growl that comes from Dan makes me take a few steps back. "She took it and spent the next two hours crying her eyes out. I've never seen her cry, man. Never."

He sits down heavily on the step. This time I keep my distance. Another punch from him is not on my agenda for the rest of the evening.

"I'm going to find whoever did this to her."

He looks up at me and shakes his head. "Good luck with that. I have a feeling she's going to get to them first."

"What's that supposed to mean?"

He chuckles lightly. "You don't know Jess like I do. She's going to get what she wants. She's wicked smart, Dirk. Whoever did this to her... guarantee she already has a plan to make them pay."

Again, I get that fucking jealousy pang. I want to know her. Damn do I want to know her. Just one tiny problem with that. Bill. He warned us, rather violently I might add, that he will disembowel anyone who touches his baby girl.

"I thought you said she was just a girl. Make up your mind." I turn around, heading towards my bike. "Get some sleep, cousin. I have a feeling we're all going to need it."

Chapter Twelve

Jesse

I wake up with a headache and my mouth feels like I ate the entire desert. The cramping in my stomach instantly reminds me of everything. I roll over taking in Dan's bedroom. He's sleeping in a chair in the corner of the room with his boots propped up on the end of the bed.

Quietly, I inch out from under the covers and stand. Oh, god. I grab my stomach, leaning over. Boots thud to the ground. "You okay?" he asks gently, coming up behind me.

I wave him away. "Yeah. Yeah, I'm fine." Standing straight, I face him. "I have things I need to do today, Dan."

He stands like a tower in front of me. "You're not going anywhere without me."

"Jesus Christ." I stomp my foot, poking a finger in his chest. "I've been taking care of myself for a long time."

"And how has that been going for you?" he asks, not budging.

After he says it, I see the regret on his face. I hold up my hand to stop him.

He gently places his hands on my shoulders. "Why don't you go shower and I'll whip up some breakfast, then we can head to the shop."

This perks me up. Yes, the shop. Some damn normalcy. I nod enthusiastically and offer him a big smile. I notice his shoulders drop. He pats me on the head like a puppy and heads out to the kitchen.

The smell of bacon and eggs waft through the house, making my mouth water. Smells good, who knew Big Dan could cook. When I get to the kitchen, Dan and William are talking quietly at the table. They stop the minute I walk into the room.

Dan stands and motions for me to take his seat. I catch William's gaze as I sit down. He tosses me one of his boyish smiles, making my heart thaw a little. Dan pushes a plate in front of me. "I'll leave you two kids to visit." He kisses the top of my head and then leaves the room.

"How are you feeling?" William asks hesitantly.

"Good. How about you?" I motion towards him with my fork.

He laughs. "Oh, Jesse. This is why I love you. Tough as nails."

I almost choke on my food. What did he just say?

His dimples come out in all their glory. "I've always loved you, Jess. Not in the way I love Penny but it's not a lesser love."

My eyes drop to my plate. I know what he means. I love him too. There are only four people in this world I've ever loved. My grandparents and the two men in this house. "I'm sorry I've been treating you so poorly. You don't deserve it."

He reaches out and takes my hand. "I understand, Jess. It had always been just the two of us, thick as thieves." I peek up at him and he winks.

"I don't want you to think I'm not happy for you, William. I am. I really am. Penny is great. You two are going to make great parents." Fuck why did I say that. Now the tears are coming again.

William gets up and moves around the table to sit in the chair next to me. He pulls me into his arms. His familiar scent calms me, but I try to push him away anyway. He doesn't let me. He keeps me tightly pulled into his chest. "I'm so sorry, Jesse. I knew Jimmy was bad news. I should have protected you. Twice now, I've failed you."

"It's not your fault. Without you, I wouldn't have made it out of Saint Mary's."

"You were the one to get us out." He pulls back to look into my eyes. "I never asked but did you purposely drop that candle or was it really an accident?" he asks, a slight smile on his face.

I smile back. "A girl never reveals her secrets, William. But she does tattoo them onto her skin." I pull up my jeans to show him the candle tattooed on my leg. A single candle, dripping blood instead of wax.

His finger traces over it. "You saved us," he whispers.

I pull my pant leg down, shifting back to my breakfast. Enough sap. "Why are you still here? I thought I told you take the money and get Penny out of this shit hole."

"I can't take the money…"

I interrupt him. "It's my fucking money. I worked hard for it, and I want you to have it. Please. I need something good to think about. You and Penny are good. Knowing you are out of here, will give me peace."

He grabs my hand and places a set of keys in my palm.

"What's this?"

"It's the keys to Sylvia. You're buying her from me."

I try to give them back to him, but he shoves his hands in his pockets.

"William, I can't take the rod. You've worked so hard on her."

"I did and now she's yours. You've been itching to tag her with your art. So, make her yours. Besides, I'm the proud owner of a mini-van and as much as that kills me, it's safer for peanut. Plus, the rod only has two seats."

"Oh, William, this is a better gift than the roller skates I've always wanted."

"Not a gift. You bought her. It's the only way I take the money." He ruffles my hair like he always does.

"Where are you going?"

"Penny has an uncle in San Diego, he works on old cars. He's offered me a job."

I bite the inside of my cheek to keep the tears at bay. I don't want him to feel guilty for leaving me. He needs to go. Things are going to get ugly around here. It will ease my mind, knowing he's happy and safe in San Diego.

Our eyes lock. "I'm so happy for you, William. This is your chance to show everyone your talent."

"When you turn eighteen, come out and live with us," he says with tears in his eyes.

I shake my head sadly at him. "I've got a lot going for me here," I tease.

"I'm serious, Jesse. You aren't stuck here. You are such an amazing artist. You can make it anywhere."

"Don't worry about me. I've got big plans." I stand and scrape the remnants of my breakfast into the trash.

"You're not going to do anything stupid are you? Stay away from Jimmy and his crew. They won't go down as easily as Father Gabriel did."

Fact is, Father Gabriel didn't go down. No, he's still preaching. Just like Rick. I'm sure he is still being a creepy asshole somewhere in this world.

"Jesse?"

"Don't worry." I dry my hands off and toss the towel at him. "Jimmy taught me a valuable lesson. No more stupid... I promise."

He narrows his eyes at me. Big Dan walks back into the room, eyeing us suspiciously.

William gives me the biggest hug before giving me a gentle kiss on the cheek. This is goodbye. He turns, briskly walking out. I don't move until I hear the screen door slam shut behind him. I close my eyes, gathering every bit of courage I have to go on without him.

A warm hand touches my back. "Let's get to the shop, doll. I'm letting you work on clients today."

My eyes fly open. "You're lying."

He fills his travel mug with coffee, looking at me out the corner of his eye. "Why would I lie?"

I jump up and down. "Let's go then. I'll drive myself." I twirl the keys to my new rat rod around my finger.

"Ah, no."

"Dan, come on. You're going to deny me taking a ride in my first vehicle?"

He sighs. "Straight to the shop." He points a meaty finger in my direction.

I put my hands together all innocent like. "Of course."

He rolls his eyes. "Go on."

I rush out of the kitchen before he has a chance to change his mind. He yells out to me as I'm walking out, "If you deviate, I'll turn you over my knee, little girl."

I laugh at this. When I get outside, I stand beside the rod, so giddy I could squeal. She's beautiful. I love her unfinished rusty appearance. Dan walks out behind me and smirks as he tosses his leg over his bike. "You going to stand there and drool over that thing all day or you going to fire her up?"

I stick my tongue out at him but then I smile and get in my new car. She purrs to life and suddenly, I feel whole again. Shifting the rear-view mirror, I catch a glimpse of the rug burn on my face. Fuck Jimmy and his crew. Sylvia and I are going to have so much fun together. We're going to paint the desert red.

Fighting the urge to drive by the trailer, I decide to behave myself and head to the shop. I really need to hook up with my guys before word gets out that I'm pedaling dope for the Devils. Getting that shit under control needs to be my number one priority. If people stop trusting Sugar, then things will get out of hand fast. I can't have that.

But Dan is being overgenerous and letting me tattoo someone besides myself and him. I'm not going to pass this opportunity up. No way. Submerging myself in my art will help me more than anything. It will give my mind a much-needed break. It's why he's giving me this. He knows my body will heal but healing my soul... well, that might not be as easy.

My heart drops as I pull up in front of the shop. There must be twenty or more bikes parked in the empty lot across the street. All the men have Rebel Skull patches adorning their backs. My eyes drop to my lap. What did I expect?

Knock. Knock.

Slowly, I raise my head, my green eyes lock onto swirling, colored ones. Eyes that have haunted me since the first time I saw them. "Go away," I yell through the dirty glass that separates us.

Yeah, he didn't seem like a guy who walks away without getting what he wants. My door opens swiftly before I have a chance to lock it. He bends his tall frame at the waist, poking his unwanted self in my space.

"Get out," I say, shoving his head with my open palm.

He wins. Not because I can't shove his ass out. No, not because of that. It's because I'm stupid. A stupid, stupid girl. One who just discovered how soft his hair is. *So, so soft.* Pulling my hand away quickly, I scoot over to the passenger seat away from him. He slides right in beside me.

"You should know that your dad has assigned me the job of being the stink on your shit." One thing that is not soft about Dirk, is his voice. It's hard, with rough edges that scrape along my skin, making it pebble with tiny goose pricks. It doesn't even matter what words fall from his lips. He could tell me to eat shit and it would sound sexy.

Christ.

What the hell is this?

Maybe it's just because I've seen him naked. Yeah, that's it. *Forget, Jesse.* Just. Forget.

Now that the image is there, it's ten thousand times worse. A hot coil wraps itself up into a tight ball in the pit of my stomach.

"Did you hear me?" he asks, leaning forward to catch my eyes again.

Well, I'm not falling for that trick a second time. I stare out the passenger window. "I heard you. What do you want me to do about it?" I manage to spit out.

"I'm not asking you to do anything about it. I'm just telling you so that I don't spook you, yeah?"

Snorting, I turn to him. Finally, praise Gabriel's god, I find my balls again. "You? Spook me? Ah, not possible."

He raises his eyebrows, tilting his head in challenge.

Oh, fuck.

What have I done?

He crowds me again. Except this time there is nowhere to slide. My hand slowly reaches for the door handle.

Click.

"You weren't spooked when I broke Ricky boy's fingers?"

Pressing myself into the door, my escape route stollen from me, I shake my head.

"No?" His one-word response whispers across my face.

My green eyes lock onto his stormy ones. The coil that has slowly been wrapping itself around my insides squeezes painfully.

What the fuck is happening to me?

A slow grin spreads across his face.

Just like a cat keeping his prey caught by a strong paw, clamped on a tiny tail, he releases me.

Sliding back into his own space, he pulls his smokes from his front pocket. He taps them in the palm of his hand, catching one that slides out between his fingers. When he puts it between his lips, I unconsciously squeeze my legs together. The movement catches his eye. He chuckles lightly before releasing the lock button.

I scramble out of the rod, bumping into Big Dan as I do. Goddammit, he is like a brick wall. One that I'm always running right into to. He catches my shoulders, stopping me. He scowls over my head, looking behind me. The tick of a lighter breaks the silence. Hesitantly, I glance over my shoulder, swallowing hard.

A challenge begins to brew between cousins.

One wants to shelter me. The other wants to blow my house down.

Dan pushes me towards the shop, guiding me inside with a firm hand between my shoulder blades. Once inside, the tension breaks.

"What the fuck was that?"

Continuing to walk towards the back, flipping lights on as I go, I answer in as steady a voice as I can muster, "What was what?"

"Don't. Just don't. You..." he points at me before turning a finger on himself, "and me, we are one hundred percent honest from here on out. No more secrets, no more bullshit. It's my job to keep you safe and I can't do that if you keep things from me."

I pull a tray out of the cabinet, setting it carefully on the counter. I know Big Dan worries about me but if these damn men think they can suddenly start calling the shots in my life, they have another thing coming. I've been on my own since I was ten. Sucking in a calming breath, I face him.

"Someone has already beat you to that job. Dirk was just kindly telling me how he is my new babysitter." I fold my arms across my chest, resting my butt against the counter.

"What?" Dan, stares at me confused.

The ding of the door announces the man himself. His head swivels from Dan, to me, back to Dan.

"What?" daddy dearest, asks.

"Oh, I was just telling Big Dan here how you have already hired a babysitter, so he's off the hook."

My dad shrugs his shoulders, not denying it. Rolling my eyes, I turn back to my task. "Well, I don't need a fucking babysitter. I don't need a dad either, so..." I bite the inside of my cheek, choking back any emotion.

No one says anything to that. When I hear the squeak of leather as someone slides onto the chair behind me, I glance over my shoulder. Oh, hell no. "No, no way." I shake my head and start clearing my tray.

Big Dan's hands clasp around mine, he tugs, spinning me to face him. "We don't discriminate at this shop. He's a paying client and you," a meaty finger digs into my chest, "wanted to work here. Welcome aboard." He shoves a file folder in my hand before walking away. "Oh, by the way, I drew that up for him after he was paroled." He opens the front door and I flip him off behind his back. "I love you too," he says as the door closes, leaving me and my dad alone.

Smacking the file against my palm, I turn my attention to my dad. "Sure, let's do this. You trust me, yeah?"

"You could tattoo a giant dick on me, and I would proudly show the world." He shrugs out of his jacket, tossing it over to Dan's empty chair.

"One giant dick it is." I ignore him while I go back to work organizing the supplies I'll need. I casually flip the folder open with one hand. Slowly, I let my gaze roam from my tray over to the open folder. It's my name and birthdate, the script flaring with Dan's amazing artistry. This isn't fair. How am I supposed to do this?

My hands shake as I lift the stencil out of the folder. I'm not sure if it's because I'm nervous or angry, probably a combination of the two. "Where do you want it?"

"Right here." Shifting to see where here is, I catch him pointing at the bare spot over his chest. "I saved that spot for the girl who stole my heart," he says, cautiously raising his eyes to meet mine.

Setting the stencil down on the tray, I push the cart over to my chair, blinking back tears. Since Dirk saved me from Rick, I've dreamt of the day my dad would come for me. Why now? Dan said something about parole. Has my dad been in prison my entire life? And if so... what did he do to get there?

As I'm placing the stencil, I feel him tense, restraining himself from pulling me into a hug. My eyes flit up to his briefly. A million words hang in the air between us. There is so much he wants to tell me, so much I want to tell him. I've wanted to belong to someone for so long. Since grandpa and grandma died, my heart has longed for a family. Even if it was one person. One parent.

Blinking back more tears, I point to the mirror so that he can check the placement. He stares at his reflection, bringing his hand up to rub under my name. Regret and remorse stare back at him.

"Is it good? I can move it, it's not a problem," I tell him with an unfazed drawl, leaning back and stretching.

"No, it's good. It's perfect." He quickly sits back down in front of me. As I'm slipping my gloves on, I let my eyes roam over the rest of his ink. He has an impressive amount of it. Some pure shit, other pieces beautifully done. I notice a slew of dates etched from his ribs, running down, disappearing under his jeans. The contrast in ink indicates the dates were all done at different times.

The man is probably mid to late forties. He definitely lifts weights, a sign of prison life, being locked up with nothing else to do. His hair is the same blue-black color as mine, except peppered with silver streaks. Seeing myself in another person is weird as fuck. Aunt Renee doesn't look anything like me, neither did grandpa or grandma.

"Ready?" I ask, smacking my gum annoyingly.

He nods, not taking his eyes off the ceiling. Something about the look on his face makes me feel bad for him. No. Fuck that. I don't feel sorry for anyone. Not even my fucking self. Even if he regrets getting himself locked up and not being there for me, that is not my problem. He made the bad decision. Him.

"I'm sorry," he says so quietly I almost don't hear it over the buzz of my gun.

And there it is.

The words I've been dreading and longing for all at the same time. Ignoring him, I continue to punish his skin. I wish the needle would go deeper, would puncture his heart so he could feel the pain I felt while hoping he would come for me.

He shifts uncomfortably. Backing my gun away from his skin, I scold, "Jesus, sit still. You act like this is your first tattoo." I wipe the excess ink away before meeting his gaze.

"I'm so, so, sorry, Jess," he says with pleading eyes.

"You must be confused. I'm an artist, not a therapist. I'm not here to make you feel better about yourself." Rising from my chair, I begin to pull my gloves off.

"No." He reaches out to stop me. "I'll shut the fuck up." He leans back in the chair and closes his eyes.

Reluctantly, I sit back down. Surprisingly, he keeps his promise, even though he periodically opens and closes his mouth like a goddamn fish out of water. I'm not looking forward to all the words that are begging to fall from his lips.

Placing a thin layer of ointment over the finished piece, I hesitantly raise my eyes. He smiles at me sadly. "Done." My feet push against the floor, sending my stool rolling away from him.

I walk out, leaving him to stare in the mirror.

The heat hits me in the face when I open the door. Dirk is leaning against the building. I lean over and snag his cigarettes out of his pocket as I take a step down. He smirks as I put one in my mouth before tucking the pack back in his pocket, patting it for good measure.

Big Dan starts towards us from across the street. "No smoking. Jesse, goddammit," he growls.

Dirk tosses me his lighter. I light my cigarette and toss it back just as Dan joins us. I stretch my arm out towards him, keeping him at arm's length as I take a long, much needed drag. "After what you just made me do, you can fuck off. I'm inhaling this entire thing."

Dan places his hands on his hips and huffs like an angry mama bear.

I roll my eyes, sharing a knowing look with Dirk. He laughs until Dan slaps him in the chest.

"So, you next?" I ask, tipping my head towards Dirk.

Without taking his scowling eyes off Dan, he answers me. "Not a fucking chance."

"Why? Do I got you spooked?" Sarcasm drips off my tongue before I can stop it.

That fucking scary eyebrow pops up on his scary fucking face, sending my heart galloping and my thighs clenching.

Why do I do that? Why?

There is something that makes me want to push his buttons. Provoke him. He makes me want to run, only to see if he'll follow. God, what is wrong with me?

Calculating, stormy eyes make their way from Dan to me. Oh god, I'm going to pay for that later.

"I've got no room for you to paint your pretty pictures, baby." He gestures down his body with both hands. My dad joins us for a smoke. Dirk and I don't take our eyes off each other.

A slow smile spreads across my face. "You've got plenty of real estate. How about that empty spot on the top of your thigh? That spot's mine, *baby*." I back away, flicking my cigarette butt at him before heading inside.

I hear my dad and Dan roar at the same time. Fucking grizzly bears.

Chapter Thirteen

Dirk

Before you get your shackles all stirred up, hear me out. Jesse isn't your normal girl. I know, I know, she's seventeen but just so you know, the legal age of consent here in the great state of Nevada is sixteen. She's a year and fucking half above that. And... she looks and acts at least a good ten above that, just saying.

Now, I'm not stupid. I've not forgotten the risk to my balls or my dick. But I'm not worried about either of those. It's my fucking heart that's got me concerned.

She is my Eve, the girl who is going to lead me down a damming path. Oh, who am I kidding? I've been on that path most of my life. However, she is a hairpin turn. I can't see what's up ahead and I'm coming in at nine-o. I need to put my foot on the brake real quick.

Bill and Dan are both in my face the minute the door closes behind her. That little bitch is going to spend a considerable amount of time on her knees for that little stunt. When she turns eighteen of course, even though we already went through all that. Besides, I never said I was good man. I'm being generous here. She is asking for it. She will be begging for it by the time her birthday rolls around.

You know as well as I do that there is something undeniable between us. The push, the pull, the sparing, it's *all* foreplay. She's good at it and the most alluring part about it is, she doesn't even know what it does to me. Not that she's naïve. No, innocent may be the better word. She reeks of it. Unfortunate for her. Because it calls to the predator in me. I want to defile her, piss on her, mark her, *make her mine*.

"Don't ask questions you don't want the answer to." I glare into the face of my best friend, my president.

Bill snarls in my face as Dan flexes his fists. I get it, they want to protect her. We're all on the same page here.

"How does she know where your ink stops and starts?" Bill grinds his molars.

I drop my cigarette to the ground between us, grinding it into the pavement with the toe of my boot. My hand rakes through my hair as my eyes take in our surroundings. Lowering my voice, and leaning into his space, I give the information he won't like. "I checked on her while she was showering and caught her clawing at herself."

His eyes instantly soften, allowing me a glimpse of his soft spot. Continuing, I push the knife deeper. "The water was so hot it was scalding her skin." I step back, reigning in my own feelings about that night. "I went in for her."

He stumbles back, leaning his ass against the concrete steps. I pause long enough for Raffe to pass behind him, heading into the shop. Raffe gives us a once over but continues inside. When Bill's attention turns back to me, I finish. "She caught a glimpse of me when I put my clothes in the dryer. That's when she took the opportunity to make her escape. Don't worry, I won't get caught with my pants down again."

"Did she tell you," he swallows convulsively, "what happened? Who hurt her?"

"If she had, we would be knees deep in blood and entrails." I motion between the three of us.

He runs his hand over his face. "Sorry to jump all over your shit."

Waving off his apology, I circle around him and Dan. He should hold off on the apology because he will most definitely be jumping all over my shit again. My skin feels itchy, knowing Raffe is inside with Jesse alone. My head knows she's too smart to fall for the charms of Raffe, but my heart is beating a war chant, preparing my blood for a fight. I point to the door, maintaining enough sense to ask Bill for permission to leave the conversation. He nods once.

When I step inside, my muscles lock down one by one. Forcing air into my lungs, I control the urge to rip my pretty friend's head off his shoulders. Her face is inches from Raffe's cock. The fucker tips his face up at the sound of my entry. He winks at me with a shit eating grin on his face, one that is soon going to be shoved to the back of his nonexistent brains.

Raffe places his hands behind his head, relaxing into her chair in nothing but a t-shirt and tight-fitting boxers. My jaw clicks against the silence as I work my teeth together to keep my war cry buried in my chest. Jesse gives me a quick glance before returning her concentration to Raffe's body. Her hand clenches around his thigh. His tongue snakes out to wet his bottom lip while cocking an eyebrow at me in challenge. I'm not sure if he's trying to make me jealous of him or her. He has never hidden his attraction for me.

They are beautiful together. Her blue-black hair, lying in ropes across his thigh. His chiseled jaw clenches with each brush of her breath over his skin. She's so close to his crotch, I bet she can smell him. He lowers one hand and hovers it over her head, not touching but painting a sinful image of his fingers wrapped in her shinny tresses. A torrent of blood gushes to my cock, spurring me further into the shop.

Narrowing my eyes at him, I stalk towards them slowly, stopping only when I've effectively crowded their space, towering over the both of them. Jesse instantly reacts to my presence. The hum in her hand halts. Her eyes climb up my frame. Slowly, I release Raffe from my gaze and focus on her. She blinks rapidly before tearing her eyes from me to seek shelter in Raffe's. Whatever she was seeking, she didn't find. Comfort, reassurance, safety?

Nervously, she pushes her chair away from us. She busies herself with the tools of her trade. My eyes go back to him, silently scolding him. He shrugs his shoulders, running his palm heavily down his dick in a punishing stroke.

His hands grip the chair as I lean over to inspect her work. The sound of approval I make in the back of my throat, triggers him to raise his hips slightly. My eyes slide to his, promptly putting him back in his place. He dips his head in submission. He clears his throat. "I told you she was an amazing artist. Dan had been doing the piece but seeing as he's letting her work on customers, I thought it would be nice to have her finish it. You know since it's her design and all." He clamps his jaw shut and focusses his stare out the window, silently hoping my attention will wane, even though moments ago he craved nothing more than my full attention.

I grab his thigh harshly, turning it to inspect every puncture to his skin. When her hand shoves mine away, I raise my head to glower at her. She snaps her teeth at me in a possessive feline way before patting his leg to draw his attention back to her. "Leave us alone, I don't want to mess up Raffe's fuckable Grecian body."

"What did you say?" I growl.

She laughs.

I look around, snatching a chair and shoving it right up beside her.

She gives Raffe an exasperated expression. "Is he always this clingy?"

Raffe wants to joke with her, I can tell. They have an easy camaraderie between them. But he is aware of my arousal. It equally excites and terrifies him into silence. She laughs nervously when he doesn't answer, her eyes darting between the two of us. Shifting away from me on her stool, she braces herself against the side of his leg. "Ignore him," she whispers against his thigh, sending goosebumps to break out over Raffe's tanned skin. He stares at me over her head, pleading with me to spare her.

Too late.

Bill and Dan enter the shop, giving the three of us a once over. Dan points Bill in the direction of his chair while storming over to us. "Jesse," he growls. His eyes peruse over her current canvas. He tips his head this way and that as if he's searching for a clue to appear in the ink. A sexy smirk appears on her face while she watches him.

"Next time you secretly ink a cock on someone, you're fired." He points at her, his finger a sliver away from her nose.

She smacks her gum and nips at his finger. "One and done. I don't have a desire to tattoo anymore dicks on anyone."

Raffe sits up straight in the chair and pulls his leg up for closer inspection.

"Not you, dumbass." She shoves his leg.

He drops his leg, relaxing in relief against the chair.

"You love dick," I state dryly.

"Doesn't mean I want the veiny things tattooed on me."

"For the record, he said I could tattoo a dick on him, and he would proudly show it off. Guess he changed his mind," she says, glaring at Bill.

Dan snaps his gloves on. His face pinches as he inspects Bill's new tat. She didn't? She glances at me over her shoulder before bowing her head over Raffe's lap. The look of satisfaction in her eyes gives me the answer

I'm looking for. I stifle a chuckle and push my chair back to give her a little space. A little.

Her tenacity makes my balls ache.

Chapter Fourteen

Jesse

Thank Gabriel's God my dad and Dan came back inside when they did. The air was so heavy with... well, I don't know exactly. Whatever it was, it caused a physical reaction that I've never experienced before. I wish Dirk would take a step the fuck back. Christ, my skin is hot and itchy. "Dan, you stingy bastard, turn the air on."

"It is on." He's trying to fix the dick I just finished tattooing on my father. Hey, he asked for it. It was intricately hidden in the ink. He wouldn't have ever noticed but Dan has an eye for these things and I'm sure he picked up on it at first glance.

Blowing a wisp of hair from my face, I try to focus on the black rose I'm constructing beneath my hand. Dirk and Raffe's eyes are caressing my skin. My teeth sear into my bottom lip. I need the pain to distract me from the scorching heat their gaze leaves behind.

A blackened hand snakes into my vision. A thumb reaches out to tug my lip from between my teeth. I keep my hand gliding smoothly over Raffe's thigh as every other part of my body convulses at Dirk's touch.

I'm too close.

Too close.

I roll my head to the side, the loud crack my neck makes, does nothing to break the spell that lingers in the air. It hasn't evaporated since Dirk decided to pounce on me. No, not just me. My eyes dart to Raffe's. He stares at me. *"Run, run now,"* they scream.

My needle pulls up as I study his expression. He's worried for me, yet there is something else. One thing I've always prided myself on, is my ability to read people. When trouble finds me, I know. Not that it's ever helped, but it does give me a heads up. I'm having a hard time reading Raffe.

Dirk's hand ghosts over my back, his hot breath rustles the stray hairs against my cheek as he hovers beside me, pretending to study my art. Raffe's eyes pull away from me, seeking Dirk's. He blinks slowly, his sexy fucking lips parting.

Jesus, they are too close.

My body twitches to run. To fight their proximity. To protect what is mine.

I don't run. I never run.

You could surrender.

The word flits like a butterfly in my chest, banging against the wall of bone that protects my internal organs.

Surrender.

Surrender.

And then, the only man in the room who could burst my lustful thoughts, speaks.

"I've been talking with Dan, and we've decided that you will stay with him during the week and stay with me on the weekends."

Raffe's eyes soften at the sight of my anger bubbling to the surface. He grabs my arm as I try to push away from him. I pry his fingers off my arm one by one, glaring at my father across the room.

"I'm sorry, Raffe. I'm done for the day. Come see me when we're not so busy."

"Sit your ass down," Dan growls.

"No. I'm done." This is ridiculous. I've taken care of myself since my grandparents died. I've got shit to do. My own agenda to fixate on. I can't let Big Dan or a wannabe father, or two painstakingly beautiful men slow me down.

"We have things we need to talk about, Jess," my dad pleads with me.

"Well, you have about five minutes while I clean up." Swiftly, I gather my things, hurrying to put everything in its proper place.

"Jesse, the living arrangements are non-negotiable. Also, you need to see a doctor."

My heart stops, then lurches forward. I need out of here and fast. As if he can sense my haste, he hurries his speech, knowing that while I may not agree, I'm at least hearing him.

"My final demand is for you to tell us who hurt you."

"Your final demand," I repeat, deadly calm.

He nods his head in confirmation. His chest pauses as he holds his breath.

I let my fingers trail down the injury on the side of my face. Where was he when my face was rubbing over the musty, dirty carpet as Jimmy held my head against the floor while ramming into me from behind.

Gulping in a shudder of breath, I steel myself. I'm not giving these fuckers my tears. "I'll go to the doctor right now." *No fucking way in hell.* Dirk stands as I pass him, assumingly to be the stink on my shit. "Alone." I turn on him fast, shooting daggers between him and my dad.

Dirk throws his hands up in front of him in surrender.

Surrender.

Aiming my threat directly at my father, I draw a line in the sand. "I mean it, keep your dog off me or you'll see just how far I'll run."

Dirk growls and bares his teeth just like a canine would.

Fuck me if that wasn't the sexiest snarl I've ever heard.

With one last glance at Raffe, I push out the door, leaving the infuriating group of men behind. I perch behind the wheel of Sylvia, waiting to see if Dirk emerges from the shop. No one followed me. I text my guys to head to our usual meeting spot, keeping my eyes trained on the mirror, watching to see if the stench follows me. Fucking asshole.

I need to stay clear of him and Raffe. Whatever the fuck that was back there, it was scary. Being caught between the two of them felt like being trapped between hard edges and sharp points. One movement in the wrong direction and it could tear my heart clean open.

Alone they disengage my senses, together they rip those suckers out and fill me back up with a darkness that promises to steal my soul.

My pulse has always quickened around Raffe. I mean, you would have to be dead not to be affected by his disarmingly good looks. And Dirk? Well, Dirk is a different story. I have to will my legs not to give out on me when he is around. I want to both run to and from him at the same time. It's confusing. My eyes don't know where to land when I look at him. He is all the dark and dirty things you know you shouldn't want but yet you do.

My phone buzzes in my pocket. I pull it out, keeping an eye on the review mirror.

"Trailer. Now." Jimmy's grimy voice invokes a fresh wave of nausea to rise in my throat.

I don't give him the respect of an answer, I just hang up. I turn towards the trailer. May as well get this out of the way.

When I get there, he hands me a bag filled with dope. "I'll give you something, girly, you are ballsy. Aren't you worried about Bill finding out about this?"

"I'll worry about Bill. You worry about keeping your guys away from me."

He tips his head to the side, studying me. "You know it didn't have to go down like that," he says, pointing at my face.

"So, you're telling me I had a choice?" I back up closer to the door.

"Yes. You could have chosen not to steal from me."

Yeah. He has me on that one. "And you could have asked me to pay it back… with cash, not my hide."

He glances around the room as if searching for something. "I know that got a little out of hand. The president changed things up, it wasn't supposed to go down like that. I know it probably wasn't good for you…."

I cut him off with an incredulous snort.

He narrows his eyes but continues. "I can make it good. Let me show you how gentle I can be." He reaches for me as I dash out the door.

Only after I pull out of the court, do I breathe again. How the fuck is this going to work? Every interaction with him drains me. The faster I pull my plan together, the sooner I'll be done with him.

A billboard of a voluptuous seventy's era stripper winks at me in approval as I drive into the broken-up parking lot to the abandoned strip club. Tate, my main seller, walks up to my window. "Nice," he says as he drags a finger through the dust along the side of Sylvia.

"Yeah, are the others inside?" I ask.

"Yep." He eyes the bag in the seat next to me. "What did you want to talk to me about?"

"Well, I need to sell this shit for the Devils. Don't ask me why, I won't tell you. Just know I need to sell it and I want it done outside of Trap."

His eyes wander over my face and then they soften as he takes in the battered state of it. "Sugar, I told you those guys shouldn't be messed with," he says quietly.

I bang my palm on the steering wheel. "I know. I know what you told me, Tate, but I have to get rid of it. Can we cut it with something better, bring the grade up and push it in Reno?"

"How long are we going to be doing this?"

"Just a few times. Until I... well, until I can get rid of him."

His eyes go wide, and he hops away from the rod as if it burned him. He grips his hair, turning in a circle. "Jesse..."

"I told you not to call me that when we're doing business."

"This isn't about business. You're going to get yourself killed, Jess."

Tate and I have become friends. I guess you could say he replaced William after he and Penny hooked up. I trust him. He watches my back, knowing the drug world is not where my strengths lie.

Tate is tall, lanky, maybe mid-twenties, with a boyish face and charm. His hair flops over his brown eyes which he is always flipping out of the way. He started selling drugs to help his mom. She has cancer and her disability checks barely cover her rent and groceries, leaving nothing for anything else.

"I'll double your money for the risk of getting it from point A to B. Please, Tate."

"I'm not worried about me. You can't just get rid of Jimmy. Even if you succeed, there will be retribution. From the looks of you, you've already experienced some of that." He squats down and rests his arms on my windowsill.

My head drops back against the seat. "I know, I fucked up. But I have to try. He will never leave me alone if I don't."

"Yeah, you know I can handle it. Just don't go getting yourself killed." He flops his hair and lays his head on his arms. "Maybe I can be the go between. That way you won't have to be alone with him."

"No. I'm already asking too much. I'll be fine, I promise."

Tate gives me a big smile and opens the door for me. "Okay, Sugar, you're the boss."

I hand Tate the bag and he locks it in his truck as I head inside.

The good news is the market for dope is never ending.

The bad news is I hate it. I hate it all.

Chapter Fifteen

Jesse

All six of my runners had already heard the rumors that I would be selling for Jimmy. Good news travels fast. I assured them nothing has changed. I didn't lie. Sometimes, honesty is the best policy. Once they heard what happened, the first time I've told anyone, they all vow to have my back. Tate is going to handle the sale of their shit and the rest of the guys will handle things in Trap. Not much will change.

Donny approaches me as everyone else heads out. He hands me a wad of cash that will go back to the residents of Trap as I see fit. "Hey, this is shitty timing after what you just told us about you and Jimmy but...." he hands me a polaroid.

I stare at the photo, blood pumps in my ears and my hands begin to tremble. My mind races back to a time when I was young, when I was the girl in the photo.

"I... I figured you might know who she is and make this right. One of our new customers dropped this as he was pulling his cash out."

I slide the photo in my back pocket, no longer able to look at it. "Where does he live?"

Donny shakes his head. "Don't know, like I said, he is one of the newer ones. I think he lives over on the east side."

"Next time he shows up, follow him. Call me with an address when you get it."

He nods. "I've wanted to rip my eyeballs out since I found it."

"You did the right thing, Donny. I'll take care of it."

"Don't forget to take care of yourself too." He taps a finger under my chin. Donny is mid-thirties. He's been selling in Trap County for over a decade. I kept him because he doesn't put up with bullshit.

"Play it cool when he shows up again. He's probably wondering where he lost this. If you do anything different, he may bolt."

When all the men take off, I crouch down beside Sylvia and throw up. The picture is burning a hole in my back pocket. I pull it out and toss it face down on the passenger seat.

Fuck!

I sit in the rod for a few minutes before calling William. He answers first ring.

"Everything okay?" he asks nervously.

"Yeah," my voice cracks on the word when I force it out.

"I'll turn around. What is it?"

"No. Goddammit. Don't you dare turn around and come back to this shit hole. I... I just remembered something."

"Jesse," he sighs. "Are you alone?"

"Yes."

"Why are you alone? You have people. Lean on them. You shouldn't be alone after what you've just been through."

"What I've just been through?" I stare at the shiny black photo on the seat next to me.

"Yes, get your ass back to Dan's. Let him help you."

"Did you ever think about killing him?" I ask William.

There is a long silence that follows my question.

"Jesse, you're scaring me. Please go to Dan's."

"Yeah, yeah. I'm headed there now. You're right, Jimmy is just in my head, messing with me. Call me when you guys get there?"

"We will." He takes a breath and as he lets it out, he finally answers my question. "Yes, yes I've thought about killing him, every single day."

"Drive safe," I whisper before hanging up.

I head over to Samuel's hardware store. He looks up when I walk in. "Hey, Jesse. How's your aunt doing?" I smile and tell him she's fine. He's always had a crush on her. But he's too nice for her. Too good of a man. Her words not mine.

When I traded him cans of paint for her phone number, I had secretly prayed that they would get together. She turned him down and blocked his number. He's an attractive man, owns his own business and is kind. He is the perfect catch, but she turned him down because she didn't feel worthy enough to date someone like him.

He helps me lug all my paint out to Sylvia. "Whatcha working on. Any murals here in town?"

He's always bragging to the other store owners in town about how much people love the mural of the beach I did on the side of his building. He's brought a lot of business my way.

"No, nothing right now. I'm just restocking my paints."

He nods, offering me a little wave as he heads back inside.

I glance around the parking lot. It's odd no one has followed or called me. Maybe Dan and the rest of them have given up on me already. I was pretty mean back at the shop. Oh, well. I've got so much going on, it's probably for the best.

Right now, I need to paint. I haven't been out to the railyard in a long time. As I get closer, my mind becomes a colorful swirl of lines and curves. I pull up amongst all the abandoned railcars. Some are occupied by squatters with nowhere else to go. Before I head to the cars I've claimed, I walk around and greet the residents of rail town. Little fires pop up as the sun sets. I hand bills to those in need of food or clothing. Once I've made the rounds, I unlock my sanctuary.

I turn the lantern on and close the door behind me. The light chases away the shadows as my hopes and dreams come out to say hello. I have two railcars. This one holds my dreams. The other one… well, let's just say the other one I haven't unlocked for a long time. It holds my nightmares.

Chapter Sixteen

Dirk

I've watched the little dot flit around on my phone all day. This girl is busy. When she went back to the trailer, I moved closer to her. She must have been picking something up because she was only there for a few minutes. Now she's at the railyard, and she's been here for hours. Hours I've waited in the dark, watching the box car for movement. She's in there alone, what the fuck is she doing? Maybe this was where she stayed when she went missing.

The door finally slides open. She emerges and locks it behind her. I watch as she stares at the car beside the one she came out of. She unlocks it and slides the door open. The light of the lantern dances across her face as she holds it in front of her to peer into the dark car. Jesse stands there, swaying slightly. She looks tired.

Her bag drops to the ground beside her, and her hand goes to her throat. What the fuck is in there? Suddenly, she reaches out and slams the door shut, frantically trying to lock it. I slide off my bike. She's scared. I take a step but in the blink of an eye, she has her bag and is jogging to her rod.

I stand there a few minutes before walking over to the box cars. It only takes me a few seconds before I've picked the lock of the first car, the one she spent so much time in. I step inside and flick my lighter. She has a lantern right beside the door. I turn it on and close the door behind me.

My gaze wanders over the vibrant colors that adorn the walls, the ceiling, the old, rotted floor. Fresh paint stands out against the older faded pictures. Most of the old pictures are of a faceless man. The new one has a face. A face and a tattoo over his chest with her name. I rub my own chest as if the tattoo is on me. Christ, this girl makes me ache. Makes me... feel. Fuck!

I flip my phone to the video setting and stand in the middle of the car, slowly I spin in a circle, stopping on the most recent image. I pause there. He needs to see this. Needs to know. A box car filled with him and all of the things she loves. Rainbows, roller skates and happiness.

As I'm locking the door, I realize what this car contains. It's her. The girl she was before her world crashed and burned. Under all that spunk and sass, is a little girl with hopes and dreams.

When I unlock the other car, I see something entirely different. This one I understand. It's ugly and scary. It's her pain. Nothing looks newly painted here. No. This happened long before she came here. Demons, religious relics, skulls... death. I hold my arms out in front of me, studying my black ink, then I look back to the walls. A dark story. Mine's on my body. Hers is here.

A thud sounds behind me. I turn, expecting to see her but it's Raffe. He's on his knees. Fucker must have followed me, following her. "No," he whispers.

"You going to help me?" I ask as I light up a cigarette.

His eyes frantically dart over the images in front of us. "We have to be careful here, Dirk."

I place my hand on his shoulder and squeeze. "I was careful with you wasn't I?"

His eyes pull away from the darkness and come to rest on my face. The corners of his eyes soften as he takes me in. He nods. I pull him to his feet and watch as he runs his hands over the dark paint. He traces a cross with his finger before sliding over to examine the flames that start on the floor of the box car and climb up the walls, engulfing the entire ceiling. Demon eyes gleam, hidden by the dark smoke between the bright orange flames.

"Shit," he whispers, holding his hands in front of the painting as if he can feel the heat radiating off the wall of the box car.

"It hasn't consumed her," I say. He turns to face me. I nod towards the other car. "It's filled with good."

He closes his eyes. I remember dragging Raffe into the light. Holding him there, forcing him to look directly into it. I couldn't let the darkness swallow him like it did me.

And now, together, we will make sure it doesn't swallow her.

Chapter Seventeen

Jesse

D an seems surprised when I show up at his place. "You don't have to knock, doll."

"Yeah, well this is temporary. It's not my space. I'll knock." He holds the door open for me.

"What's mine is yours. We grilled some burgers. I saved you one in the fridge." Dan sits down on the couch and pats the spot beside him. "He waited you know."

"I know. I waited too... until he left." I lean against the wall and pick at the paint on my hands.

"How long are you going to beat him up?"

"Seventeen years sounds about right."

"Jesse, he didn't want to be away from you. It wasn't his choice."

"We all have choices, Dan." I push off the wall and head towards the back of his house. "I'm beat. Care if I shower and hit the hay?"

"Did you go to the doctor?" he asks, leaning forward and resting his arms on his knees.

I pause beside the couch. "What do you think?"

"I'll go with you," he says, holding as still as he can, like I'm a scared rabbit that will bolt. His face relaxes when I take the seat on the opposite end of the couch.

Biting my lip, I pull my feet up on the couch and shift to face him. "What do you see when you look at me?" I ask.

He tips his head in thought. "Someone I love, an amazing artist, a business partner."

I blush and drop my head so that my hair covers my face. That was not what I was expecting. I wanted to know why he looks at me different. He looks at me like Will does. It's... it's nice. It's safe. They don't see what other men see.

Dan slides down the couch, his thigh brushing my toes. He lifts my head with a knuckle under my chin. His eyes scan my face. "What's this about?"

"I'm sorry I've been such a pain in the ass. What a mess I've made of your life."

"Life is messy, Jess. Doesn't mean it's not worth it." He scans the rug burn on my face. "Let me take you to the doc in the morning."

I nod my head yes.

He smiles wide. "That's my girl."

"I'll warm your food up while you shower," he says, getting up from the couch.

"Thank you for everything. If you hadn't let me hang out at the shop the last three years I…" my words trail off.

He nods, he knows. While I'm grabbing some clothes from my bag in his room, I hear him on the phone with my dad. *My dad.*

Leaning against the wall in the hallway, I listen.

"I'm taking her in to see doc in the morning." He pauses. "What did she say?" Another pause. "Well, that's great news, one less problem. You never doubted she was yours and I didn't doubt it either. She has your fucking attitude." The microwave dings and I hear him shuffle around. "She'll come around, Bill. You can't push her. Let her come to you."

I push off the wall and head to the bathroom. Evidently, the paternity test came back a match. I have a match. A parent. What I've always wanted. But now… shit, I can't think about that right now.

There are bigger problems to deal with, one being the picture burning a hole in my pocket. Someone will die because of it. I just hope I have the guts to do it when the time comes. I will. I have to. No matter what kind of memories it conjures.

Chapter Eighteen

Raffe

Bill's jaw clenches as he watches the video Dirk is showing him. The one that will prove to Bill that his little girl is still there, she's just buried under her anger towards him. Question is, will Dirk show him the other video.

I told him I thought it would be a bad idea. That car was filled with her demons. Demons she alone will have to slay. I'm speaking from experience.

When I was thirteen, I ran away from home. It wasn't a bad home, but I was stupid. I thought something better was waiting for me. Their rules stifled me, or so I thought. Looking back, I see that my parents loved me. Their rules were there to protect me.

A friend of mine met a man who was going to help her break into the modeling world. So, one day her and I packed our bags and hitchhiked our way to the big city. When we got to the apartment on the business card the man had given her, it all seemed legit. We were both so excited. She was truly a natural beauty.

Anyhow, I don't need to go into details. Just know it was the last time I saw my friend. We were tossed into an underground world. Trafficked. It's not what you think. Not really what you even see on the news. I was trapped even though I walked free. Until I met Dirk. He saved me. He will save her too.

Bill sets the phone down and walks away. Dirk shuts the video off and pockets his phone. "We need to talk," he says, drilling me with cloudy eyes.

"Do you want her?" I bite my lip, clamping down on everything else I want to say.

Dirk's tongue runs over the ring in his lip, and he nods. I tamp down my jealousy. Dirk isn't into guys, much to my disappointment.

"Do you want her too?" he questions.

"I do."

He sits back in his chair. "We've got to get her out of the hell we saw back in that railcar before either of us have a shot."

"I'll let you lead." I lean forward, lowering my voice, "You have got to go easy though, man. You are one intense motherfucker."

He chuckles. "You love my intensity."

I narrow my eyes at him. He pisses me off sometimes. He flirts but that's it. It never goes beyond that. "Anyhow, we play bad cop, good cop?"

"That could work. You nurture her light while I stomp on her monsters." He tips his head side to side as if weighing his thoughts.

"Think it will work?" I drum my fingers on the table nervously. I'm worried for her. Dirk will scare the monsters out of her for sure. He did mine. She has one thing I didn't though. Me. I'll be there to tend to the open wounds he leaves behind.

"It has to. She's wound so tight, if she springs, she's going to explode."

"God, this sucks. This sucks!" I bang my hand on the table, making all the empty beer bottles bounce. "I of all people should have seen it. Should have seen how lonely she was. How hurt…"

Dirk stands up, coming over to stand by me. He grips the back of my hair and pulls my head back so that I have to squint into the morning sun. "What the fuck did I tell you about blaming yourself for shit that is not yours?"

I swallow hard. He lowers his face to mine. "If you can't handle this… you need to step the fuck aside." He lets go and shoves my head away from him.

God, he is such a fucking asshole. A beautiful asshole.

His phone buzzes, he glances at it. "Let's go. She's on the move."

Partners. We are partners. Normally, I'd be giddy as a fucking schoolgirl about that. I need to remember we are only partners because we both want the same thing. Her. The smart-mouthed, black-haired beauty that seems to be stealing everyone's heart.

I make the sign of the cross, *please forgive me, Lord, for what we're about to do*.

Dirk tips his head back and laughs. "What are you so worried about, Raffe. I'll take good care of you both."

Chapter Nineteen

Jess

Poked, prodded, violated. If I would have known what that appointment was going to include, it would have been a hard pass. Whatever. It's over. Big Dan stayed with me for the most of it. The least embarrassing part of it that is. Times like this, I miss grandmama so much. The doc gave me some sort of birth control shot, so at least there's that. Let's keep our fingers crossed that it won't be needed anytime soon. Jimmy better keep his end of the deal because I just can't. Not again. Not ever again.

Anyway, I got a clean bill of health, so I can at least breathe a little easier on that front. Also, Dan is so happy that I went to the doctor, he let me off my leash early. I told him I had to go see a friend. It was a true story, so I don't even feel guilty about it.

When I get to Jenny's trailer, the smell hits me before I even reach the door. Fuck. I knock on the door and Jenny's daughter, Katie, peeks through the window before slowly opening the door for me. "Hey, sweetie, is your mama home?"

She nods, her dirty hair falling in front of her face. She points to the bedroom at the end of the hall. My eyes take in the state of the trailer.

There's food left out, flies galore, dirty dishes piled high, and a mountain of dirty clothes shoved in the corner of the kitchen. Shit, she's using again. We don't sell to her. She has a kid and an addiction the size of Texas. I helped her get clean after I informed her she would not be getting any more dope in Trap County. She's been clean for a year, or I should say was.

Unfortunately, she's been getting it somewhere and I think I know where. I pull a candy bar out of my bag and Katie's eyes light up. "Why don't you go sit in my rod and enjoy your candy while I talk to your mama."

She takes the candy bar but pauses before walking out. "Mama's been sleeping for three days. She won't wake up."

"It's okay, hun. Go on. I'll get her up."

I watch until I see her open the door to the rod. She gives the steering wheel a tug back and forth, pretending to drive. Katie is in second grade. I've had to set a few kids and teachers straight at school for bullying her. It's amazing the girl gets herself to school every day. From now on, I'll be picking her up. She notices me watching, she gives me a shy wave before ripping the wrapper off her treat.

Blinking back tears, I make my way to the bedroom. When I open the door, the stench takes me back. Oh, my god. Jenny is sprawled on the bed in her underwear, she is breathing but she has puke in her hair. The sheets are covered in god knows what. Little baggies are scattered over her nightstand along with uncapped needles. Most of the baggies are marked with a black x, the crap the Devils sell. But there are two baggies with my skull logo on them. My heart sinks.

You know what you got to do, Jesse. *Sometimes, you have to get a little mean.*

I grab both of her ankles and yank hard, pulling her off the bed. Her head slams to the floor with a thud, that wakes the bitch up. She starts hollering and flailing her arms around. I drag her all the way down the hall to the bathroom, grab her under her arms and haul her over the edge of the tub. She is screaming at me, still confused as to what is happening.

When the cold-water douses her, she begins to sober up. She sputters and chokes. "What the fuck?" she yells.

I reach down and shut the water off. She tries to get out of the tub, but I push her back down. I wipe my hands down my jeans, then pull the polaroid out of my back pocket and shove it in her face. She pales and begins to tremble. Well, I guess I have my answer.

"Please don't call CPS," she begs.

I ignore her plea. "So, I know how you got my stuff. Who's selling to you from the Devils?"

"I haven't spent any money on drugs. I swear."

Like that makes any of this any better.

She continues spewing words like vomit. "Jimmy. It was Jimmy. I'm so sorry. He was asking lots of questions about you. I didn't tell him anything at first. But then he showed up with some of his guys and they held me down. I didn't want it. I really didn't want it." She shakes her nasty hair back and forth. "Once I start, I can't stop."

That's how he found out I'm Sugar. Jesus Christ.

"When he quit coming a few weeks ago, I...." she stops, unable to say the words.

"You traded Katie for your fucking fix," I finish for her, spitting in her face.

"Oh, god. I know. I'm so sorry. I'm so, so sorry," she wails.

This is my fault. Jimmy got her hooked again because he was looking for who stole his drugs and then when she couldn't get her fix from him, she sold her daughter.

What am I going to do?

"You have three fucking days to get this place cleaned up and to get your head screwed on straight. I'm taking Katie with me to keep her safe."

"O... okay," Jenny's chin wobbles as she accepts her fate. "I'll try, Jesse. I promise."

"Don't try, do it. If I can't be certain she is safe with you then I'm not bringing her back."

She nods.

I turn without another word. I'm shaking all over as I wash my hands in the sink. What the fuck am I going to do? I glance out the window, Katie is leaning her head out, watching the trailer with nervous eyes. Quickly, I grab a trash bag and go to her tiny closet sized room and dump the few clean clothes that are in the dresser into the bag. As I'm walking out, I turn back to look at her bed and see a fluffy teddy bear lying on her pillow. I place it in the bag carefully and toss it over my shoulder.

Katie pushes the car door open as I walk towards her. "Are you leaving now?" she asks sadly.

"Your mama isn't feeling well. What do you think about coming to stay with me for a few days? Your mom said it was okay with her."

She smiles big and nods her head. I push the bag behind my seat. "Do you want to go tell her goodbye?" I ask.

"No, thank you," she says quietly. She scoots to the passenger seat and buckles herself in.

When the suit lady took me from the Ditsworth's and then from St. Mary's, I felt relief. That's what I see on Katie's face. My heart hurts. It hurts more than it ever did for myself. She's so tiny. So vulnerable. I have no idea where to go from here. I don't have a home to take her too. Big Dan has done so much for me, I can't ask him to do this too.

"Do you want to go play at the park for a bit? I have a few calls to make, then we will go get something to eat. Sound good?"

She agrees, then reaches over and puts her tiny hand over mine. She whispers, "You haven't been at school all week." I can't decide if it's a question or a statement. Her eyes dance over the burns on my face.

She's worried that whoever hurt me might hurt her too. "I fell off a ladder when I was painting, so I took a few days off. We'll go to school together on Monday, okay?"

She smiles big.

When we get to the park, she runs to the equipment. She's probably thankful to be away from the trailer.

I sit down with a sigh on the bench. The world suddenly feels so heavy. What the fuck am I going to do? I can't call CPS, I just can't. The suits will move her from place to place. Good or bad, they don't care. I can't leave her with Jenny. What. Am. I. Going. To. Do?

Think Jesse, think.

I bury my face in my hands, overcome with Katie's situation, with memories of my own…

Someone sits down next to me. In one smooth motion, I have the knife in my boot out and pressed against the man's throat. Just as quickly, someone behind me places a knife at mine.

Raffe's beautiful, toothy, white smile breaks through my tear clouded vision after a few seconds and I drop the knife. The one at my throats

126

retreats as well. Dirk comes around from behind and sits on the other side of me.

"You can't sneak up on me like that," I say angrily, panting slightly from the surge of adrenaline. My eyes dart to Katie. She's oblivious to what just happened. Her legs pump back and forth as she glides into the sky on her swing.

"Who's the kid?" Dirk asks, lighting up a cigarette.

"Go. Away," I demand, glaring at him.

Raffe's hand runs over my back, enticing me to focus on him.

"Seriously, Raffe. You guys need to go."

He shoots me a sad look. What is he trying to tell me?

"Raffe and I aren't going anywhere. We have some things to discuss." He sends smoke rings swirling above our heads. "Are you babysitting or something?" He points his cigarette in Katie's direction.

Katie has stopped swinging and is staring at us nervously. No. Oh god, no. She doesn't think...

My brain rapid fires. I can't handle the look of fear on her face.

"Stay here a minute," I tell them.

Katie's muscles tense and I'm afraid she'll run as I rush towards her. "Hey, sweetie. Those guys are friends of my dad's, they aren't going to hurt either of us."

Her eyes focus past my shoulder to the two bikers perched on the park bench.

"I know they look scary, but they aren't. I promise."

Katie's gaze moves back to me. "You have a daddy?" she asks.

I nod. "He would thump them on the head if they hurt us," I tell her.

She giggles. "Will your daddy be home when you take me there?"

"He... well, my dad just found me. It's all kind of new, Katie. It's hard to explain."

Her eyes go huge. "You're big. If your daddy just found you, then maybe there is a chance mine will come find me."

And just like that, my heart breaks into a million little pieces. Katie reaches out and twirls a piece of my hair around her dirty little finger. "Do you think your daddy would thump someone on the head for hurting me?"

I shake my head yes. I already know the answer to the question, but I need to ask. She needs to tell someone. I've never told anyone what happened to me. I don't want her to carry that load. "Has someone hurt you, Katie?"

She nods and a tear runs down her cheek, leaving a dirty streak. I pull her into my arms. "He isn't going to hurt you ever again. I promise."

She leans back, wiping at her eyes. Her strength shining brightly against the dull desert landscape. "Pinky promise?" she asks.

I've seen girls do it. It always seemed a silly thing to do until right at this moment. I hold my hand up and wrap our pinky fingers together. She hugs me tight again.

"I'm going to go talk to my friends for a second and then we'll go."

Her little head bobs and she scoots herself back on the swing. I give her a few pushes before turning back to Dirk and Raffe.

128

They both squint up at me when I approach. Choking back tears, I ask for help. Something I haven't done since I asked Dan if I could borrow his drill. "Can you call him for me?"

Raffe takes my hand and pulls me to sit between them. "What's going on, sweetheart?"

I shake my head, unable to speak.

Dirk stands up. "I'll call him."

He takes a few steps away. Katie is watching me. I smile at her, she smiles back. Raffe looks from me to Katie and then back again. "Jesse." When I turn at my name, his eyes bounce over my face. "It's okay, Jesse. We have you. Both of you." He wraps his arm around me, and I sink into him.

Dirk walks back and gently pushes the phone up to my ear as he sits next to me.

"Jesse. Baby girl, what's wrong?" my dad asks calmly in my ear.

I press my lips into a thin line. I'm scared. I need him to be my dad right now, really be my dad. Swallowing my pride, my anger, I ask. I ask for her and maybe a small part for me. "I need help," I manage to squeak out.

"Oh, baby. I'm on the way." I can hear the wind as he heads outside.

"Wait. I was thinking maybe I could come…" my voice trails off. I don't know how to say it. I haven't had a place that felt like home in so long.

"Give the phone to Dirk, baby. I'll see you in a little bit, okay?"

"My friend, Katie…"

"Dirk told me. She can come too. We'll talk when you get here."

"Thank you," I say on a sob. I shove the phone back to Dirk, pulling away from Raffe. I take a few steps away from them, gasping for air. Once I've pulled myself together, I walk over to the swings and take Katie's hand in mine.

After I get her buckled in, Dirk leans through the window. "You okay to drive?"

"Yeah, sure. Katie and I are going to swing through a drive-thru before we head out of town, if that's okay?"

He nods slowly, studying my face intently. "Of course. We'll follow you."

I avoid his gaze and fire up Sylvia. He steps away. My eyes trail him in the mirror as he walks back to his bike.

"Ready?" I ask Katie.

"Ready for takeoff," she responds in a cute little robot voice.

We giggle.

While Katie is munching on her fries, I decide to call Dan.

"Hey, doll," he answers. He is at the shop. I can hear the faint buzz of the gun in the background.

"Dirk and Raffe are taking me to see him."

The buzzing stops.

"I figured now was as good a time as any." I drum my fingers over the steering wheel. "I'll be back Sunday."

"Jesse, that's great. Bill is going to be over the moon."

"Yeah, I guess."

"Do you want me to come down after I close?"

"You don't have to." I keep my eye on the Rebel Skull patches guiding me. They keep me moving forward. My outward appearance is calm, for Katie. But inside I'm screaming, kicking, and fighting. I want to turn around. Go back to what is familiar. What is safe. I sigh. It's not safe. Actually, it's not safe anywhere.

"I know I don't have to. Answer the damn question, Jess."

"Yes."

"See you tonight then. Anything you need me to bring?"

"Maybe the black duffle bag on the chair in your room."

"Got it. You're doing the right thing by giving him a chance. Have I ever steered you wrong?" The buzz starts up again.

"No." I pause. "Thank you."

He grunts and hangs up.

The good news is Katie is fed, happy and away from the people who hurt her.

The bad news is it's my fault she got hurt to begin with.

Chapter Twenty

Jesse

We travel north for a few hours and then head west, the dusty scenery changing before our eyes. Katie points out the window. "Look, Jesse, it's a lake!" she exclaims, bouncing in her seat.

I smile at her. I'd be just as excited except my nerves are getting the best of me. She rolls her window down and the smell of pine and fresh dirt permeates the inside of the rod, chasing away the smell of fast food. The air is cool here in the foothills.

We turn off the main road and head closer to the lake. A large warehouse comes into view on the west side. Bikes are scattered on the asphalt in front of the building. Dirk and Raffe park amongst the other bikes, pointing me to park up in front of a smaller building. The bay doors are pushed open. A couple of guys working on their bikes glance our direction before going back to work.

I shut the engine off and stare at the little girl in my passenger seat. Her eyes are wide. Maybe this wasn't the best idea. I forgot my dad is the president of a biker club. He lives here, with other people from the club but then she squeals, a high-pitched noise that confuses me. "Your daddy lives in a castle!"

My eyes go back to the warehouse. A castle? *Through the eyes of babes*, my grandmother used to say. I wish I could see the world the way she is seeing it. She's a brave little girl.

However, her enthusiasm changes the minute we are out of the rod. She presses her tiny body into the side of mine as Dirk and Raffe approach us. They seem to understand the situation and hover a few feet away as I pull the trash bag from behind my seat.

Wrapping my arm around her tightly, we follow them inside. When we step across the threshold, my mouth falls open. This is… wow, holy cow. It looks like we stepped inside a lodge. It looks nothing like I thought it would. I almost want to step outside to make sure we haven't stepped into an alternate world or something.

I glance up at the open balcony above us and there stands my father. He quickly heads for the stairs and jogs down to greet us. He doesn't take his eyes off me. Dirk stops him and whispers something in his ear. My dad's face softens, his gaze never leaving me. He nods, pats Dirk on the back and makes his way towards us. He slows when he is a few feet away.

"I'm so glad you're here," he says.

"Katie, this is my dad, his name is Bill." I squeeze her tighter. "Dad, this is my friend, Katie."

My dad lowers himself to one knee so that he is eye level with her. "It's nice to meet you, Katie. That is such a pretty name."

She blushes and rubs her dirty face over my shirt. "Hello," she replies quietly.

"Have you both eaten?" he asks, rising to his feet.

133

"Yeah, we picked something up and ate on the road."

"Let me show you to your room. It's upstairs."

"Yeah, it's been a long day," I tell him. He nods in understanding and turns for the stairs. Katie and I follow. When I pass Dirk and Raffe, I mouth a silent thank you. Both men nod.

Bill leads us up the stairs and to a room at the end of the hall. This place looks more like a hotel than a warehouse. He opens the door. The space is warm and cozy.

"I've saved this room for you for years. It's kind of surreal you're finally here," he says, walking over and pulling the curtains back. "I always thought you might like a room with a view of the lake. Maybe tomorrow we can go fishing or something?"

Katie lets go of me and hesitantly makes her way to the window. My dad stands perfectly still as she approaches him. I see a smile form on her face through the reflection in the glass. "Pretty isn't it?" my dad says.

He points to something outside. "See that wooden dock over there?" he asks.

She nods.

"That's my favorite fishing spot. I could sit there all day. Have you fished before?"

Katie looks up at him. "No, but it sounds fun," she whispers.

He smiles kindly. "Well, why don't you and Jesse get some sleep and then tomorrow after breakfast we'll head down there."

She nods, her eyes going back to the lake. A look of longing on her face.

My dad comes to stand by me. He points to a door. "There's a bathroom right there. I had one of the women pick up a few things I thought you both might need, she left it all in there. I'll leave you two to get settled. My room is right next door if you need anything."

"Dan is on his way. He's bringing my bag," I say, biting my bottom lip nervously.

"I'll have him bring it up when he comes." He opens the door to leave.

"That's okay. I'll come find you after I get her settled."

His eyes go to Katie and then settle back on me. "I'll be right next door, Jesse."

I drop my head and nod. The door closes quietly behind him.

Once my dad leaves, Katie goes back to her chatty self. "I can't wait to go fishing tomorrow," she says to the glass. I dump the trash bag out on the bed to find something she can change into for the night. She comes and sits down on the edge with me.

"I grabbed a few things out of your bedroom. If you need anything else maybe we can go shopping tomorrow." I watch her out the corner of my eye for any signs of distress as I sort through her things.

She latches onto the teddy bear and hugs it to her chest. "You brought Cricket," she says.

"Is that his name?"

"Yeah, I named him Cricket because he makes me feel the way the crickets do. I like the sound they make at night."

My throat tightens. "I think I know what you mean. I've always liked the way trees sound in the wind. They make me feel warm right here." I press my hand against my chest.

She nods and buries her face into the teddy bear.

I find a t-shirt and a pair of shorts that look soft. "Why don't you take a bath and then I'll tuck you in for the night."

"Are you going to sleep with me?" Her eyes roam up the bed.

"If that's okay with you. If not I'll sleep on the floor, and you can have the bed."

She shakes her head no. "I want to sleep here with you," she pats the bed.

I turn a few lights on in the room as dusk turns to dark over the lake. I pull the curtains closed after one yearning look from myself, then we head to the bathroom. Inside, we find a large clawfoot tub. Katie gets in and lies down, giggling. "It's so big" She stretches her arms over her head to show me just how big it is. I laugh with her, happy that she is happy.

On the counter are bags and bags of stuff. I find a big pink bottle of bubbles. "Do you want a bubble bath?" I ask.

Her head bops up from inside the tub. "Yes!" She scrambles out and starts stripping out of her dirty clothes.

I busy myself, filling the tub as she climbs in. She scoops a big handful of the bubbles that are piling up around her and blows on them, sending them into the air. I leave her to play in the tub while I finish unpacking the rest of the supplies. Everything a girl or woman might need.

Once Katie becomes wrinkled like a prune, I help her wash her hair and then get her dried off and into her clean clothes. "Come brush your teeth," I tell her.

She rubs her finger over the bright pink toothbrush on the counter, suddenly becoming quiet.

"What's wrong, sweetheart?"

"Nothing," she says, picking up the toothbrush and sticking it in her mouth.

"You know you can tell me anything?"

She nods, bubbles dripping down her chin. I wipe off her mouth after she spits in the sink. I grab a brush and we head out to sit on the bed. As I'm running it through her curly brown hair, someone knocks on the door. She jumps a little and slides behind me. I pat her leg to let her know she is safe. I won't let anyone hurt her.

"Come in," I holler.

Raffe opens the door but doesn't cross the threshold. He's holding a book with a plate of cookies resting on the cover. "Thought you could use a little bedtime story and cookies," he says, winking at me.

The butterflies I've always felt around him pound at my rib cage. "Awe look, Katie. Cookies."

She peeks around my torso, narrowing her eyes at him. He holds the plate out. "They're chocolate chip," he encourages.

She slides off the bed and takes the plate and book, quickly returning to me. She sets them on the bedside table and takes her position behind me.

"Goodnight, Katie," he tells her.

She waves but doesn't look at him.

"Good night, Jesse." His fingers tap over his heart twice and then he pulls the door closed.

Two minutes later, another knock sounds at the door. "Come in," I mumble around a mouth full of cookie.

Dirk pushes the door open. He leans against the door frame with two glasses of milk in one of his big hands. "Raffe is a dumbass. He forgot the milk."

I tip my head in warning and point to Katie. "Language, Dirk."

He smirks and Katie giggles. "You coming to get this milk or not?"

"Why don't you bring it in? We don't bite," I tease.

"Bill has forbidden anyone from entering the princess's cabin," he says lazily.

Katie giggles again. I turn and look at her. She peeks at Dirk from behind me, a clear interest on her face. She doesn't look scared of him at all. Which surprises me because he is a scary looking guy. They all are, but especially Dirk.

He winks at her and then his attention goes back to me. He holds the glasses out. I leave Katie on the bed to retrieve the drinks. When I try to pull them from his hand, he pulls back, tugging me closer to him. "We need to talk, soon," he says in a serious tone.

"Okay," I sigh, not taking my eyes off the milk in his hand.

He tips my chin. "I mean it."

I nod. "Tomorrow?"

"Tomorrow. Find me after breakfast." He lets go of the milk and walks away.

I hand Katie a glass as I sip on the other one. Katie is studying my face. "What?" I ask.

"You're so lucky. You have a daddy who lives in a castle, and he protects you by not letting anyone come into your room. And you have two boyfriends."

138

I spit milk out of my mouth. Quickly, I grab a towel and pat myself dry. "Katie. I don't have any boyfriends."

She giggles and slides under the covers. "I like the one with the tattoos best but the other one is really pretty."

"Katie, they are not my boyfriends."

I shut the light off and slide in next to her. She snuggles into my side like a little kitten. Sleepily, she murmurs, "Two boyfriends are better than one."

She falls asleep three seconds later. My fingers run through her curly hair. I have to protect her. She reminds me so much of myself. I don't want her to have to fight for everything by herself. I want to save her from all the ugly in the world. Katie can't get hurt again.

I run different scenarios through my head of how to help Katie. Only one ensures her safety. Killing the bastard who hurt her. One thing worries me though. After I kill him, who will try to hurt her next? I couldn't keep myself safe. I can barely keep my own head above water. How am I going to keep us both floating safely? Eventually, I doze off to the sweet scent of Katie's strawberry shampoo tickling my nose.

Chapter Twenty-One

Bill

When I was in prison, I would wake up sweating, shaking, terrified for my baby girl. I was helpless. All I could do was hope that someone was taking care of her. It was fine the first ten years until Tammy's parents died. I'm fairly sure I know who killed them. I haven't voiced my fears out loud. Their deaths were listed as accidental. Supposedly, there was a gas leak.

Jesse was the one who found them. She came home from school to find them dead in their recliners, or so I was told. I frantically tried to get her into a home of someone in the club, but no one listens when you are a prisoner. After that, it was hard to get any information on her.

Jesse's grandfather used to send me one letter a month. It simply outlined her growth, her accomplishments in school, when she learned to ride her bike, things like that. He also sent a photo. I lived for those letters.

Without the letters, I went crazy with worry. Who had my baby? Did they read to her? Did she have food? Clothes? Love…

Years I've dreamt of this. Having her home. When she didn't come find me, I checked on her. She was curled up, sleeping with Katie. She had her arm around the little girl, protecting her in their slumber. I'm not sure what has happened or who the girl is to her but whatever is going on, I can tell it's serious. So serious she came to me.

I haven't been her favorite person lately.

When Dirk called me and told me she wanted to talk to me, my heart burst. When she asked to come here, it burst again. And now she's here. For the first time in seventeen years, I feel whole.

Dan, Raffe, Dirk and I are all sitting here in silence, drinking from the top shelf. We started as a celebration of Jesse finally finding her way home. After a few drinks and discussion of what led to her being here, we have settled into a tense silence. She didn't come here on happy terms. She came because she is frightened. For Katie? For herself? We don't really know. Seems Jesse is a bit of a mystery. She has friends but no one seems to really know her beyond their own relationship with her.

Dan and she are close. I see it but even he knows little about the Jesse outside the tattoo shop. "Another bottle, boys?"

They all nod. I get up and head over to the open bar but stop as I pass the entrance to the hallway. Jesse is standing at the end of it, watching me. I turn to go to her but stop dead in my tracks as she runs to me. She throws herself at me. I open my arms to catch her, taking a step back to steady myself as she barrels into me.

An anguished cry escapes her. Her face buries in my neck, my beard shielding her from the world. "Hey, it's okay, baby girl. I got you," I whisper into her hair.

My baby is in my arms. Oh, god, how I've waited for this moment. She's so small, so fragile. She smells like heaven. I never want to let her go. Never. The guys quietly sneak out of the room to give us privacy. Dan gives us one last glance. He offers me a look of encouragement before turning away.

We embrace each other for a long time, then she gently pulls away. Her eyes say everything. She has forgiven me. I hope she sees the genuine regret in mine. We stare at each other, each of us really taking a good look at the other for the first time since our initial meeting.

"Do you want to talk?" I ask hesitantly, hoping that speaking out loud doesn't break the reunion that seems to be going better than any other I've tried.

"Sure," she says quietly, walking over and sitting down on the couch.

"Do you want something to drink?"

"Water is fine, thank you."

I grab a bottle of water for each of us and sit down beside her. She pulls her legs up and turns to face me. "Thank you for letting me bring Katie here."

"This is your home. You can bring anyone you like here," I tell her as I twist the cap off one of the waters and hand it to her.

She takes a sip and then drops her head. "I've made such a mess of my life," she says into the bottle.

"Jesse, whatever is wrong, please let me help."

"A friend of mine found a picture of Katie. Someone dropped it." She worries at her bottom lip before continuing. "Her mom is an addict."

My heart beats wildly in my chest. Jesse's mom was an addict too.

She reaches into the back pocket of her jeans and pulls out a photo. "This... this is hard to look at, but I can't say it out loud," she starts to cry again, the photo shaking in her trembling fingers.

Slowly, I reach for it. Jesse reluctantly let's go when I give it a gentle tug. One look and I see red. I turn it over and set it on the coffee table.

"I couldn't leave her there, Dad."

Dad.

She called me dad.

"And I can't call CPS. She would end up..." Jesse stops talking and scoots away from me a few feet.

"Like you," I finish for her.

She nods. I know she isn't saying this to hurt me. She's saying it because it's the truth. CPS did not do right by her. She doesn't want Katie to experience what she did.

"Does her mother know where she is?" I ask calmly.

"She knows she's with me. I told her she had three days to get clean. You should have seen it, dad. It was awful."

I scoot next to her, and she doesn't move away. "We will figure this out, together. Okay? We won't let anyone hurt her anymore."

"How can we do that? How can I keep her safe? I can't even..." She turns away from me.

"Jesse, please talk to me. I know someone hurt you too. Please, trust me."

Her wall comes up. "We just need to stay for a few days until I figure things out."

I lean back against the couch. She's shutting me out again. "I'd do anything for you."

She quickly stands. "Thank you. I'll see you in the morning." Jesse rushes out of the room before I can respond.

I rub at my eyes.

Please, let me in, Jesse. Please.

Chapter Twenty-Two

Dirk

I found Bill passed out on the couch this morning. I also found a disturbing photo of Katie on the coffee table. That explains why Jesse brought her here. My tongue snakes out to flick the ring in my lip. I can taste death in the air. Whoever took the photo is a dead man walking.

Jesse's been avoiding me like the plague. She can't run forever though. Bill took the girls down to the lake after breakfast. Her eyes flitted to mine before they walked out. She can run all she likes. What's going to happen is going to happen. She can't stop it. Raffe can't stop it. Not even Bill can stop it.

I'm a patient man but I'm also persistent. Jesse will show me her demons. How do I know this? Well, I'll tell you. I'm an exorcist. Ask Raffe. He'll fill you in. I cracked him clean open and sucked the poison straight out of him.

I can do in a week what would take a therapist years to do.

Is it painful you ask?

Yes.

Very.

No one gets through life without pain.

I watch them out the window. Bill is helping Katie toss her line out. Jesse is leaning against a pole on the dock, staring into the dark forest. The guys are all talking over each other behind me. Bill left instructions before he left. Find out who Katie's mom is and who sells to her.

"Why don't we just have Raffe go over there and fuck her. It would save us a lot of time. Thirty minutes with him and she'll spill everything Bill wants to know."

"Yeah, I can do that," Raffe says on a long-drawn-out sigh.

"He doesn't do that shit anymore."

The room goes silent. I turn to find them all staring at me, Raffe included.

"It's fine, Dirk. I got this. No big deal," he says, narrowing his eyes in question.

"I. Said. No."

"Like, never? Or just with this job?" Jared, asks.

My head slowly turns to him. "Jared. Your dick is up next. Go find out what Bill wants to know."

Jared nods quickly and rises from his chair. Before he leaves, I answer his question. "Raffe keeps it in his pants from now on. No more jobs. Ever."

Everyone nods, getting out of the room as swiftly as they can. I guess they can sense my foul mood.

146

Raffe stays in his chair. When everyone is gone, he turns on me. "What the fuck, man?"

"Is it really that hard to understand. You will no longer be doing jobs that involve your penis. Do you need me to spell it out for you?" I blow smoke towards him.

"Why?"

"How long are you going to let people use your dick?"

"Club business is different," he runs his fingers through his hair, leaning back in his chair.

"Is it?"

He doesn't answer.

"You want a chance with her? You gotta be clean. No other way."

"I thought... you said you wanted her and now you're trying to help me? How does that work?"

"Are we in competition?"

He stares at me.

"You know what I'm going to do to her. She is going to need both of us. In the end she's probably going to hate me. That leaves you."

"I still wanted you after what you did to me," he says, his eyes flitting over my face. He still wants me.

"We'll see," I say, leaving him to his thoughts. I decide to head down to the lake.

Jesse blinks up at me as I tower over her. "Got a minute?" I ask.

147

She looks nervously down the dock towards Bill and Katie. "Um, I'm sure they are about ready to go in. Can't it wait?"

I point to the forest and then walk into the trees. My confidence doesn't allow me to look back to see if she is following.

When I stop, I listen to her footsteps. Leaves crunch before she stills and the only sound that remains is her nervous breath. I turn to face her. She backs up against a tree. "What do you want?" she asks, struggling to control her breathing. She puts on a hell of a good show, I'll admit. But I can see through her air of nonchalance. She is terrified right now.

I take two wide steps, stopping toe to toe with her. She hugs the tree behind her as if she can meld herself into the bark.

"You're going to tell me everything I want to know."

She laughs nervously. "I'm not telling you anything." She shakes her head as if she is trying to convince herself of her statement.

"You will. We can do this the easy way or the hard way."

"What exactly do you want to know?" she asks, pressing her hand to the center of my chest. She gives a little test push before letting her gaze drift to mine.

I tip my head back and forth as if weighing my options. When my head stops, she cringes. She's good at reading people.

"No." She shoves hard now. I don't budge.

She needs to know. This is the trailer, the prequel for what is to come. My eyes follow hers as she tries to look anywhere but directly at me.

"I'm not telling you anything. Let me go."

"Tell me, Jesse, when did it start?"

148

She huffs and puffs. "When did what start?" she asks angrily.

"When did the hiding start?"

Jesse's chest rises and falls, rises, and falls. "I'm not hiding."

"Hmmm." I tap her head. "You're up here. Hiding behind a red velvet curtain, frantically trying to set the stage for the next scene."

She doesn't say anything. Her green eyes blink once. Twice.

"You see there are those in the audience who only care about what is playing out in front of them. They don't give a shit what goes on behind scene."

Her tongue darts out to wet her lips. The wind blows the leaves above us. The sun cuts across her face, the light bringing out the gold flecks hidden in the green of her eyes. A whole treasure is buried there. It will be mine.

"You've done a good job at keeping that stage set but it's getting harder and harder isn't it?"

"I don't know what you're talking about. Did you fall and hit your head this morning?"

I cradle her face in my hands. "Talk to Raffe. Prepare yourself. The three of us are going to take a little trip over spring break."

She doesn't say anything, her eyes never leave my chest. I kiss her forehead before leading her back to the lake. Jesse lowers herself back to her spot, leaning against the post. Katie and Bill are having such a good time fishing they didn't even notice she had left.

I take the post opposite of her. "Catching anything?" I holler down to Bill.

He turns towards us, smiling. "No, but that's not the point."

Jesse's focus goes back to the dark tree line. I wonder what is going on in that pretty little head of hers.

Chapter Twenty-Three

Jesse

Spring break begins this Wednesday. Four days. I have four days to prepare for a trip with Dirk and Raffe. I don't know where we're going or what we are going to be doing. I'm nervous. I'm excited. I'm terrified.

My life is getting more and more complicated. I really don't have time for Dirk and his mystery trip. I need to monitor Katie's well-being. Then there's Tom. He's probably wanting to visit his daughter in Phoenix. He goes every few months to see her and he depends on me to take care of his dog, Teddy. Then there is the shop. Dan just started letting me tattoo actual people.

On top of my schedule, there is Sugar's. She has a business to run. Funds to distribute. Product to secure. And of course, we can't forget she still has Jimmy to deal with.

I'll talk to Raffe and tell him whatever they are planning, I just don't have time.

Katie and I are sitting at a picnic table on the brick patio behind the warehouse while the guys are grilling steaks for supper. Katie watches as

I scratch out a drawing of her holding a fishing pole. "It's really cool you can draw," she says in her sweet little voice.

I rip a sheet of paper out of my sketch book, handing it to her. I give her a charcoal pencil. "Here you go. This is how I started, by putting pencil to paper."

She smiles brightly. "What should I draw?"

"Most of the time I draw my secrets," I whisper to her like we are two sisters sharing a private moment.

Her tiny hands spread over the paper. "Do I have to show anyone?"

"Nope. That's the best thing. You can keep your drawings all to yourself if you want to." I tap the end of her nose.

She starts to draw, her tongue sticking out between her lips in concentration. I chuckle and go back to my own drawing.

When the guys begin to tote the food out to set the table, she turns her drawing over and slides it under my sketch book. "You can look at it if you want," she says sadly then she looks longingly at the group of children who are gathering at the kid's table. Biker wives and girlfriends are getting them set up with watermelon and hotdogs. "Would you like to sit with the other children?"

She nods shyly. I walk her over and introduce her to the other kids. "This is my friend Katie. Can she join you guys?"

They all nod and a girl close to her age scoots down the bench and pats the spot beside her. "My name is Ally," she tells Katie.

Katie smiles at me like she can't believe the other children are letting her sit with them. Ally grabs her hand and pulls her down beside her. "After we eat you should come on the treasure hunt with us. It's going to be so fun. Uncle Bill even made us a treasure map." She pulls it out of her pocket and all the kids huddle around to study it, Katie included.

My heart warms. At home Katie is shunned. For being dirty. For her clothes. For her mom. For things Katie has no control over.

As I'm gathering my art supplies, the guys start to crowd around me. "Damn, I'm fucking hungry," Raffe says. I chuckle but as I turn Katie's drawing over, I stop mid laugh. A bought of nausea rolls through me. Of course, Raffe notices.

"You okay? Here let me get you a plate, you need to eat." He hops up but I stop him.

"No. I just remembered something. I... I have to go back to town."

Raffe studies my face closely. "I'll go with you."

"Don't be silly. I forgot I have a project due and was supposed to work on it with a classmate. I'll run over, finish it up and get back before Katie has to go to bed."

He waves Bill over to the table. My eyes dart to Katie. She is laughing with the other kids. I take a deep breath.

"What's up?" my dad asks.

"Raffe is making a big deal out of an assignment I need to finish for school. I'm just going to buzz back over to town and finish it with a classmate. I'll be right back."

"You're just remembering this now?" he asks.

"I was a little distracted with Katie. Can you keep an eye on her? I'll be back before she goes to bed."

He turns and looks at Katie sitting with the other kids. "Yeah, I can do that. I'm sorry I forget you are still in school. You seem so much older." He tucks a stray hair behind my ear. He wraps me up in his arms.

I bite the inside of my cheek hard to keep my emotions in check. "Drive safe, okay?"

I nod, tightening my squeeze on him.

"Get something to eat first." He motions towards the table of food, then becomes distracted by one of the guys and turns away from me.

Raffe narrows his eyes. I shrug my shoulders. Looks like I won this one.

Katie smiles as I approach. "We are going on a real-life treasure hunt," she tells me, full of excitement.

"That sounds like so much fun." I run my fingers through her curly hair. "Hey, I need to go to town quick to finish some homework, but I'll be back before bedtime. My dad is going to keep an eye on you. So, if you need anything, you ask him. Okay?"

She nods, her curls bouncing around her face. "I like your daddy. He's nice."

My dad comes over to the table. He places his hands on Katie's shoulders as he talks to the entire table of kids. "Get eating kids. There's treasure to be found in them there hills," he says in his best pirate voice.

They all laugh. "Are you going with us, Uncle Bill?" a little boy with red hair asks, crumbs falling from his lips.

"Sure am."

Katie stares up at him like he is the best thing since sliced bread. I guess I'm kind of staring at him like that too. Is this the kind of father he would have been with me? All of these kids call him Uncle Bill even though he isn't really their uncle. It's a term of endearment. One he obviously deserves.

"I'll be back soon," I whisper to Katie, giving her a quick hug.

My dad winks at me. Before I get too far away he hollers, "Don't forget to wear your seatbelt."

I wave without turning around. I don't want him to see how much that simple statement affects me.

Dirk and Raffe are nowhere to be seen when I leave. Thank god. I'm going to do something I should've done long ago. If I would have, Katie wouldn't have been hurt. Her picture was of a man dressed in black and a cross. What are the odds?

When I get to town, I stop at Tom's to change.

"I thought you'd gone and found yourself a boyfriend. Haven't seen you much," he says.

"No, just super busy with school and stuff. I'll try to get over more. Are you planning another trip to see your daughter?"

"No, honey, I'm too tired to make the trip. Maybe next month. That girl could come to see me, the road runs both ways."

Teddy gives me lots of sloppy kisses before going over to settle in front of Tom who has dropped into his old green recliner for the evening.

I change into her, Sugar, as quickly as I can. My heart pounds in my ears. This is it. I'm going to kill a man. I remember when I was little, my grandfather told me that he had killed men. He said once you kill someone it changes you forever. I asked him how many men he had killed. He didn't answer. It's all right here he said, running his hand over his tattoos.

Sugar stares back at me. Her sunken eyes and the hollow of her cheeks gives me confidence that she can handle this. I might not be able to, but she can. She has to. For Katie.

I sneak out the back door and hide my face until I get to Sylvia. When she purrs to life, I take a deep breath. I drive another hour, pulling up in front of the rectory just as the sun begins to set. Father Gabriel's car is gone. I checked the website before driving over. He's still the priest here.

Still here.

Still evil.

For now.

Soon, he will find himself where he really belongs.

I park a few blocks down and make my way through the alley until I end up in his back yard. The house sits in the shadows of the church. Its peak looms over me. It stretches for the heavens, the sunset painting it a pale pink color. The cross catches the last bit of sun, blinking at me.

Will Gabriel's god forgive me?

Do I forgive him?

If he truly exists, why did he let this happen to Katie?

To me?

To William?

Pulling my leather gloves on, I push on a few windows, finally finding one unlocked. I throw my bag over my shoulder and climb in.

Now to set the stage.

My breath catches at the thought. Maybe Dirk knows more about me than I thought. I push Dirk out of my mind and begin my search. When I find Gabriel's box of sins, which was hidden in the back of his closet, I sit down at the long dining room table.

My hands shake as I peel back the lid. Carefully, I pick up each photo, faces of broken children stare back at me. Eventually, the face that stares back is my own. The fear I felt that day rushes through my system. I didn't even remember that Gabriel took pictures of William and I until I held the one of Katie. The look on William's face breaks my heart into a thousand pieces.

There will be no more photos. It ends tonight.

I toss a length of rope on the floor near the door that leads to the attached sitting room and then I go to the kitchen, grabbing the most expensive looking bottle of wine I can find. I pop the cork and toss it into the trash.

Waiting in the dark, I pour a generous amount of wine into my mouth, careful not to let my lips touch the rim. The house is quiet, the only sound the tick of the grandfather clock in the hallway and my own breath. As I drink, I allow my mind to reunite with my memories from that night.

The good news is I'm about to rid the world of one sexual predator.

The bad news is there's more than one.

Chapter Twenty-Four

Raffe

Dirk and I stare at each other as we wait in the dark. She climbed in through a back window. We followed. She spent a fair amount of time upstairs but now she's in the dining room. It's quiet. She's waiting. For what? Or should I ask, for who?

I knew something was bothering her. She put on a good face for Bill, and he bought it hook, line and sinker. That's something Dirk is going to need to address with her. She can't be doing that. We can't let her begin her relationship with her father by manipulating him. She needs to be honest with all of us. Most importantly, with herself.

Keys jingle in the lock, the only other sound a soft click, the sound of a safety being turned off. God dammit, Jesse, what is going on? When the light flips on in the dining room, a man gasps loudly and begins to chant a prayer under his breath.

"Good idea," Jesse says smoothly. "But I hate to tell you, prayers don't work. Bad things happen no matter how much you pray for them not to."

"Who are you? What are you doing in my home?" The man asks, his voice rising along with his adrenaline. He's scared. Why is scared of Jesse?

I take a peek around the corner. Holy fucking Christ.

Okay, I see why he's scared.

I nod my head for Dirk to take a look. He does and his jaw flexes when he takes her in. These two are going to kill me. Could there be two more sexier people?

"You don't remember me? I thought I meant more to you than that." She fake pouts, the skeleton on her face turning sad.

The man studies her. "I'm sorry, with the makeup…"

His voice trails off as she shoves a photo in his face. "Jesse?" he chokes on her name.

She shoves the photo in her back pocket. "Have a seat, Gabriel. I can call you Gabriel, can't I?"

He nods and sits down in the chair she has placed a few feet away from the table. He glances at whatever is laid out on the table and pales. He sways to the side as she perches herself on the edge of the table so that she is staring down at him.

"How have you been?" she asks casually.

He grimaces and drops his head. "What do you want?"

She sighs and places her foot between his legs. His head bops up. Slowly, she slides her foot until the heal on her boot is digging into his junk. He tries to squirm away, but she digs in deeper.

"Let's just say I left feeling a little unsatisfied last time." She eases her boot back slightly, letting the threat hover over his dick.

"Jesse, you don't have to do this. Let's talk," he scrambles to reason with her.

159

She pours wine down her throat as he watches, then she leans forward, tipping his chin with her gun, the other hand holds the bottle over his face. "If I remember right, you like to celebrate with wine. Go on, open up," she seethes, her voice doesn't even sound like it belongs to her.

She pours from the bottle into his mouth. He chokes and sputters before she pulls it away, leaving the white on his collar-stained red.

"I'm sorry," he begins to plead.

"How are your legs? The fire didn't mess you up too bad I see."

"Jesse, please."

"I found your photo of Katie."

Now he truly looks confused. "I don't know any Katie. I don't know what you're talking about."

She grinds her heel into his pelvis. His scream echoes through the big old house.

When she pulls her foot back, he begs her, "Please, Jesse. I don't know a Katie."

"Get on the floor." She stands and points to a spot in front of a closed door. I notice the rope lying on the ground the same time the priest does.

"Jesse. Let's talk. I promise you I don't know anyone named Katie."

She points her gun at his face, sending him scrambling to the floor.

"Take off your pants." She motions with the gun towards his legs. "All of it. Underwear too," she orders, turning her head away to avoid looking at his nudity.

The priest begins chanting again. She ignores him as she ties a noose around his neck, securing it to the doorknob.

Oh my god. She is going to strangle him and make it look like he was getting off and choking himself.

Her hands shake as she finishes tying him up. Dirk slowly rises beside me, pulling me up with him. He whispers in my ear. "I can't let her do this." I nod and follow him from our hiding spot.

Jesse turns towards the doorway as we make our presence known. Her eyes widen. The priest notices us at the same time. "Oh god," he wails.

"He's mine," she says defiantly.

Dirk walks the length of the table, taking in the photos carefully laid out against the crisp white cloth.

The priest begins to beg us for his life. "Please. She's crazy. She set me on fire once!" he screams.

Dirk jerks to a stop. He glances at me. We both come to the same conclusion. The fire she painted in the boxcar represents one of her demons. One sitting pitifully on the floor in nothing but his black socks and shirt.

My eyes roam down the man's legs. The skin is puckered and waxy. Holy hell, if she set him on fire, she did a thorough job of it.

Dirk takes two big steps towards the man. The man thrashes around but it only tightens the noose around his neck. Dirk grabs his ankles and pulls him away from the door. The priest's eyes bulge as his oxygen is cut away. "Any last words for him?" Dirk asks Jesse.

With the slightest of movement, she shakes her head no, staring into her abuser's face. Dirk jerks him lower as the priest fights for air until everything becomes still. The priest. Jesse. Dirk… myself.

Tick. Tick. Tick.

161

Jesse is the first to move. She pours the rest of the wine down her throat, not stopping until the bottle is empty. She places it on the table and turns, walking out the back door without another look at the dead priest hanging from the door handle.

Dirk nods his head. "She isn't driving. Take her to Dan's. I'll get someone to pick up your bike."

I start to walk away but he stops me. "Tie her up, Raffe."

"Dirk."

"I mean it. If she runs, she will do something stupid. She's in way over her head. This is proof. He isn't the one that hurt Katie and we both know it. Jesse is about to hit rock bottom; you need to be the cushion to her fall."

"Don't worry. I know what it's like to fall without one." He pulls me into a hug. I breathe him in. It's been a long time since he touched me this intimately. Dirk has always been my rock. Now he will be hers.

I jog to catch up with her. She is slowly making her way back to the rod, her eyes pointed heavenward. When I get beside her, she doesn't acknowledge my presence. Jesse's lips are moving but no sound is coming out. She trips on a broken piece of concrete. I catch her before she hits the pavement.

Her glassy eyes try to focus on my face. I pick her up and carry her the rest of the way to the car. I place her gently in passenger seat and then slide in beside her. She wants to argue but she doesn't have it in her. She sighs and leans back against the seat as I pull away from the curb.

When we get to Dan's, she looks out the window to his house before turning to stare at me. Tears are streaming down her face, blurring the lines between white and black, turning her face a shade of grey. I run my finger through the heavy makeup, following a tear down her cheek.

"What do you see when you look at me?" she whispers.

"I see a fellow survivor."

She blinks. Her long eyelashes flutter against her cheeks, sending another string of tears racing down her face.

"What do they see?"

They.

Not him but *they.*

I know exactly what she means. It's something I've asked myself a million times.

"They don't see you at all," I answer honestly.

Chapter Twenty-Five

Jesse

"They don't see you at all," Raffe says.

They don't see me at all.

"Dirk and I are going to help you, Jesse. I've been where you are. It will get better," he tells me.

He said he saw a fellow survivor. Someone hurt him too. Who? I want to kill them. I want to kill all of them.

"Let's go in and get you cleaned up," he coaxes gently.

"I need to get back to Katie. I promised her."

"I know, sweetheart, but you can't go back looking like this." He points at my face.

Oh shit.

My hands fly to my cheeks. Oh, god. They've seen me as her.

"Jesse, hey. Please don't panic and run. You can shower and then we will get back to Katie. Everything is okay."

Once inside, I go straight to the bathroom. I'm about to shut the door but he stops me. He shakes his head. "Leave it open a crack. I want to be able to hear you."

"There are no windows in the bathroom. It's not like I can sneak out."

He leans against the door frame. "He told me to tie you up."

I take a step back.

"I'm not going to, but you need to understand something, Jess. This is no longer something you are going to handle by yourself. Neither Dirk nor I are going to let you pretend tonight didn't happen. That Jimmy didn't happen."

"I'm not doing this," I say, crossing my arms over my chest.

He shakes his head, staring down at his boots. "Not now but you will."

I push on the door. He steps back into the hall. I don't shut it all the way because I can't stand here and argue with him all day. I need to get back to Katie. Katie is who I'm worried about, not myself.

Turn the water on. *Don't think*. Wash my face. *Don't think*. Hair. *Don't think*.

Don't think about it. Don't think about it. Don't think about it.

When I get back to Dan's living room, Dirk and Raffe both stand up.

"We need to get on the road. Raffe is driving you," Dirk orders.

"I can drive myself." I shove past him.

165

He grabs me and spins me, so my back is pressed to his chest. His arms encircle me, so tight I can't move. "I'm all for choices. You can either let Raffe drive you or you can ride on the back of my bike. Choose."

My heart is galloping out of my chest. His breath is hot on my neck. His voice in my ear. It would be so easy to surrender. Surrender, my mind screams. But that's not who I am. I don't need them. I don't need him. I don't.

But it would feel so good to turn in his arms. To burry myself into him. Let him take care of me.

"What's it going to be, Jesse?"

"I'll ride with Raffe, but I'm not talking."

Dirk releases me. Immediately, I hate the loss of his strong arms.

"One more thing. Where's the photo?"

"What photo?" I try to shove past again, but he drags me close to him. He presses my head into his chest while his other hand presses against the small of my back. I squirm around, trying to break free.

I still when I feel Raffe's body heat against my backside. He begins to frisk me. I panic. Not because they scare me. Not because I don't like the feel of their hands on me. I do. More than I should. But because I'm terrified of how they will look at me once they see the photo of William and me.

When the picture is slipped from my pocket, I let out a sob. Dirk tightens his grip on me. His mouth presses against the top of my head. He places a kiss there. "I know everything feels out of control right now." He pushes me back so he can look into my eyes. "It's not. It just feels that way. Take a deep breath." His mood ring eyes glide over my face. When he's satisfied I'm as calm as I'm going to get, he lets go of me.

My head drops when Raffe hands the photo to him. I'm so ashamed. He shoves it in his pocket. "We will talk about this later. Right now, we need to get you back to Katie and Bill."

"Please don't show that to Bill," I say quietly.

"I won't." He places his hand at the small of my back and guides me out to the rod.

Before I duck my head to get inside, I pause. "Or Dan."

"I won't show anyone, Jesse. I'm just going to hold onto it for you. I'll give it back soon."

For most of the trip I lean my head on the door frame, watching Dirk's headlight behind us in the side mirror. Raffe doesn't push me to talk. Eighties rock plays quietly on the radio. Raffe taps his fingers against the wheel to each tune.

"Dirk says we are going somewhere over spring break. I can't leave Katie, so I need you tell him I can't go."

He doesn't say anything. Raffe stares straight ahead at the road.

"Raffe. I can't go. You know this. Please make him understand."

Finally, his eyes leave the road. He glances at me before returning his gaze to the highway. "Jesse, this is going to sound crazy to you but I'm going to give you a piece of advice."

I nod. "Go ahead."

"Stop trying to think ahead. I know you've got a lot going on in your life and in your head, but you need to focus on the now."

"I am but I have school. I have responsibilities." I throw my hands up in the air.

"Goddammit, Jesse," he says, grinding his teeth. I've never seen Raffe angry before. "All you need to worry about is being there for Katie and your schoolwork. Everything else we will handle together."

"Together as in you, me, and Dirk?" I scoff.

"Yes."

I shake my head and pull my feet up on the seat, hugging my legs to my chest. "You have no idea how complicated my life is."

"No idea? I watched you almost kill a man tonight. I think I have a good idea of how complicated things are."

I have no argument for that.

I'm used to doing things my way. Right or wrong. Raffe might know about this, but he doesn't know about the million other things I'm currently juggling.

My phone rings. I glance at the screen. I answer it, turning away from Raffe. "Hey, what's up?"

"That guy just left. You know the one who dropped the picture of the little girl."

My heart drops into my stomach.

"I followed him. You're not going to believe this."

I sit up straighter in the seat. No. I know who it was. It was Gabriel. It had to be. The photos and Katie's drawing prove it.

"He went to your fucking aunt's trailer."

"Who was it?"

"It wasn't Jimmy. He's a member of the Devils though. He was wearing their jacket."

168

I close my eyes, swallowing convulsively. Shit, a black jacket with a fucking cross logo on it. I was wrong about Gabriel.

"You all right, sweetie?"

"Yeah. Yeah. Call me the next time he shows up."

"Will do, Sugar."

Raffe's head is spinning back and forth from me to the road as I hang up. "Everything okay?"

"Is it ever?" I lie my head against the seat.

Chapter Twenty-Six

Dan

When one of the guys pulls up with Raffe's bike on the trailer he's pulling, I know something is wrong. I stop him at the door. "Where's Raffe?"

"Don't know. Dirk called and asked me to pick up the bike, he didn't elaborate on why and it's not my job or desire to question anything that man tells me."

An hour later Raffe and Jesse show up, Raffe driving her rod. Dirk pulls in behind them. What the hell now?

Dirk shakes his head at me before I get to them. I slow my steps. Jesse gets out. When she sees me, she wraps her arms around herself. I open my arms to her, and she quickly steps into them.

"You good?"

She shakes her head no.

"Okay," I say, then I say it again. "Okay."

The look on Raffe and Dirk's faces tell me she's definitely not okay.

I place my arms around her and guide her inside. Katie comes running the minute we step inside. Immediately, Jesse changes.

"Come help us," she grabs Jesse's hand and drags her over to the table where Bill and she have been working on a puzzle all evening.

Jesse laughs and lets the little girl pull her along. Bill watches them, his eyes never leaving his daughter. When she sits down next to him, he drapes his arm over her shoulders and pulls her in, giving her a kiss on the forehead.

She smiles at him. Not a hint of "not being okay" on her face. Dirk and Raffe stand next to me, taking in the scene.

"What happened?"

"We caught her in the midst of murdering a priest," Dirk says.

My head swings towards him. "What?"

"Remember when I found Raffe in Los Angeles? I'm going to need the same amount of time with her. You going to help me get Bill to see this?"

"Why was she trying to kill a priest? Please tell me she didn't do it."

"I finished the job for her."

My head bounces back and forth between Raffe and Dirk. "What the hell are you two thinking?" I shove them into the conference room and close the door behind me.

"Dan, this is her story to tell, and she is never going to tell it if you don't help me get some time with her."

"You tell me."

"No." Dirk stands toe to toe with me. "I don't even know the entirety, but I will and then if she chooses, you will hear it from her."

I push him in the chest, sending him stumbling against a chair. He rights himself, glaring at me. "I've known her a hell of a lot longer than you, cousin," I growl.

He holds his hands up in front of him. "Dan, I'm not pretending that I know her better than you. That is exactly why it needs to be me. She wants you to see only what she wants to show you. She wants you to see her as the smart mouth, tough girl that hangs out at your shop. Not because she doesn't trust you. But because she loves you, man."

I drop into a chair. Three years ago, that smart mouth popped into my shop, wanting a tattoo. Little did I know how important she would become to me. She's my friend, my fellow artist, the daughter I never had.

Dirk's right. Jesse has been in fight or flight mode her entire life. She hasn't noticed that there are people in her life who care about her, who will help her. She stomps around, keeping people at bay with her sharp wit and wicked mouth. She's used to fighting her battles alone, always hustling to stay ahead.

Jesse needs to slow down and let herself heal.

Dirk saved Raffe from self-destruction, maybe he can save Jesse too.

The thought both terrifies and gives me hope. I want to meet the whole Jesse. Is the girl that got left behind still there? Or did she get buried while trying to survive this dog-eat-dog world.

Chapter Twenty-Seven

Jesse

Everything is falling apart. Everything. Let's just start with the fact that I had the wrong man killed. Gabriel wasn't the one who hurt Katie. Now, I have to kill someone else.

"You want to see my treasure?" Katie squeals after she puts the last piece of the puzzle in place.

"Treasure? You guys found it?" I ask, following her over to a box on the coffee table.

My dad laughs. "Katie is a smarty pants. She was the one who figured out most of the clues I gave them."

I glance over my shoulder at him, smiling. She opens the box, shoving it in my face.

"Oh, wow," I gush over her newfound treasures. The box is full of candy, beaded necklaces, and a plastic tiara which she plucks out, placing it on my head.

She cups a hand over her mouth and leans in, whispering into my ear. "I told you your daddy lived in a castle, and you are his princess." She giggles, pulling back to look at me.

"I'm too old to be a princess. How about you be the princess of the castle." The tiara catches in my hair as I try to remove it before placing it on her head.

She dips her head and rubs a finger under her nose, sniffling.

"Hey, what's wrong, sweetie?"

Shyly, she looks up at me, then glances at my dad before turning her eyes back to me.

"It's okay. You can tell me anything, remember?"

"I don't want to go back."

Pulling her onto my lap, I hug her tight. "I'm going to do my best to keep you safe, Katie. I'll figure something out."

Ally, the little girl that Katie sat with at supper comes running down the hall. Her mom following close on her heals. I notice the mom bumps my dad with her hip as she passes him.

"Do you want to sleep in a tent with me?" Ally asks, grabbing Katie's hands and swinging them in the air.

Katie jumps off my lap and turns to face me. "Can I?" she begs. She looks so adorable batting her eyelashes at me.

Ally's mom introduces herself to me. "Hey, I'm Candice." She holds her hand out and I take it.

"I'm Jesse," I reply.

"Everyone around here knows who you are. Bill has talked nonstop about you." She offers me a kind smile and glances at him. "Is it okay if Katie joins us. A few of us are camping here this weekend. We have the tents set up by the lake. I'll sleep in the tent with Katie and Ally."

Katie looks at me with pleading eyes.

"Yeah, that's cool," I say. Candice pats my leg and walks over to chat with my dad. Katie and Ally squeal and jump up and down, hugging each other.

I'm so happy that Katie found a friend. My eyes roam over to Candice, her and my dad are blatantly flirting with each other. Candice gives him a playful punch in the arm before calling for the girls.

Katie gives me a big hug and then runs over to give my dad one.

After they walk away, my dad perches beside me on the couch. "Did you get all caught up on your homework?" he asks.

At first, I'm not sure what he's talking about and then I remember my lie and… I'm about to lie to him again. "Yeah, all finished." I snap my fingers and rise from the couch. "Shoot, I left my bookbag in the rod. I'm going to go grab it. I'll be right back."

"Maybe we can watch a movie together or just talk tonight?" he asks, his eyes full of hope.

My mind is racing, there is so much I need to do. I rub at my face. Did I get all the makeup off? My heart grips in terror as I think about the picture Dirk has in his possession. What if he shows my dad? What if he shows Dan? I spin around, looking for them. They were all here a minute ago.

"Jesse? Are you okay?" My dad places the back of his hand against my forehead.

I can't breathe.

I nod and turn away from him. "I'll be right back."

As I'm stumbling for the door, my dad's eyes glued to my back, I hear the guys come into the room. "Where's Jess going?" Dan asks.

Not waiting for his reply, I rush out into the cool night air. Quickly, I make my way to Sylvia so she can take me away. Somewhere I can breathe. Oh god, I'm not going to make it. My hand grips at my chest. I finally make it to my rod. With shaky hands I try to open the door, but I'm too far gone. I slide to the ground, pulling up my knees, gasping for air.

Dirk crouches down in front of me, resting his inked hands on my knees. I try to stand but Raffe kneels at my side and pushes my head down gently between my knees. "Breathe, Jesse."

Slowly, the tightness in my chest eases and air fills my lungs.

"That's it, nice and slow," Raffe says, running his hand slowly up and down my back.

Dirk sits back on his heels, lighting up a cigarette. His eyes swirl with mixed emotions. His attention is pulled towards the warehouse, he stands quickly. My dad and Dan rush towards us. Dirk tries to push them back, but my dad is having none of it.

He lowers himself to the ground in front of me, studying my face, concern all over his. I can't speak. I can't move. I can't anything. He doesn't ask me to. He pulls me towards him and then lifts me in his arms. Once we are inside, he gently lays me on my bed. I roll away from him.

The door clicks shut before I feel the bed shift as he sits down beside me. "Is this about Katie?"

I don't say anything.

He sighs. "Jesse, I know you probably don't see me as your dad yet. I want you to know that I see you as my little girl. You will always be my little girl. Please tell me how I can help you."

"I can't do this anymore," I whisper.

"What can't you do, hun?" He leans over me and brushes strands of hair from my face.

"Anything." I roll over to face him. "I'm so tired."

"Let me take care of you… and Katie."

"I have school and…"

He cuts me off. "I'm going to handle all of it. You just rest." His hand rests against my cheek.

"Okay," I whisper, giving in.

He stands to leave but I grab for his hand and pull him back down. "Can I ask you something?"

"Anything."

"What do you see when you look at me?"

"My beautiful, smart, baby girl."

I offer him a small smile.

He shuts the light off, pausing at the door. "Goodnight, Jesse."

"Goodnight, Dad."

He places his forehead against the door jamb. "I'm going to do right by you. I'll make everything right. I promise."

Sleep doesn't come easy to me. I toss and turn. Eventually, I wander to the window. There are a few adults sitting around a fire by the lake, but it looks like everyone else is tucked away in their tents. I hope Katie is okay. What if she gets scared?

The door to my room opens and Raffe peeks his head in. When he sees I'm standing in front of the window, he steps inside, closing the door behind him.

"I thought no one could enter my room," I tease lightly.

He stands beside me, both of us looking down at the lake. "He sent me here."

My head swivels towards him. He slowly turns to meet my eyes, he isn't lying.

"I'm fine," I say, getting back into bed. "You can report back that I'm in my bed safe and sound."

He pulls the only chair in the room towards the head of the bed and takes a seat, staring at me quietly.

"I'm not talking about tonight, Raffe," I say, stubbornly crossing my arms over my chest.

"Good thing I didn't come here to talk about that," he says, giving me one of his panty melting smiles.

I roll my eyes. "Then why are you here?"

He leans over, resting his forearms on his knees, his hands clasped in front of him. "Things are going to change and it's going to happen fast."

My fingers dig into the blanket. Raffe's words sound ominous.

"When I was thirteen I ran away from home. I thought my parents were assholes with too many rules. So, I ran away with a friend. We both

178

thought we were going to make it big in L.A. We were going to be models. She had been approached by an agent. But you know what we found instead?"

I shake my head back and forth, entranced by his story.

He laughs lightly, hanging his head, his hair flops over his eyes. It takes everything in me to keep my hands from reaching out and brushing it away with my fingers. He glances up, his piercing blue eyes glowing against the moonlit room. "The only thing we found in the city of angels were a whole lot of devils."

My mind immediately goes to the Desert Devils. The entire group of them are nothing but pure evil.

"You were hurt?" I ask hesitantly.

He nods. "It's a long story. One I'm willing to share with you but that's for another time. Right now, I just want you to hear how it ended."

He leans back, running his hands through his unruly blond hair. My wide eyes focus on him, hanging onto every word.

"One night, a man had me pinned against a brick wall in an alley behind a club. The bricks had rubbed the entire side of my face raw." He pauses to watch as I trail my fingers lightly over the injuries on my own face.

His eyes drop closed, his jaw tightens. I notice his chest expand as he takes a deep breath. When he releases it, he continues, "One minute he was behind me and the next he wasn't."

My breath catches. *Dirk*

"When I turned around, I found the most frightening man, pummeling the one who had held me to the wall." Raffe tips his head back over the chair to stare at the moon rising high in the sky through the window. "He took me."

"What do you mean he took you?"

His head drops back, his eyes locking on mine. "Dirk. He took me."

My head pulls back. Slowly, I pull the covers up over my chest. I don't want to hear anymore.

"He's going to take you too," he says, deadly calm.

My heart races. My dad won't let him take me. What does that even mean? Like he's going to kidnap me?

Raffe tips his head as he watches my reaction.

"I don't understand. What the fuck do you mean?" my voice rises to an embarrassing level.

"I'm going to put this the way he put it to me all those years ago."

I nod quickly, gripping the blankets to my chest.

"If you were to get bit by a rattlesnake and Dirk found you, he would first prevent the poison from spreading to the rest of your body." His eyes darken, he slides forward in his chair, resting his hands on the edge of my mattress. "Then he would make a small cut near the bite and suck out the poison."

My heart full out stops. What? Slowly, I edge off the other side of the bed.

"Jesse, you have to get the poison out or it will kill you. I know you are scared but I'm going to be there with you." He sits perfectly still. He doesn't try to reach for me.

"My dad isn't going to go for this. No way. Dirk can't just take me."

I back towards the door, away from Raffe. He may be beautiful but right now he is scaring the shit out of me.

A sliver of light cuts across my floor. My muscles tense. Raffe's eyes refuse to let me go.

Dirk wraps his arms around me from behind. His gravelly voice whispers in my ear, "The easy way or the hard one? Choose."

I stare at Raffe. This is not fucking happening. My dad is here. Dan is here. If I scream, they will come and stop this insanity. Raffe slides his gaze to Dirk's. He nods to him at the same time I open my mouth to scream. A needle sliding into the side of my neck stalls the sound in my throat.

What the fuck? Dirk releases me and I stumble to the bed, my hand flying to the sting in my neck. I feel more betrayed than I have in my entire life. Raffe climbs on the bed with me. "Don't be scared. It will be fine. Everything is fine," he repeats over and over, I think more for himself than for my benefit.

I glare at Dirk as warmth spreads through my body, lulling my muscles to relax. I hate him. I hate him. His calm mood ring eyes are the last thing I see as I fall into a deep sleep.

Chapter Twenty-Eight

Dirk

You're probably wondering how I got Bill to agree to this.

You see Bill hates anything meth.

I'll break it down for you in simple terms:
1. Meth killed Jesse's mom.
2. Bill killed a Desert Devil because he sold bad meth to Jesse's mom.
3. Jesse is now an orphan because mom is dead, and dad is in prison.
4. Jesse goes to live with grandparents.
5. He believes grandparents are murdered by the brother of the meth dealer he killed.
6. Jesse gets hurt in the first foster home.
7. Jesse gets hurt at St. Mary's.
8. Jesse gets hurt at her aunt's…. assumingly, by one or god forbid, more than one Desert Devil.

Now, here comes the real kicker.

As I'm relaying to Bill that his little girl was trying to murder a priest tonight, dressed full out like a goddammed skeleton, Jared comes back from his time with Katie's mom.

The bitch was so messed up she spilled everything. She rambled on about Jesse and how sometimes, she isn't Jesse.

I don't have to spell this out for you, do I?

As soon as we put two and two together, we discovered Jesse is the one and only... she is the Sugar that supplies all of Trap County with meth.

Not much surprises me but I'll be honest, this shocked even me.

Bill blew his fucking lid.

You know I'm sure there is a good explanation for all of this. He can't see that right now.

I can.

So, here we are.

Jesse was coming with me either way but having his blessing makes this much easier. For me anyway. Not so much for her.

Jesse is starting to stir, so I sent Raffe out for a walk. It's best she learns what she is in store for from me. I'm in charge here and she needs to know that.

She rolls onto her back and stretches leisurely. Her raven hair spreads over the pillow, a sharp contrast to the white of the sheets. Jesse's mind must be catching up, she stills and then bolts upright. Her eyes snag on mine.

"You," she growls low from the back of her throat. Her eyes narrow as she pictures all the ways she wants to be mean to me.

I don't say anything. Keeping my eyes leveled on her, I don't allow her a glimpse of the fire burning in my blood. She is the sexiest damn woman I've ever seen. Her anger only enhances her appeal.

"How dare you fucking drug me."

Slowly, I lean forward in my chair. "Says the woman who drugs all of Trap County."

Her anger vanishes, replaced by guilt. Which gives me my first answer. She didn't want to sell drugs in Trap. None the less she did. Yes, that is past tense. No way in hell is she getting near that shit again.

"I don't know what you are talking about," she says, not meeting my eyes.

I stand, sending her shuffling back against the headboard. I toss the little baggies with her logo on them at her feet. She stares at them, her hand unconsciously rubbing over her face, searching for left behind makeup.

Sitting at the end of the bed, I watch her closely. She sighs in defeat. Her eyes hesitantly seek mine again.

"It's not what you think."

"I'm not thinking anything."

Nervously, her eyes roam the room. "Where are we?"

"My cabin."

"Which is where?"

"In the woods."

Her eyes narrow again. "You can't keep me here."

When I don't say anything, she scoots off the bed cautiously, keeping her eyes on me. She edges to the banister that overlooks the living room. She gasps as she takes in the view out of the floor to ceiling windows. She spins to face me. "What the hell, Dirk?"

I get up and jog down the stairs. She follows but instead of following me into the kitchen, she heads towards the front door. "There's nothing but trees and things that would like to eat you for miles. So, unless you want to be something's dinner I suggest you don't go out unless you are with Raffe or myself."

She pauses with her hand on the doorknob. Jesse glances around, assumingly looking for Raffe.

"He's taking a walk. Don't worry, he knows what he's doing. He's been here before."

She hugs herself, defeat creasing her forehead.

"Come eat." I push a plate of fresh fruit and toast across the breakfast counter.

"Dirk," she says, choking on my name. Her face contorts at the emotions she is struggling to keep at bay. She breathes deeply before continuing. "Please, take me back. Katie needs me, my friends need me."

I sit down opposite her plate, pointing to it.

She must think if she complies that I will let her go, because she rushes over and sits down, shoveling food into her mouth. Maybe she thinks she can talk some sense into me. Sorry, not happening. When she takes the last bite, she gazes at me expectantly.

After several awkward minutes of silence, she tosses her napkin onto the breakfast bar angrily. "Now what?"

I put my cigarette out in the ashtray, blowing the last bit of smoke into her face. She waves it away, visibly annoyed with me. I chuckle lightly.

"Well?"

"You tell me what I want to know."

"Fine. Sure. What the fuck do you want to know?" She rolls her hands to hurry me, like she has somewhere to be.

"Why haven't you asked Bill where he was all those years?"

"Because I don't care."

I tap my lighter on the counter. "Why not?"

"Does it fucking matter? He wasn't there. Period."

"Do you think things would have been different if he had been?"

"Duh, of course things would have been different." Her eyebrows crease together. Suspicion is creeping up on her.

"How?"

"Dirk, Jesus Christ. I don't have time for this." She stands up but there is nowhere for her to run.

"Sit down."

She doesn't. I slowly rise from my seat. That makes her think twice and she parks her ass back in the chair. I drop back into my own, throwing the picture of her and William onto the breakfast bar between us.

She grimaces, turning away.

"Do you think that would have happened if he would have been there?"

"We both know it wouldn't have," she says quietly.

"And you're angry at him for that?"

"I'm not angry anymore."

"No?"

"No."

"What exactly did the priest make you and William do?"

"I'm not doing this, Dirk."

"You are."

She shakes her head back and forth frantically. "You can't make me talk."

"Let me rephrase. What did you hate most about it?" I place my hands behind my head, waiting for her response. I don't really expect her to answer much today. She'll fight me for a few days until she realizes we aren't going anywhere. That's the difference between me and a therapist. They don't give a shit if takes you ten years to get all the shit out of your system. Every appointment puts dollars in their pocket.

She bites on her bottom lip, battling with herself. There is a natural desire to purge yourself of the poison. It's embarrassment and fear of rejection that keeps people silent. Predators know this, it keeps their victim a prisoner in their own minds.

She surprises me by answering.

"I hate that William felt... feels guilty about it."

Jesse is something else. Always worried about someone other than herself. "What do you feel about it?"

She thinks about it. Her eyes raise to the ceiling as she stumbles around in her memories. "Confused," she simply says.

I nod, giving her space to explore that feeling.

She levels her eyes on me. "What do you see when you look at me?"

This is a question I've been expecting. She's asked Raffe, Dan, Bill and now me.

"What do you really want to know?" I counter.

"I want to know what the fuck you see." She bangs her tiny fist on the counter.

"No, you don't. You want to know why men keep hurting you."

Her body tenses. Bingo.

"Let me ask this. When you meet a man like the ones who have hurt you, do you know before it happens?"

"Not with Rick but the others... yes." Her eyes bounce over me.

"So, you think since you can sniff them out, that they are somehow doing the same to you? That they know you're a victim."

She nods, the first of many tears begin to pool in those beautiful green eyes.

"You're a smart girl, Jesse. You know they see the exact same thing everyone else sees. The same thing you see when you look in the mirror. The difference is the rest of us look beyond that. They don't."

Her head tips to the side, her lip trembling.

"When those fucks look at you, they see a beautiful young woman with curves in all the right places. Big green eyes filled with tears. Tears they love because they know they are for them... because of them."

She squirms uncomfortably, her arms wrapping around herself to hide the attributes I pointed out.

"Raffe was right though. They don't see you." I get up and walk around the bar, crouching down in front of her. "You." I jab a finger in her chest.

"When I look at you, I see the beauty they see but I see so much more. I see the way you bite your lip when you're nervous. I see the tiny gold flecks hidden in the green of your eyes. The light freckles across your nose, letting me know how much you enjoy being outside. I see the way you study the world around you. I see you noticing colors and lines. I see your mind creating images. I wish I could take a peek in there just to get a glimpse of the beauty you're imagining."

Her cheeks turn pink at my words. She blinks, forcing tears to spill down her face.

"You're not the problem. They are. You are nothing special to them. They hurt you because you crossed their path. Unfortunately, that's the way it works."

"Wrong place, wrong time," she whispers.

"Or you could change the way you look at it. Could it be the right place at the right time? If none of that would have happened, would you have been there to save Katie?"

"I didn't save Katie." She leans away from me, turning her face to stare out the windows. "She got hurt because of me."

"It wasn't the priest," I tell her.

"I know it wasn't. It was one of them," she spits the word as if it were poison on her tongue. She closes her eyes. "Jimmie went to Katie's mom to dig up information on who had stolen a case full of his meth. They were in Katie's home because of me. I did this."

"We'll put pressure on the Devils. Crow may be an asshole, but he won't want a pedophile in his club." I grab her hands as I say this.

"Wait, who?" She tries to pull her hands out of mine, but I tighten my grip.

"Crow. He's the Devil's president." I watch her closely. She is about to answer an important question without me having to ask.

Chapter Twenty-Nine

Jesse

row.

Crow.

Black Shirt, black pants, black soul.

Silver chain with a silver crow bouncing off black cotton.

Pain.

Hushed dirty words.

Jimmy's laugh.

The silver crow bouncing over my face.

"Hey, Crow, is she as good as her mom?"

"Yeah, and she's better than yours too."

More laughter.

"Jesse. Jesse," Dirk shakes my shoulders.

I blink as the memory evaporates. *Oh god.* No. No, no, no.

"I'm going to be sick," I say, pushing myself off my chair.

Dirk grabs me around the waist, hurrying me to the sink.

He holds my hair out of my face. My hands shake as I brace myself against the porcelain sink. Breathing in through my nose and out my mouth, holds off the wave of nausea. After several minutes, it passes but the tightness in my throat remains.

"I'm okay."

He drops my hair, running his fingers through the strands to smooth it over my back. Dirk corrals me between his arms. His hands come into view, bracing against the counter. His hot breath on my ear. "Do you know Crow?"

I don't answer. "Do you want to know why I haven't asked where Bill was?"

"I want to know the answer to both questions."

I trace over the skull on his hand with my finger. *Surrender.* I'm so tired of carrying everything by myself. Why not give him what he wants. He's strong enough to take it. He will absorb it and spit it out. "I know where he was, that he was in prison. I haven't asked about it because I'm scared to find out what put him there."

"And Crow?" he asks.

"Did he know my mom?" I counter, placing my palm over his.

His forehead drops to the back of my head. He nods against it.

I quickly turn in his arms. "Crow mentioned her…" my words fade as they leave my mouth.

Dirk cups his black hand over the side of my face, his thumb rubbing slowly back and forth over my cheek. "I'll tell you everything you need to know about Crow, Bill, and your mom if you tell me who did this to you." The fingertips of his other hand rain lightly over the scabs that have formed on my face.

"You'll be disappointed in me."

His eyes turn the deepest color of the ocean. A dark blue that makes me want to fall into them and drown. Dirk uses his thumb to trace over the seam of my lips. I bite my tongue to keep it from sneaking out to taste him. His eyes reel me in. "You could never disappoint me." He leans in so close I think he's going to kiss me.

My eyes fall closed as his thumb fades away, making room for his mouth. The sensation is so intense my legs give way, the only reason I stay upright is the press of his body against mine.

I breathe in deeply as he presses his lips against mine. He smells like a warm summer breeze. He coaxes my lips to part, his tongue hesitantly seeking mine. The moment they touch, the kiss deepens. His hands slide around the back of my head, pulling us closer. My heart falls into my stomach at an alarming rate.

My hands fly up to his chest. I don't know if I should pull him closer or push him away. Holy hell, he's solid. My heart gives in. I abandon his chest, exploring higher. My palms roam over his shoulders, climbing his neck, reaching the sexy dark scruff that covers his cheeks.

I grab his face, pulling him closer. He moans into my mouth as I do. The sound vibrates to the deepest parts of me, awakening the woman who's been sheltering herself in the darkest parts of herself. That woman wants to come out and see if the sun still chases the moon.

Dirk's kiss makes me believe in the possibility of seeing the sunset the way I did when I was ten, with chalky hands, a grumbly tummy, and dreams of roller skates.

He pulls away slowly, my body sways towards his as if we're magnetized. When the force lets go, he stumbles back. We stare at each other for several minutes until our breath slows and our hearts return to a normal tempo.

He smirks, licking his lips, stopping to give his tongue ring a flip. Holy, holy mother of god.

Raffe comes in, stomping his feet on the rug to knock the mud off his boots. When he looks up from his task, his eyes bounce between the two of us. "Everything okay in here?" he asks, my ears picking up on the hint of jealousy.

I swivel to face the sink, grabbing a glass from the dish rack. I fill it, watching the water rise, listening for any signs of what's going on behind me.

"Things are great. She's been talking and we just had our first kiss. I think it's rendered her speechless."

The glass slides out of my hand, dropping into the sink with a loud clank. Dirk reaches around, taking the glass from me. He fills it and walks away. I hear him set it down on the breakfast bar. "Have a seat, Jess. We are just getting started."

Raffe comes to stand by me. He takes my hand in his and guides me back to the breakfast bar. He takes a seat and pulls me onto his lap, keeping me wrapped in the safety of his arms. Dirk sits across from us. His eyes slide over the two of us, contentment resting over his features. He leans forward, narrowing in on me. "Tell me about Crow."

I pull the glass of water to me, slowly taking a drink. Stalling the inevitable. As I set the glass back down, I ask, "What happens if I don't talk?"

194

"Oh, you'll talk. We aren't leaving this cabin until you do. You have quite a bit of freedom right now. You're able to move around the cabin freely, but if silence becomes the norm, that freedom will dwindle until you have no choice but to give me what I want."

"Which are my words?" I shift on Raffe's lap. Images of being tied up with the two of them makes me feel a little funny.

"No. Your pain."

Crossing my arms over my chest, I sit up straighter on Raffe's lap.

"What's stopping you, Jess?" Raffe asks, running his hand over my stomach in circles.

That's a good question. What is stopping me? Obviously, Dirk knows a hell of a lot more about me than I thought. He already knows about the drugs. He's seen the photo of William and me. He killed the priest for me. *He killed for me.*

"Does my Dad know I'm here?"

Dirk nods.

"Did you show him the picture?"

"I told you I wouldn't show anyone." He flicks his lighter, sending it sliding across the table. It stops in front of me. He pushes the ashtray into the middle and sets the photo carefully inside. He nods his head towards it.

Raffe lets his hands fall to his side. I pull the ashtray towards me and stare into the eyes of a scared little girl, clinging to the first boy she felt safe with. A boy I helped get out of here. A boy who will soon be a father.

Gabriel is dead. William is safe and happy. And I'm....

195

I'm safe.

I'm safe.

My eyes connect with Dirks. Raffe sits up, pressing his chest into my back, his chin rests on my shoulder. Slowly, I turn my head. He smiles, his hand caresses my cheek. He drags our faces close, pressing his lips to mine in a single warm kiss. He pulls away, smiling. Boyish dimples deepen along the edge of his beard, giving him a youthful appearance.

My heart beats hard in my chest. Raffe kissed me. My head swings to Dirk. He kissed me too. When my eyes snag on his, I realize he's not jealous. And maybe Raffe wasn't jealous either. Did I read him wrong?

Raffe picks up the lighter, placing it in the palm of my hand. "Let's do this. Listen to Dirk. He helped me and he will help you too."

He pulls my hair away from my face, holding it in one hand. "I know all your reasons for wanting to keep it bottled up inside. I do. But you will never be free if you don't let it go and I don't just mean from this place." He swirls his finger in my face. "I mean free in here." He taps my forehead before continuing, "I'll be here to hold your hand through the storm. I won't let go. You won't get blown away. You won't get lost. I promise."

So, with shaky hands I set flame to Gabriel once more. Only this time, I'm not alone. I won't have to keep running. I'll be able to breathe and process because someone will be watching my back while I do.

As I watch the flames consume the religious man's sin, I tell them about that night. They do nothing but listen. When I'm finished with the tale from my childhood, I raise my eyes to Dirk.

"Katie drew a man in black and a cross. Automatically, my mind went to Father Gabriel. Because of the photos…" I let my words trail.

"He deserved what he got," Dirk states matter of fact. His finger jabs into the table to drive his point.

"Crow was there that weekend."

Raffe tenses beneath me. "What weekend, sweetheart?" he asks.

"The weekend you found me and took me to Dan's."

Dirk pulls his chair around the table to sit directly in front of me.

"Was your aunt there that weekend?" he asks.

"No. I hadn't seen her for an entire year, but she still left for work. A weekend client. She left me alone with him." I take a deep breath. "I hadn't planned on staying, even though the suit lady told me I had to. I knew what type of man he was, but I fell asleep waiting for Renee to leave."

Dirk looks over my shoulder to Raffe. "Why don't we take a break," he states more than asks.

"I'm worried about Katie. I need to get back to her. I have school tomorrow," I say impatiently. I'm willing to spill everything. I just want to get it over with and get back to my life.

"We're taking a break. Go outside and listen to the trees," he orders, pulling me off Raffe's lap. He pushes me to the door. I look back as he shuts it in my face. Raffe hasn't moved. His face is buried in his hands. He's upset.

"Dirk," I try to push my way back inside. My focus on Raffe.

"Listen to the trees. I'll take care of him," he whispers firmly in my ear.

"You said there were things that wanted to eat me outside and now you're shoving my ass out there?"

He smirks as he closes the door. The lock clicks.

Grrr… asshole!

I stomp over to the windows. My heart stills. My anger immediately dissipates in the cool mountain air. Dirk is on his knees in front of Raffe, staring into his eyes. He grabs the back of his head and pulls their foreheads together. The act is so intimate, it makes me ache to be a part of it.

Why is Raffe so upset? What did I say?

My gaze drifts over my surroundings as I back away from the windows. I walk down a little path until it opens to the most spectacular view of the mountains, and it steals my breath away. Suddenly, I feel ridiculously small in world.

I find a tall tree, and sit down, leaning against its trunk. My eyes climb high above me, taking in the height of the thing. Holy cow, it is amazing here. It's vastly different from Trap County. I breathe deeply, listening to the trees like Dirk instructed. Did he know that was what I was doing while my Dad and Katie were fishing?

There aren't trees like this in Trap. It's like they speak to me. I love it. A hawk flies over the expanse in front of me. Wow. If I were Dirk, I would never leave this place. It's beautiful.

It gives me time. Time to reflect on everything. The rat race of my life never gave me a minute. I don't think my mind has had a break since the day I found my grandparents dead in their chairs. The only time my mind has come close to having a moments peace, is when I'm creating art.

I close my eyes and listen. Katie's voice whispers on the wind. *I don't want to go back.*

I don't want to go back either.

Hours pass as the tree shelters me from the sun and I learn that the sun does indeed still chase the moon. My eyes drift shut as the gentle breeze whisks me away to a dreamworld. When my eyes open, I blink a few times, trying to decide if my dad is real or a remnant of my unconscious mind.

"You were sleeping so peacefully, I didn't want to wake you," he says, smiling.

Using my palms, I rub my eyes, then I try to stand. My stiff body protests louder than it should for someone as young as myself. Christ, how long was I out? Once my cracking bones bring me upright, I notice my dad is still sitting against the tree opposite to mine. *My dad came for me!*

"I knew you would come for me," I say shyly, brushing my hair away from face as the breeze teases it against my cheeks.

"Oh, baby girl." He runs his hand over his short dark hair.

"I told Dirk I had school. I don't know what he was thinking, dragging me up here."

He pats the spot beside him. I lower myself back down, reluctantly. He pulls up a knee and rests his arm over the top of it. He takes a deep breath before he speaks. "I'm not here to take you off the mountain."

My eyes bounce back and forth over his face. What is he trying to tell me? I have to go back. I have school. I have Katie. I have Sugar.

He laughs as he runs the tip of his index finger between my eyebrows. "Your mama used to scowl at me just like that."

"Did you have someone kidnap her too?" I pull my head away, turning away from him.

"Actually, yes."

When I glance at him, I see he isn't teasing. He actually had my mother kidnapped.

"Only once when she was pregnant with you. I kidnapped her. No matter what I said, she couldn't keep the needle out of her arm. I did it for you. To keep you healthy. It was the only way."

My mouth forms a perfect little o, but no words follow.

"I can't let you go back there," he says while watching me struggle for words.

"What do you mean? I live there."

He shakes his head. "Not anymore. You live with me." He points up the path towards the cabin. "I brought you a laptop and everything you will need for the online classes I enrolled you in."

I stare blankly at him.

"The school counselor helped me get it all set up. She said that you had enough credits you could have graduated at the end of last year but that you had wanted to continue your education on through your senior year." He stops, waiting for a response from me.

When I don't offer one, he continues.

"Dan is getting you set up with a work area at the warehouse. There are plenty of clients right in our own club. You can flex your tattooing skills on them." He's tiptoeing now. He knows he's treading in dangerous waters.

The slow thud of my heartbeat is picking up speed with each word out of his mouth. "I… I don't understand," I mutter, pulling my legs up and hugging them to my chest. "I'm talking, isn't that what you wanted? Isn't that why I'm here? I'll tell you whatever you want to know."

He reaches out and tucks my hair behind my ear. "I know you are, baby girl." His hand drops away. The mountain draws his attention away from me. He stares out for a long time before turning his eyes back to me.

"I'm sorry I wasn't there. I left you with your grandparents. I thought you would be safe."

"I was," I murmur quietly.

He smiles sadly. "I know you were." He picks up a stick, scratching absentmindedly in the dirt. "I tried to petition the state to give Candice temporary custody, but I couldn't get anyone to listen to me. Your mother didn't put me on your birth certificate." He stabs the stick in the dirt. "It was all one big cluster fuck. I was young and stupid. I failed you."

"It's fine. I survived. I need to go back to Trap, dad. There's so much…"

He raises his hand, cutting me off. "No. Let me finish."

I rest my chin on my knees, shutting my mouth. The scowl creeping back on my face.

"I'm so proud of you, Jesse. You did survive. You fought your battles with the bravery of a true Rebel Skull. You may not have known you were one of us, but your heart did."

My cheeks heat not from his compliment but from my own thoughts. I've always wanted to be one of them since the day I met the scary man with pictures on his skin. The same day my heart melted for mood ring eyes. I didn't know he belonged to a biker gang then, but I wanted to be a part of his world, whatever that was. And then I met Raffe. I've watched his beautiful body slip in and out of his Rebel Skull jacket since I was fourteen years old. My pulse spiking at every smile, wink, and kick start of his bike.

"So, why are you taking everything away from me? Why are you punishing me?" I try to push myself up off the ground, he pulls my hand out from under me, making me totter back on my behind.

"That's not fair, Jesse. I'm not trying to punish you. I think you've been punished enough for one lifetime."

I close my eyes, blocking out the beautiful sky as dusk settles over the mountain. "I want to go back to Trap."

"It's just not happening, Jesse."

I open my eyes slowly, silently begging, pleading with every drop of my soul. "Dad, please."

He shakes his head. "This is the only way, baby girl."

I tuck my face and hug my knees tight, curling up into a tiny ball. His hand rests on the small of my back.

"You're selling drugs, Jess. I'm not judging you, but I can't let that continue."

When I don't say anything, he lifts himself up from the hard ground.

Suddenly, my anger spikes. I jump to my feet. "You are judging me. I can hear it in your tone." I step away from him. "You're a fucking hypocrite. You were in prison for how many years?" Tossing my hands in the air, I storm up the path.

His boots thump, following closely behind me. He grabs my arm, spinning me to face him.

"Jesse. I'm trying to be a good father for once in my pathetic life."

I cross my arms over my chest as he pulls me close to him.

"God, Jess, I only want to see you smile. I don't want to make you angry, but I've got to give you some tough love here."

He holds me tight. I swallow big gulps of air, trying to shove the new feelings I'm having down. With a last-ditch effort to hang on to my past, to go back to the only life I've ever known, I beg pitifully... tears, snot, and all. "Dad, please. I can't just stop. My guys are going to wonder where I am. The people I help in Trap need me. Old man Tom, Jimmy..."

He growls and tightens his hold on me. His mouth lowers to my ear. "Stop. It's over, Jess. I'm taking care of everything. You're going to stay here and learn how to breathe again. When we think you're ready, you'll come home. Get right with this so you can get back to me." He tugs me in hard. "You belong with me. I don't give two craps about anyone in Trap County."

I cry harder, my anger turning to shame. "I'm sorry. I'm so, so sorry. I... I don't know what I was thinking when I started selling. Part of me wanted to get even with Jimmy for taking the door off my room and part of me wanted to help people. I didn't spend the money on myself, I promise. I gave it back to the people..." I stop, unable to go on I'm crying so hard.

"It's okay, baby girl," he shushes, rocking me in his arms. "You're looking at this like it's a bad thing. Getting away from that godforsaken hell hole is not a bad thing, Jesse. It's a fresh start for you... for me."

He holds my arms, pushing me back so he can see my face. He wipes my tears and snot away with his bare hands, brushing them off on his jeans. I give him a small cockeyed grin. Only a parent would willingly stick their hand in snot.

"So, what do you say? Are you ready to go back? Dan and I brought pizza." He bites his lip, trying to sweet talk me back inside.

I shake my head yes, earning me a handsome smile. He takes my hand and steers us back up the path. I glance over my shoulder as the last bit of light is chased out by the night. For the first time in my entire life, I feel like I belong. My dad is holding my hand, watching my back, and guarding my heart. He smiles down at me as we walk.

The good news is it's getting easier and easier to smile back.

The bad news is an ominous black crow shrieks at us from a nearby bush. A sign that bad things are still coming for me.

Chapter Thirty

Jesse

The rest of the evening goes smoothly. The guys are out on the deck, having few beers while I sit on the couch, clicking away on the computer. I run through my new "online" classes. Sighing, I resign myself to the fact that this is how I'm finishing out my senior year. It's fine. I didn't have any friends at school anyway. They either thought I was a stuck-up nerd, or they were afraid of me. My counselor was right. I had enough credits to graduate last year but why? I like learning new things.

I'm engrossed in my studies when Dan sits down beside me, draping his arm along the back of the couch behind my head. "You're handling this way better than I thought." He smirks before bringing his beer bottle to his mouth.

I tap my pencil on my chin. "Oh, I'm sorry, did I have a choice in the matter?"

He laughs and runs his hand over his eyes. "I'm going to miss your smart mouth."

"Bill says you are setting me up at the warehouse so I can tattoo there," I whisper, biting my lip to keep from crying… again.

"I'll set it up just like at the shop so that you know where to find everything." He looks away from me.

I close my laptop, setting it on the table. "Dan, you don't have to do that. I don't want to tattoo there. It won't be the same," I curl myself up into a small ball and snuggle into his side. He drops his arm around my shoulder, pulling me in closer. "I don't want to do it without you."

"Awe, Jesse. Jesse, Jesse, Jesse," he sighs.

And now I'm fucking crying again.

I hear the door slide open, the rest of the guys are coming in. Quickly, I pull my shirt up over my face, trying to wipe the evidence of my weakness from my face.

Dan tugs it back down over my stomach. "Stop, you can let people see you're fucking human, Jesse."

I hide my face in his shirt instead. He chuckles, making his big body shake. "Always got to be difficult."

My dad sits on the coffee table in front of us. I peek at him from behind my hands. "Dan and I need to get going. We'll see you soon, no need for tears."

"Easy for you to say. You're not giving up your entire life," I snip.

"He did once," Dan says, grabbing my chin and forcing me to look at him. "He gave up his entire life for you."

"Dan it's fine," my dad waves his hand in the air like he can wave away all the bad mojo from the past.

"No, she needs to hear this."

I sit up straight. My eyes briefly flitting over Dirk and Raffe before landing back on my dad.

"I was in prison for killing a man. He was president of the Devils at the time."

Slowly, I uncurl myself.

"He had always been in love with your mom. She didn't love him back, but she did love his drugs. He was very jealous when your mom and I hooked up. Shortly after you were born, he gave your mom some bad shit… it killed her." He pauses, his gaze drifting past my shoulder as he remembers that day. "He was arrested but the charges were dropped. I'm sure he rolled on someone. Anyhow, as I was getting on my bike to leave the courthouse, he pulled up beside me. He said he was coming for you next. He laughed and said he would wait a few years… until you were old enough to enjoy…" he struggles to get the rest of the story out. He takes a deep breath and sits up tall. "Until you were old enough to enjoy him and his drugs."

I look down at my chest. Where's the blood. I pat around, sure that there is a hole somewhere. Dan touches my elbow lightly, drawing my attention away from the pain piercing through my heart. "You're not to blame," he says quietly.

"What was his name?" I ask. I'm not sure why I need to hear who is to blame for both of my parents being torn away from me because the man is dead but for some reason it seems relevant.

Dirk's voice growls from across the room. "She's not ready."

My dad turns away from me to face him. They stare at each other for a fat minute before my dad turns back. "Another time. It's getting late." He stands, pulling me with him. Quickly, he presses his lips to my forehead. "I love you, baby girl." Then he's gone.

Dan hands me my backpack. "I refreshed your paint supply in case this place gives you some inspiration." He gives me a hug and then follows behind my dad.

I stand in the middle of the room with a gaping hole in my heart, unable to speak, unable to breathe.

Dropping the backpack, I trail after them. I follow the red lights of their bikes, eating the dust that follows them until I fall to the ground, exhausted.

I barely notice when strong arms pick me up and carry me inside.

My thoughts are bouncing from one thing to the next.

No wonder my dad let Dirk and Raffe take me. My mother died from drugs… from the Devil's drugs. Well, I guess all drugs are considered evil and therefore the Devil's drugs, but you know what I mean.

My dad went to jail to protect me. He killed for me.

Crow.

Where does he fit in all this?

Katie… what about Katie!

Dirk pulls my socks and shoes off, bringing me back to my reality. Water is running in the next room. Raffe walks out, wiping his hands off on a towel.

"I got the tub filled for you. Go soak." He nudges my knee gently as he sits down beside me.

I briefly glance at the bathroom door. "I'm so selfish, I forgot to ask about Katie. What is Bill going to do with her? She has school tomorrow too," I say sadly.

208

Dirk places both of his hands on my knees, crouched in front of me. "He talked your social worker into helping him. Katie's mom signed paperwork to give Candice temporary custody. It's a start. If Katie's mom doesn't clean up her act, then we will petition the court for full custody."

"Candice?" Wait, my dad said something about wanting Candice to have custody of me when my grandparents passed.

"Ally's mom. You met her at the warehouse," Raffe reminds me gently.

"So, so she's at the warehouse with Candice?" My brain has overheated. Everything is coming to me slowly.

"With her and Bill," Dirk says, pulling me off the couch and walking me to the bathroom. "Don't worry about Katie. They are taking good care of her. Bill and Candice are enrolling her in the same school Ally goes to in the morning."

I stop dead in my tracks. "Bill and Candice… are they?"

Dirk shakes his head. "I don't know what they are, Jess. I only know they are good friends. They lean on each other."

I sigh, dropping my shoulders. I'm so goddamned tired all of a sudden. "Katie will be happy. She didn't really have any friends at school," I say quietly.

Dirk tugs on my arm. "Did you?" he asks.

"No," I simply state before closing the door behind me.

After taking a warm bath, I'm truly exhausted. I climb out, dress in the clothes Raffe laid out for me, then stand at the door. I don't have the energy to do anymore talking or thinking for that matter. I take a deep breath and open the door. Raffe and Dirk have made beds for themselves on two of the couches.

Raffe jumps up. "You want a snack, a drink, anything?" he asks, dipping his head to catch my eyes.

"No. Just sleep," I murmur, rubbing my eyes.

Dirk walks over and gives me a gentle kiss on the lips, whispering a quick goodnight in my ear before stepping away. Raffe takes my hand and guides me upstairs.

"If you need anything, just holler." He tucks me into Dirk's bed, leaning down and planting a soft kiss on the tip of my nose. He winks before heading down the stairs. "Sleep tight, sweetheart."

My eyes blink sleepily as I listen to their hushed voices. I smile, secure in the fact that no one is going to take what's mine tonight. Not with the two scary, sweet men downstairs. Tonight, I don't need to sleep with one eye open.

Chapter Thirty-One

Dirk

Giggling is what stirs me from the best sleep I've had in some time. All of us being under the same roof probably has a lot do with it. I hate admitting that. Does it make me weak? Probably.

What the hell are they up to? When I sit up and look over the back of the couch, the visual that greets me is straight out of a fucking Hallmark movie. Raffe and Jesse are covered in flour, their heads bowed over a bowl. Raffe is stirring whatever is in it with a large wooden spoon. Jesse is supervising, a beautiful smile on her face.

They are so goddamned beautiful together it makes me question whether I should join them or get up and walk out the door right now. Jesse sense's my scrutiny, her eyes meet mine across the room. Her smile widens.

"Hey, sleepyhead." She gives me the cutest little wave in greeting.

Raffe's gaze joins hers, his eyes twinkling with mischief. His dazzling smile mirrors hers. Could it be we all just needed a good night's rest? Or is it that we're finally where we belong?

I've been trying to sort this shit out in my head. Ever since I saw them together in the tattoo shop, I can't get the image of either of them out of my fucking head. Raffe has had an interest in me since we met but I wasn't into guys back then and I'm not sure I am now but... god, I can't deny that there is something about seeing the two of them together. Man, I don't know. I just don't know.

Raffe and I have been friends, brothers for so long. Can feelings change? Can they grow or have I been in denial about who I am?

No. Fuck that. I know who I am. I'm the person who drags you away from your demons and then I devour those motherfuckers. That's what I did for Raffe and that's what I'm going to do for Jesse. It's not that I have been in denial... it's that I'm seeing Raffe in a different light. Him with her is a side of Raffe I haven't seen. It's sexy as hell.

From the day I met him, he's been a playboy. Something that the traffickers conditioned him to be. While I may have saved him from them, helped him overcome the larger obstacles, those deeply engrained ideas of himself remain.

But this is new. Maybe seeing how Jesse has survived is changing him. Made him realize he is good for something other than his dick.

"She's trying to teach me how to make pancakes." His laugh is lighter than I've ever heard it.

"I'm going to shower," I tell them.

They both nod and go right into the next Hallmark scene.

As the water runs over me, I let me head drop, staring at the ink I've encased myself in. It started on the playground when I was ten years old. Same age as Jesse when I met her.

The day we met, I shared the lesson I learned at ten. *Sometimes, you have to get mean to protect what is yours.*

Sugar and Skulls

My sister and I had been home for a week by ourselves. We needed out of the house, so I walked her down to our local park. Our parents were both working. Always working. I turned my back for two minutes... maybe less. Long enough to fill her water bottle. As I was walking back, I realized she was gone.

The panic tingles up my spine even now. It's never evaporated. It never will because I still don't know where she is, what happened to her. So, I got mean. I will break, burn, and murder to protect what's mine. I embraced the dark, lived it, breathed it... became it.

It's why I became a Skull. The Rebel Skulls embodied what I wanted in life. Protect those who cannot protect themselves. Yeah, we are scary motherfuckers and now you know why. No different than a grizzly protecting it's young.

The scent of pancakes and bacon greets me when I step out of the shower. Inhaling deeply, I check to make sure my heart is rock solid... I have more dragons to slay today.

But when I step out, the rock cracks. Raffe is sitting down, stuffing his beautiful fucking face while Jesse hugs him from behind, her arms wrapped loosely around his neck. She bites her perfectly pink bottom lip in anticipation, waiting for his critique of the pancakes. "Mmm," he moans, closing his eyes for effect.

She squeals in delight at his appreciation. Her lips press against the blond stubble of his cheek before she turns back to the griddle. I clear my throat, letting them know play time is over. Time to get to work. Two set of eyes land on me. Raffe shifts nervously. Jesse smirks. She points to a chair with her spatula. "Bout time, I thought you drowned," she smarts off.

"Oh really, I didn't see you coming in to check on me," I flip back. I plop my ass in the chair she didn't point at. She cocks an eyebrow at me. I return the look. She swallows slow, her head dropping slightly. Yes, little girl, I'm still the one in charge.

She turns back around to finish the pancakes. When she returns to the table, she has two plates one for me and one for herself. She sets mine down in front of me. Her mischievous eyes do their best to hold mine hostage. She sits down between Raffe and I, reaching for the syrup bottle. Good god, the girl has a sweet tooth. She has more syrup than pancake.

Jesse flips the syrup upright, running her thumb along the edge, catching the excess sugary liquid. When she pushes her thumb into her mouth and her cheeks hollow, I lose it. Jesus Christ, I've never gotten hard so fucking fast in my life. I force my focus to Raffe to see if he's watching the way this vixen is torturing me. He is. His lips are pressed into a thin line, caught between his teeth. His hand is pressing painfully down on the growing bulge in his pants.

I turn back to find her grinning at me. So, I toss my eyebrow up, tilting my head to the side. Instead of being intimidated like the look intends, she laughs and ignores me for her pancakes. This little shit.

Fine, she can have this one. I pick up my fork, ready to dig in... what? I roll my head back and forth. I don't even need to look over to see her trying to stifle her laughter. I can feel it shake the entire table. She can't hold it in. Her voice breaks past her lips. "Oh god. Your face. Priceless. Priceless," she says through tears of laughter.

A snort escapes Raffe. Oh, I can't wait until she turns eighteen. "You do know I'm keeping a tally," I say, driving my fork into my hilariously dick shaped pancakes.

"You thought it was funny when I tattooed one on Bill," she says, wiping her tears away with a napkin.

"Bill deserved a certain amount of animosity but me. Why pick on me?" I ask, taking a bite, stopping myself from moaning in appreciation like Raffe had done earlier.

"Oh, I pick on you for an entirely different reason." Her cheeks turn pink as she shifts her gaze from me to Raffe.

"Why don't you pick on him?" I point my fork towards my friend.

She smiles sweetly, reminding me of her innocence. "Well, I guess I kind of look at him as a partner in crime." A cute little giggle finishes her sentence.

Raffe fucking straight up blushes, his beard unable to contain the effect her words have on him. What the hell? He wipes his mouth off with his napkin before speaking. "Yeah, we're teaming up to see if we can crack you," he says hesitantly, a small smile on his reddened face.

Her grin widens as she turns to face me. Both of them looking at me like I hung the stars and moon makes me... extremely uncomfortable. "Just eat your fucking pancakes," I order gruffly. "There will be no cracking *me*. Today is about *you*." I turn my fork on her.

Her smile fades, instantly making me regret my words and my gruffness.

"I know," she says sadly before straightening in her chair, a look of confidence chasing the melancholy away. "I'm going to tell you everything."

I toss my napkin on the table. "Okay, let's hear it."

She slides back in her chair, her eyes bouncing around the room.

"Dirk," Raffe warns, softly.

"No. I want to hear it. I want to hear her say it out loud so we can move forward." I slide my eyes from her to him.

"It's not that easy, Dirk," Raffe says, playing good cop. At least that is what he's supposed to be doing.

"All seven ranking officers and one prospect," she says quietly.

Raffe and I both snap our attention to Jesse. Darkness whips across the floor like a deadly serpent. It wraps itself around my ankles, infiltrating me with a hate I've never felt before. The entire fucking club will burn. Mark my fucking words.

With extreme restraint, I keep my ass glued to the chair. My breath is coming in short pants as I reign myself in. Raffe is doing the same. How the fuck do we respond to that.

She takes a deep breath and raises her head like a motherfucking queen. My queen. "The worst was Crow." Her gaze wanders between the two of us. "He wouldn't shut up. He whispered in my ear the entire time. He wouldn't let me block him out. He wanted more than in my body. He wanted in my mind."

I place my hands on my knees, willing them to stop shaking as I listen to her.

"I didn't understand until yesterday. Last night, when I was lying in bed, I put it all together. The man my father killed was related to Crow wasn't he?"

"Brothers," I answer. This girl is too smart for her own good.

She nods. "I tried to block that weekend out of my mind but when you said his name yesterday..."

"It dislodged the blockage," I finish for her. I had my suspicions it was Crow. Just like I've had my suspicions he was responsible for her grandparent's deaths. I knew if I mentioned him, and he had hurt her, it would be impossible for her to hide a reaction. What I didn't expect was this. How the fuck did she walk out of that trailer in one piece after being assaulted by eight men?

Jesse draws out an exhale, trying to decompress. When she inhales, her spine straightens. "So, how are we going to do it?" she asks, her head held high. The florescent light above us reflects a crown of blue over her jet-black hair. A queen I tell you. She has a resilient spirit to match my own. Eat or be eaten. There is no other way.

"Gotta bring the whole club in. Something this big will require a vote," I tell her.

Her eyes trail to the windows. "I'm going to go listen to the trees." She turns back to me, seeking approval. I simply nod.

"Don't go far," I warn.

"I won't," she says as she walks out, pausing to pick up the backpack of paints Dan brought for her. She doesn't give us or her uneaten breakfast a second glance.

When she walks out, Raffe jumps to his feet. "Jesus Christ, Dirk. Could you have pushed her any harder?" he growls.

"We aren't fucking here for pancakes and sweet syrups."

"No. We're here for her." He points to the door.

I stand up, pressing my knuckles into the table. "And you don't think I'm here for her?"

"Dammit, Dirk. I know you are but…" He rips at his hair. "I'm sorry, I just want to hurt someone, and you are the only motherfucker in the room." Raffe falls into his chair, throwing his head back to stare at the ceiling.

"I just lanced the fucking wound, Raffe. You know how this works. It will get better from here." I sit down in the chair beside him.

"Do you think I should go to her," he asks.

"Finish your breakfast, give her a little time, then yes, go to her. I'm going to ride into town."

"Why don't you just call him? She's going to hear the bike."

"You think it's a good idea to tell him over the phone?" I ask, grabbing my jacket from the couch.

"No."

How am I going to tell Bill what happened to his baby girl? I really hope that Dan is still around. It might take the both of us to keep him from going on a rampage and knocking off every single one of them by himself. He's mean enough to do it but going in without a plan would be sloppy and we cannot risk him getting locked up again. Jesse needs him.

Chapter Thirty-Two

Raffe

I give her a few hours by herself before packing a simple lunch for us to enjoy outdoors. She didn't eat much this morning. I head out with the basket swinging in my hand. A tiny fox catches my eye. Wait, that isn't a fox. I crouch down in front of the bottom of the tree where the bark has broken off. It's painted to look as if it's hollowed out with a small brown fox peeking out. Did Jesse do this?

Continuing down the path, I find more sweet creations. A woodpecker adorns another large tree stripped of bark from a lightning storm. On a large rock in the middle of the path, I find rainbow-colored ants forming a trail behind each other. A plant with large green leaves is covered in tiny painted butterflies.

A hissing noise catches my attention further up the path. I pick up my pace, coming to an abrupt halt when I see Jesse crouched over two large rocks. On the side of one she has painted a small deer. On the rock that lies flat she is painting a pool of blue water, the deer's reflection rippling through the paint.

Jesse is a badass no doubt. She has Skull blood pumping through her veins but deep down, a curious little girl still exists. She scratches her nose, leaving a streak of blue behind. As she leans forward to grab another can of paint, she notices me watching her. "Hey." She starts to pack up her paints.

"Don't stop on my account," I tell her, looking for a place to park my ass.

"You sure? I lost track of time."

I find a clear spot and pull out the blanket I had tucked in the picnic basket. She watches as I lay it out. "Positive," I assure her. "When you finish, we'll eat lunch." I pat the picnic basket beside me. The smile that breaks out across her face makes me happy I thought of it.

"I am getting hungry," she says, shyly tucking her hair behind her ear before getting back to her painting.

"Your art sure does brighten up the path. It's whimsical. I like it."

She talks while continuing to paint. "I see things where nothing exists." She shrugs like it's nothing.

"So, is it the same when you tattoo?"

Jesse blushes and nods. How curious? I decide to press the issue.

"Do you see something when you look here?" I pull up my shirt, baring the left side of my torso.

She wipes at her forehead with the back of her hand, staring at my bare skin. Her eyes slowly roam up and latch onto mine. She nods again, her green eyes piercing a hole in my heart. "I've had a plan for that spot for quite some time," she admits. Her tongue skates along her bottom lip. Quickly, she diverts her eyes back to her painting.

"Is it something cute and whimsical or is it dark like the skull and rose you are doing on my leg?"

Her face flushes again, her head dipping to face away from me. "It's…
it's not cute, or whimsical, it's …" Jesse stops and begins to toss her paints
into her bag, evidently finished with her painting.

"It's what?"

"It's nothing." She shoves me in the arm as she sits down beside me
on the blanket. Her face heating to an alarming level. "I'm hungry," she
states, flopping her hands in her lap.

"Okay. Don't tell me. Maybe I'll have Dan fill in that space," I tease,
opening the basket and pulling out two sandwiches.

She narrows her eyes at me in warning.

"No?" I laugh

"You're mine now," she tells me.

I toss her a bottle of water. "I like the sound of that."

Jesse hides behind her hair. "I heard Dirk leave. Is he going down to
tell my dad?"

"Yes," I answer, shooting straight from the hip. She inhales deeply,
staring at the sandwich in her hand. "You need to try and eat something."

She nibbles at the corner of the bread. I glance at her painting. It
blends in seamlessly with the natural surroundings. "Where did you learn
to paint?"

She shrugs. "I've always liked to doodle. It keeps my mind busy. I
guess you could say I was self-taught."

"It's beautiful." I watch her cheeks pinken at my compliment. "How
do you do it? How do you stay so positive despite everything you've been
through?"

"I learned early on I could not control the bad things, but I could control me. I can control the way I interpret things. So, I might feel bad for a time but then you have to dust yourself off and get back on the horse."

"Yeah, but how many times do you get bucked off before you quit getting back on?" I ask.

She looks up at the sky, contemplating my words before turning her sparkling green eyes my way. "You never quit."

I take a minute to absorb her words. "You believe that don't you?"

"With all my heart." She takes a bigger bite of her sandwich, a smile forming on her face. "When I came to Trap, I imagined I would rule over it. A group of misfits banned together by unfortunate circumstances." She laughs lightly. "Ah, the musings of a young, naïve girl."

"I don't think your naïve at all."

She stares at me. "You did once." Her head tips to the side as she waits for me to remember... and remember I do.

"Oh shit, Jesse. I'm so sorry. I didn't know."

Jesse surprises me, moving fast, her lips press to mine. She mumbles against them. "Don't." Her lips part, granting me permission to experience more of her. Oh, god. Her lips are the sweetest thing I've ever tasted. Quietly, in the breeze, we softly explore each other. When she pulls away, a lightness settles over me. The taste of sugar remains on my lips.

She smiles as she settles back in her spot.

"Jesse you are... you are..."

"One of a kind," she finishes for me.

I nod once. Her smile spreads across her entire face, illuminating the entire mountain. My heart swells in a way it never has before. Jesse doesn't look at me like other women do... or men for that matter. "What do you see when you look at me?" I ask her the same question she asked me a few nights ago.

Jesse cups her hands over her heart, letting me know she's touched I asked a question she's been asking most of her life. "I see you, Raffe." Her eyes drop away for a moment. When she returns her gaze to me, it demands I listen to her next words closely. "A kindhearted, beautiful man. Someone who would do anything for his friends, for his brothers. Someone who would put himself at the back of the pack to ensure that everyone makes it safely to other side. A man who would sacrifice his body or soul, to save those he loves."

I hang to every word as it falls from her lips. Her words aren't idle musings, they are said with so much emotion I know she has looked at me deeper than anyone ever has. Oh, god, why did I tell her I saw a fellow survivor? I see so much more than that when I look at her.

Her final words seal my fate, my future with this woman.

"When you said you saw a fellow survivor, I knew you saw me and for the first time you saw yourself. You and I are the same." She takes my hand in hers. "You know how?"

Numbly, I shake my head no.

She climbs on my lap, straddling me. "We know what it's like for someone to take what's ours. To steal a piece of us. So, we guard what is left in ways others cannot understand. By controlling what we can. Me by selling drugs and giving the money to those in need and you by using your body to help your club. Both we control."

Jesse stares into my soul, drawing leftover poison to the surface.

She combs her fingers through my beard. "So, when we give a piece of ourselves over willingly, it's the most precious thing in the world."

Again, her lips find mine and I feel her gift, a piece of her she is handing over voluntarily.

When she ends the kiss, she tucks her face against my neck. "You're the first person that I've initiated a kiss with." She curls into me. Her vulnerability seeking comfort. I wrap my arms around her, holding her tight.

Quietly, in the middle of nature I float, not fall, in love with the kindest, strongest creature I've ever met. Jesse Miller came into my life, taking nothing from me, asking for naught but in this moment she has given me everything."

Chapter Thirty-Three

Jesse

The roar of a bike brings me back from the quiet place I've been floating in, in the safety of Raffe's arms. I trace over the tattoos I've watched Dan etch into his skin over the years. I don't move, neither does he. Several minutes later, Dirk's boots crunch along the path, stopping beside us.

He crouches beside me, his big hand running over my hair. "It's time to go home, sweetheart," his gravelly voice wakes up that thing deep in my core that rouses every time I find myself caught between these two men.

I lift my head and lean over while still on Raffe's lap, I grab Dirk's scruffy face and pull him close. His eyes widen as I place a kiss on his lips. It throws him off for a minute, but he recovers quickly, taking over.

As Dirk kisses me thoroughly, Raffe stirs under me. I pull away and turn to him, offering him a taste of the heat left behind from Dirk's lips. Raffe moans deep as we connect. Dirk doesn't abandon me. My hair is quickly wrapped around his fist, his lips grazing the back of my neck as soon as it's exposed to him.

Something inside me swells with an unbearable heat. I want to feel my skin on their skin. I want to feel my heart sync with theirs. I want to taste them. I want them to taste me. I can't get enough. I need more. More. More.

As soon as it starts, it ends. Dirk stands, taking a step away. Raffe gently scoots me off his lap. What is happening? Why did they stop? I want more of them.

"This can't happen right now," Raffe tells me as he gathers up the picnic we never finished.

"Why not?" I hustle to my feet, suddenly feeling very insecure.

My eyes dart around, an overwhelming urge to flee comes over me. Dirk grabs my arm and pulls me close to him. "Don't even think about it."

"I don't understand..." I shake my head, trying to focus on what the fuck is actually going on.

Dirk grabs my chin, forcing me to look at him. "I want you, Raffe wants you and from what I can tell you want us both." I try to turn away, but his grip only tightens. "The fact you don't understand is exactly why we are stopping."

"It's... it's wrong I want you both?" I ask awkwardly. What am I asking? Of course, it's wrong. Of course, it is.

He shakes his head. "No. It's not wrong but I don't think you're ready for one of us, let alone two."

Raffe stands beside Dirk. "It would be easy for us to take advantage of you right now. We aren't going to do that."

"What about what I want?"

Dirk smirks, his scary as fuck eyebrow cocks in amusement. "Well, Jesse, you can have whatever you want when you turn eighteen."

I squint at him, defiance bubbling through my veins. "Oh, I see what this is. Poor little Jesse, all abused and shit. She's so wounded she can't be trusted with her own desires. Too young to take care of herself. Too young to understand the big bad world. Too young to know what she wants." I shove away from them both.

"Jesse, come on. We don't think that. But you're seventeen and we are considerably older. We have to think about what this might look like to others. What about Bill?"

Laughing, I grab my stomach with exaggerated amusement. When I right myself, wiping at my eyes, I pointedly declare war. "Good luck keeping up your act of nobility."

They glance nervously at each other. "What the hell does that mean?" Raffe asks.

I start up the path, letting my words trail behind me. "You boys haven't met Sugar yet, but you're about to."

When I hear Dirk pick up his pace behind me, I run. He's angry. I run all the way inside and up the stairs, only to realize that there is no door on his bedroom because it's a loft. Fuck. I back up as he walks towards me.

"There is no Sugar," he warns with a look of determination on his face.

I want to defy him.

I want to spit in his face.

I want to kiss him.

I want him to hold me.

Oh.

Oh.

In this moment, I realize that I've been acting mean to keep people away. To prevent people from taking what's mine. To ensure everyone stays at arm's length. Until now. That's not what I want from Dirk... from Raffe. I want them to hold me. To love me. Oh god.

He reads the emotions playing out over my face like an open book.

I turn away from him and crawl on the bed, concealing my face in a pillow. I'm so embarrassed and confused. Something breaks inside of me. I don't know if it's my will, my heart, or my strength, because right now I don't feel I have any of those things.

"Jesse," the bed shifts as Dirk sits beside me. "Raffe and I cannot give you what you are wanting right now. I didn't say it would never happen."

He lays his hand gently on my back.

"Talk to me, Jess."

"I'm sorry. I know all this is wrong. I'm wrong. There is something wrong with me. Wrong. Wrong. Wrong," I hiccup through my tears.

"There's nothing wrong with you." His hand continues to tenderly caress me. "I think it best if we go back to the warehouse. Your dad is missing you."

"I don't want to go back. Just leave me here," I mumble into the pillow.

He climbs over me so that he can stretch out beside me on the bed. I keep my face buried.

"We can stay if that's what you need."

"I need things to make sense."

He chuckles lightly. "The world rarely makes sense, Jesse."

I turn my head, laying my cheek on my folded arms. "I don't want to be mean anymore."

"Awe, Jess." He closes his eyes. When he opens them again, they are a calm blue. "You don't have to be mean with Raffe or I. You don't have to be mean to anyone in the club. No one is going to take anything away from you. Okay?"

Nodding, I roll on my side to face him. We stare at each other for a long time. This Dirk is different from the one I normally see. He dropped his mean. Maybe I can drop mine.

"I can't tell anymore."

"What can't you tell?" he asks, brushing my hair away from my face.

"Who I can trust and who I can't. Sometimes, I think the world is after me. I don't know what it is about me."

His eyes roam over my face. "It's not you. It's them. They are sick. You just happened to walk into their sights." He rolls onto his back, staring at the ceiling. "You have a natural instinct, Jesse. Think about it. You knew to trust Dan. You knew your friend William was good, despite what that priest asked him to do to you. You knew, Jesse." He turns back to me. "You know."

I sit up and hug my knees. "If I hadn't met you that day in the school parking lot, I don't think I would have survived. There wouldn't have been anything left of me for my father to find. Every time I had to do something hard, I thought of you."

Dirk swallows and turns his eyes back to the ceiling.

"I keep trying to be mean, to be tough but I'm so tired."

"Then stop fighting. Let us take the wheel for a while. It doesn't mean you're weak."

They've already taken the wheel. I'm fighting just for the sake of fighting at this point. Dirk flicks his lip ring while waiting for a response. God, he's hot. I drag my eyes away from him. "Are you and Raffe taking care of me because of my dad? Because of the club?"

He reaches for me, using my locked arms as leverage to pull himself to a sitting position. His eyes level with mine. "I don't do anything I don't want to. I *want* to take care of you."

I blink a few times, trying to look away. There's that funny feeling again. Like a moth to a flame, I'm drawn to this man. "I don't understand this..." I motion between the two of us.

He smiles. "You were made for me, Jesse. The only woman in the world who is worthy of standing by my side. I knew it the minute you fell out of Dan's window."

I turn my head away. "I didn't fall. I climbed out gracefully."

"Whatever helps you sleep at night."

Laughing, I let my gaze fall over him again.

"When you smile, it breaks through all this." He motions over his dark ink. "It's like feeling the warm summer sun after a long dark winter."

My laughter falls away as I study him. I'm having a hard time associating the words with the man. Words that don't match the pictures on his body.

"And... and Raffe?" I ask, puzzled how we're all supposed to fit. I want them both. I know it's strange... taboo. But my heart wants them both.

He drops his head, his dark hair falling in front of his face. "I don't know, Jesse. This is new for me too." Dirk takes a deep breath and faces me. "I like seeing him with you." He falls back on the bed. "This is confusing. I just know that I want you both with me. Maybe it's because I've seen you both at your purest form, vulnerable, and hurt. But when you are together you both seem relaxed, happy."

"Partners in crime," I tease.

His eyebrow pops up. "Oh, the things I'm going to do to you... someday."

I bite my lip, wiggling on the bed. "Dirk, I've taken care of myself for a long time. I'm not a child. I don't understand why we have to wait."

He sits up, mirroring me. "We wait not because something magical will happen when you turn eighteen. We wait because it's the right thing to do. You deserve to be waited for.... no one else has done that for you, Jesse. I'm not just going to take from you. I'm going to woo you Jesse Miller."

Should I laugh or should I cry? His words hit me hard. He's right. Everyone has just taken what they want from me. No one has worked for it, earned it. "Okay, scary tattoo man, let's see what you got in the wooing department."

"Are you making fun of me?" he asks, his eyebrow hitting a forty-five-degree angle.

"I am." I lean over so that my nose is inches from his. "But thank you."

The good news is I think it's safe to drop the mean.

The bad news is... come to think of it, I don't have any bad news.

Chapter Thirty-Four

Jesse ~ 7 months later

Today is the day. I'm nervous, excited… I don't know if I've ever been more anxious to begin a new day. Raffe and Dirk have been so sweet. Late night bike rides, lazy days by the lake, teasing… lots of teasing. My life may have been a shit show for a few years but finally, I'm right where I belong.

I get out of bed, stretching in front of my window. Just like every morning, I find Katie and my dad down fishing. It's become their thing. He asked me one day if it bothered me. It doesn't. My dad and I missed times like that together, but it doesn't mean Katie has too… or him for that matter.

Candice and my dad announced a few months ago that they are getting married. Their wedding is only a few weeks away. I'm happy for him, for both of them. I like Candice. We've become friends. I wouldn't say that it's a mother daughter relationship but that's okay. I'm learning that love comes in many forms.

I graduated a few months ago. My dad threw a big bash here at the warehouse. I'm so lucky to have such a big family. I didn't accept it at first. Some days, I fought harder than others. Being on my own had become engrained in my very being.

As I'm taking a shower, I think about the last few months. The club has basically cut off all sources of income that the Desert Devils relied on. We've heard a lot of them left, joining other clubs. It's just a small band now. We also decided that we couldn't take them all out and risk Katie's adoption. So, we let them live... except for one. The man that hurt Katie. Dirk took him out quietly. No one missed him.

The guys haven't let me step foot in Trap County. My dad eventually did let me call my guys and Thomas, to explain that I had moved and would not be back.

I miss three things about Trap County. Thomas, his dog Teddy, and Big Dan's Tattoo shop.

When I get downstairs for breakfast, I'm a little disheartened. It's empty. I try not to be disappointed. Maybe everyone is busy this morning.

I make myself some toast and eggs before heading back up to my room.

Still no one.

I glance out my window. Dad and Katie are gone.

Maybe no one knows it's my birthday.

That can't be true. I tattooed it right on my dad's chest.

A knock on my door pulls me from my thoughts.

"Hey, you want help me on a job today?" my dad asks, poking his head in the door.

I sigh loudly before answering. "Yeah, sure."

233

He pats the door frame a few times. "Good deal. I'll meet you at the truck. Dress comfortable."

I nod, fighting back stupid tears.

It's just my birthday. Just another ordinary day. I don't know why I'm letting my emotions rule me. I've spent the last eight without anyone acknowledging it, so what's the big deal? I didn't sit on my pity pot then, today is no different.

As I walk through the warehouse, I search for any sign of Dirk or Raffe. Nothing. I didn't specifically tell them when my birthday was. It hasn't been something we've talked about much. We've been focused on getting to know each other. There have been times things have heated up between us, but they always pulled away before it got too far.

My dad is waiting for me when I get to his truck. "Did you eat breakfast?" he asks.

"Yeah." I take one last glance around the yard for Dirk and Raffe.

We drive over to the town I grew up in. It's only about thirty minutes from the lake. I haven't been here in years. My dad is chatting away about the changes he's made to the club. He's making everything legit. Not much illegal is going on anymore. Besides doing bike repair, the club has invested in real estate. Maybe that's what we're doing today, collecting rents.

I search the streets for my grandparent's old house. It's sad I can't even remember where it is, the town has changed so much. He pulls into a driveway. I stare through the windshield as my heart drops into my stomach.

He shuts the engine off and turns towards me. "Your grandparents left you everything. It's been in trust until you turned eighteen." Slowly, I drag my eyes from the house where I grew up. When they land on his, he smiles. "Happy birthday, baby girl."

"I thought you forgot," I say shyly.

"I've spent every year wishing I were with you on this day. Today I am." He reaches over and squeezes my hand.

"So, there's no job?"

He laughs and shakes his head. "Want to go in?"

"Yes, oh my god, yes." I nod enthusiastically.

We both get out and walk up the steps. As he is unlocking the door, he tells me that he had a cleaning service come over after my grandparents passed. He hired someone to keep an eye on it for me as well. They've kept up on the yard work and repairs.

It's a simple three-bedroom, ranch style home, with a big fenced in backyard. When we step inside, I'm immediately thrown back to another time. It's exactly like we left it. A sob escapes me as I stare at my grandparent's recliners. My dad hugs me around the shoulders.

I came home from school and thought they were asleep. When I couldn't wake them, I ran back to school and told my teacher. I haven't been back since that day. The suit lady picked me up at school and took me to my first foster home. I didn't even get to pack my own things. She gathered what she thought I needed and that was that.

I make my way to my bedroom, my dad following close behind. He stands in the doorway as I run my hand over everything. I grab my jewelry box off the dresser and sit down on the bed. When I open it, the little ballerina twirls to life and the clang of musical notes filter out. My dad sits down next to me.

With shaky hands, I reach in and pull out my mom's mood ring. I laugh as I stare at the cloudy color of the stone. I slip it on my finger, and it turns a beautiful blue.

"I remember that," my dad says.

I look at him. "Thank you for taking care of all of this for me." I motion around the room.

"It was the least I could do. I wish things could have been different."

"We have each other now. That's all that matters." I bite my bottom lip to keep it from trembling.

He pulls me into a hug. "I love you so much, Jesse. You are the best thing that's ever happened to me."

"I can still live at the warehouse though, right?" I ask hesitantly.

He laughs. "Yes. The warehouse will always be your home, even when you decide to leave and go out on your own."

I sit up straight an idea popping in my head. "Why don't you and Candice live here with the girls?"

"Jesse, no. This is your place. Someday, you will have a family of your own. Besides, Katie loves living in a castle."

"You're right... about the castle part anyway. Katie does love it there." I laugh lightly, my mind drifting to Raffe and Dirk. I do want a family, someday. How will that even work? For the first time I worry about our dynamic.

"What's wrong? I lost you there for a minute." My dad tips my chin, studying my face for answers.

I haven't told my dad that my relationship with Raffe and Dirk goes beyond friendship. I know he likes to think of them as my uncles. What will he think? What will the world think?

"Jesse?" he asks again.

"Nothing, I'm just feeling a little melancholy I guess."

He gives me a gentle squeeze. My dad places the keys to the house in my hands.

We spend the morning going through old photo albums. I show him the swing that grandpa tied in a tree in the backyard for me. He insists I sit, and he pushes me. It's nice to share this with him.

As I swing, he tells me how my grandfather sent him letters each month. "I lived for those letters, Jess."

"Why didn't they ever tell me about you?"

"I murdered a man. They didn't feel that was a quality they wanted in their granddaughter's life. I don't blame them. I'm sure if the roles had been reversed, I would have done the same," he answers thoughtfully.

We lock up and he takes me to lunch.

"This has been nice, dad. Thank you for everything," I tell him, buckling my seatbelt. My belly is so full, I think I might need a nap.

He grabs something out of the back before getting in. He sets the present on the seat between us. "Now, I know this is a little late... but..."

He picks it up and sets it on my lap. "How can it be late? Today is my birthday, you know."

Tapping his finger over his tattoo, he says, "I know, baby girl. You'll see."

I rip the paper off carefully so that I don't rip any of it. It's wrapped in black paper with skulls that have bright pink bows on their heads. He sighs impatiently but let's me go at my own pace. This is the first birthday present I've gotten since my tenth birthday. I'm going to savor it.

When I take the lid off the box, my heart stops. My hand flies to my mouth, tears filling my eyes. I turn to him. "How did you know?" I whisper, wondering if I'm dreaming.

"The last letter your grandpa sent said you had been begging for roller skates for your birthday. He never got a chance to give you a pair."

I push the box to the floor and throw myself into his arms, crying for all the things I've lost and all that I've gained. "I love you, dad. Thank you!"

He chuckles. "I didn't know roller skates would make you so happy."

Leaning back, I stare into his handsome face. "You've made me the happiest girl in the world."

I slide back into my seat, picking up the box. "They're even my size."

"Did you think I would buy you skates that didn't fit?" He laughs, tugging at his beard. "You want to go try those bad boys out?"

Nodding happily, I busy myself lacing them. They are perfect, just like the pair the Ditsworth girls had. My dad drives us across town to the roller rink.

"Oh, bummer. They looked closed." There's not a car in sight.

"Oh, surely someone is here," he says, hopping out, undaunted by the vacant lot.

I grab my skates and follow him. The door is unlocked but once inside we realize it's probably not open because it's dark. I can't see a fricking thing past the front doors. My dad looks at me sadly.

"It's okay, dad. Another time." I punch him in the arm and turn to head back out into the warm summer sun.

Suddenly, the lights come on. I spin around to find the entire skate floor filled with the whole gang. "Surprise!" they all yell together.

I look at my dad with my mouth hanging open. "Dad," I choke.

"Happy eighteenth, baby," he whispers in my ear as he hugs me.

"You didn't have to go to all this trouble," I tell him, wiping my eyes.

Katie comes running up to us. "Happy birthday, Jesse!" she says excitedly, hopping all around us.

"Did someone feed you jumping beans for breakfast?" I ask, laughing.

"I'm just so excited!" She wraps her arms around me. "I've never been roller skating before," she tells me.

"I bet you're going to be a natural." I bop her on the nose before turning to accept all the birthday wishes from our friends who have gathered around.

My gaze searches the group for two pairs of eyes. When I find them, I offer them the brightest smile I can muster. Raffe taps two fingers over his heart, giving me a sexy smile. My gaze slides to Dirk. His eyebrow is at an alarming angle. His tongue snakes out, flicking his lip ring, making my thighs clench on their own accord. God, he makes me feel funny things.

Someone grabs me from behind, hosting me clean off my feet. "Goddammit, Dan," I yell, slapping at his tree trunk sized arms.

He chuckles in my ear. "Happy Birthday, doll." Dan sets me back on my feet, turning me to face him. "I have a surprise for you. Come find me when this is over, yeah?"

"Yeah, okay." I smile and hug him tight.

I find my dad sitting with my guys. Raffe is the only one lacing up a pair of skates. I sit next to him and get busy with my own. "Not skating?" I ask Dirk.

He shakes his head no.

"Party pooper, come on," I beg.

"I like my feet firmly on the ground. That's why I have this guy, to keep you company," he drawls lazily, tossing a thumb out towards Raffe. He turns back to his conversation with my dad.

Raffe winks at me and whispers, "He doesn't know how to have fun."

As I finish with my laces, I think about it. Dirk doesn't know how to have fun. He's always serious, always business. He doesn't even smile... he smirks but it's not the same thing as a smile.

Raffe rises from his seat and pulls me up with him. "I'm going to knock your socks off with my mad skills," he tells me, spinning in a circle.

Together, we take off and hit the rink. After a few laps, my muscle memory takes over. Raffe and I help Katie and soon she is doing great on her own. Everyone is having a great time. This was a perfect way to celebrate my birthday. It's great family fun.

My eyes wander to Dirk. Every time I glance at him, he's watching Raffe and I with a look of longing on his face. After a while, Raffe and I go our separate ways. I leave the rink and head over to Dirk. My dad and him both look up.

"Having fun, baby girl," my dad asks.

I kiss him on the cheek. "The best. Thank you."

My eyes slide to Dirk. "What size shoe do you wear?"

"I said no, Jesse." He tries to intimidate me with his scary face.

"I will help you. Come on. It's my birthday and I want this more than anything in the whole wide world." I stick my bottom lip out for affect and bat my eyelashes.

My dad laughs. "Get your ass out there. My girl gets what she wants today. That's an order." He tips his beer towards Dirk.

Dirk gives me a look, letting me know I will definitely be paying for this one. He tells me his size. I quickly grab him some skates from the counter and head back to him. Reluctantly, he takes off his boots and lets me help him lace up the skates.

I stand and nod once. Proud of myself that he at least has them on his feet. "Okay, now take my hands."

Hesitantly, he reaches for me, and I pull him to his feet. The look on his face is priceless. He is used to be in control, and he is definitely not in control... the skates are.

Slowly, we make our way to the rink.

Once we are on, we take it slow. He scowls at me. "This is not fun," he informs me.

I laugh. "We are just getting started."

And then we fall. Him on his butt and me square on top of him. When our eyes meet, he smiles.

Not a smirk. Not a half smile. A true, genuine, freely given smile.

My heart melts.

"I give up," he says, still smiling.

"No. People like you and me, we don't give up." I rise and try to pull him to his feet.

Every time I almost have him up, we fall again. Soon, we are both in hysterics. "Oh my god. I'm going to pee my pants," I cry, tears of laughter running down my face.

This is the first time I've heard Dirk laugh and it's wonderful. It makes my heart happy in ways I didn't know it could be. Eventually, we get to our feet and continue on. As we pass the sitting area, I notice Raffe is watching us. He offers me a small smile as we pass.

I wouldn't say Dirk is a natural but in the long run, he gets the hang of it. He's able to let go of at least one of my hands, allowing me to skate beside him, instead of having to skate backwards.

As the skating winds down, we gather in the food court for pizza, then we have cake and I open my presents. This is a day I will never forget. I've never felt more loved.

Everyone heads home, offering me final birthday wishes. Dan finds me and asks if I'll ride home with him. "Yeah, just let me tell dad."

I hug my dad and the guys, telling them I'm riding with Dan. "He has a surprise for me." I jump up and down on the balls of my feet, excited.

They all chuckle.

"You guys already know don't you?" I ask, accusingly.

"Go on now," my dad says. He turns me and pushes me towards Dan's bike.

Dan is waiting, he hands me a helmet and off we go. However, we don't go far. He parks on main street and hops off before holding out his hand to help me. "Okay, close your eyes."

I clap like a little kid and then close my eyes, a big smile plastered on my face. He laughs lightly and then guides me down the sidewalk.

When we stop, he spins me to face the buildings lining the street. "Ready?"

I nod like an idiot.

"Go ahead and open your eyes."

"Dan," I whisper.

"I decided it was time for me to get out of that godforsaken county too."

I turn to face him, tears in my eyes.

"It..." he drops his gaze to the ground and kicks a rock, sending it skittering across the pavement. "It wasn't the same without you."

My eyes go back to the neon sign blazing over the building. *Big D and Little J's Tattoos*. It flashes brightly in the evening sky.

"I... I don't know what to say," I whisper.

"Jesse Miller at a loss for words. That's new." He smirks.

I rush him, throwing myself in his big arms. "Oh, Dan. You're one of the best things to ever happen to me," I cry.

He pats my back, keeping me cradled to his chest. "So, what do you say? Are we partners or what?"

"Yes, yes," I answer, pulling away from him. I wipe my eyes on the bottom of my t-shirt.

"No tattooing dicks on people though," he warns, a big smile on his face.

I draw an x over my chest. "Cross my heart," I promise.

"Happy Birthday, Jesse," he says as he tosses me a key to the business.

Once inside, I see everything is set up similarly to his shop back in Trap. "I have one more surprise. I left him back at the warehouse though."

Stopping dead in my tracks, I narrow my eyes at him. "Him?"

"Can't get nothing by you, huh?"

"Nope." I cross my arms over my chest.

He sits down in one of the chairs. "Old man Tom paid me a visit. Wanted to know if you'd be willing to take his dog. Said he was moving in with his daughter in Phoenix. Seems he was tired of Trap too."

My eyes shoot to my hairline. "Teddy? How did you get him to the warehouse without him taking your leg off?"

"Oh, his bark is worse than his bite," he says, smirking at me.

"Maybe he can just sense good people," I tell him.

He shrugs his shoulders, blushing at my compliment.

"I love you, big guy."

"I love you too, doll."

Chapter Thirty-Five

Jesse

When I get back to the warehouse with Dan, my dad is waiting for us. He smiles when we walk in. We visit for a short while before I head upstairs. "Well, I better go check on Teddy."

"That dog is a sweetheart," my dad says. "Looks meaner than all get out, but he's a softy."

"Really?" I ask, confused. I can't believe Teddy has let so many people near him. He's usually a grouchy, old dog.

"Yeah, and good luck finding him in your room. I do believe Katie has snuck him into hers." My dad and Candice moved Katie and Ally to a room across the hall from us.

I stop by their room before checking my own and sure enough Teddy is lying on Katie's bed, down by her feet. He bops his head up when I open the door, his ears high and on alert. When he sees it's me, he jumps down and comes to me, wagging his tail. I pet him for a few minutes, whispering how good of a dog he is. Once he gets enough pets, he jumps back up on the end of her bed. Seems Teddy has a new job, as Katie's personal bodyguard. Could this day get any damn better?

Smiling, I make my way to my room to shower. When I get out, I glance at the clock. It's getting late. I thought for sure I would get some alone time with my guys. It was a long day though, so maybe they went to bed.

I stretch out on my bed, thinking about all the wonderful things the day brought. This was my best birthday ever.

Tink.

I sit up and listen. What was that?

Tink.

Jumping from my bed, I scoot towards the window.

Tink.

I jump a foot as I near the window. Something is hitting the glass.

Peeking out, I see Raffe down below. He smiles when he sees me and gestures for me to join him. Giggling, I pull on a pair of shorts and a t-shirt. I should have known my guys wouldn't disappoint me.

Tiptoeing, I make my way out the backdoor. He's waiting for me on the patio. I take the seat next to him. "Where's Dirk?" I ask, looking around.

"He'll be here shortly." He tucks my hair behind my ear, his eyes taking me in. "I have something I need to talk to you about before he gets here."

I shift nervously. "Okay."

He looks away. "This wasn't something I planned to do on your birthday. You know I would never purposely hurt you right?"

Raffe raises his gaze to meet mine. Now, I am nervous. "Yes. What is it, Raffe? You're scaring me."

He takes my hand in his. "I've enjoyed getting to know you these past few months, but I think it's time for me to step away and let you and Dirk explore your relationship without me."

A burning pain starts to throb right where my heart used to be. "What? No. No. Raffe, now that we're free to start something more, you are giving up before we even begin?"

"Do you love me?" he asks, calmly.

"Yes. You know I do."

"Do you love Dirk?"

I turn away from him. "Yes."

He grabs my face, turning me so he can look into my eyes. "You see? It's different. You felt something else entirely, even though the question was exactly the same.

"But I do love you," I say quietly, a tear slipping down my cheek.

His bright blue eyes bore into me. "And I love you. That will never change but our love is one of friendship. It's not the same as what you feel for Dirk."

I try to pull my face away from him, but he won't allow it.

"I'm not mad, Jesse. I'm so fucking happy for both of you. But it can't include me. I'm not going to take this to the next level, and have it spoil what I think could be an incredibly special relationship between the two of you."

"Dirk loves you, Raffe. How could you spoil it?" I ask with a tad bit of sass. I'm angry. He isn't even giving us a chance.

He sighs, letting go of me. "Today, when I saw you two together, it woke me up. You need Dirk and Dirk needs you. I don't fit into that, Jesse. It's not fair to me and it's not fair to either of you. And once we take the next step, it will eat at him. He will always see you and I together, he won't be able to erase it from his mind."

Raffe puts his arm around me. "Remember when you told me that when I saw a fellow survivor in you, I was finally seeing myself?"

I nod, brushing tears away from cheeks.

"I realize that I deserve a lot more than I've let myself have. I deserve the kind of love I see between the two of you. It's okay to let me go. It's what I want. Don't feel bad about it. I don't. I've had a blast with the two of you. It's been nice having love with no sex. Do you know what I mean?"

Thinking about it, I trace invisible circles on his jeans. I do know what he means. "I think so." I let my eyes connect with his. "When I first met you and you smiled at me, I thought how nice it was. It didn't make my shackles come up. Is that what you mean?"

"Yeah, something like that. People have always looked at me and never saw beneath my devilishly good looks," he jokes. "You and Dirk will always..." He shakes me. "Always, be my very best friends." He looks longingly out at the lake. "Someday, I'll find someone who looks at me as if nothing else exists in the world."

We sit quietly for a few minutes.

"You know that's how you look at each other, yeah?"

I shrug my shoulders.

"Do you know that today was the first time I've heard Dirk laugh. I mean I've heard him laugh at people for being stupid, he's laughed at dirty jokes but today he laughed because he was free. He's free with you, Jesse. Dirk feels safe with you, safe enough to step out from behind all that dark ink he's shielded himself behind."

Dirk told us about his little sister going missing. He told us that was the day he turned mean and vowed to use it to protect those who couldn't protect themselves.

"I'm sorry," I say.

"Jesse, there is nothing to be sorry about. I'm glad I saw it before we went any further. You both need this. I'm going to be your biggest cheerleader. I'll help Bill and the others understand when the time comes, I promise."

"I don't know how I got so lucky, Raffe."

He smiles, squeezing my shoulders. "Because you, Jesse Miller, are one of a damn kind."

I laugh lightly. My heart is happy and sad all at once. It's a confusing feeling. "I'll always love you, Raffe."

"I know you will, and I'll always love you." He suddenly gets serious. "Now, I've got a special birthday surprise set up for you just past the dock about 100 yards in the trees." He pulls out a flashlight, handing it to me. "This will help light the way."

"Wait. What?"

He stands, pulling me with him. "Don't worry, Dirk will be along shortly." He glances at his watch, then raises his eyes, winking at me.

My heart starts thumping loudly in my ears. Oh. Oh god. It's my birthday. I'm eighteen and I'm about to be alone with Dirk. "I... I can't do this without you."

He tips my chin. "You both have been using me as a buffer. It's time you do this alone. The both of you. You feel safer having me around because he makes your heart beat a little faster and it scares you. He feels better when I'm around because he thinks I can give you something he can't. He thinks he can't be gentle and caring but he can."

My eyes dart to the warehouse.

"No. You're doing this. You know here..." he pokes his finger over my heart, "that he will only go as far as you're ready to go. So, go on and enjoy the last few hours of your birthday. It will be worth it. I promise."

He kisses me on the forehead and shoves me down the path to the dock. I glance back at him before entering the tree line. With the light of the moon, I see him tap two fingers over his heart before walking away.

I choke back a sob and straighten my shoulders for what awaits me in the darkness of the forest. I shut the flashlight off when I reach my destination. A tent. I crawl inside and find little white lights strung along the top and side posts. It's filled with pillows and blankets. I laugh when I see a cooler with a happy birthday sign on it. I crack it open finding fruit dipped in chocolate and drinks.

When the flap to the tent suddenly opens, I jump a foot. Dark temptation crawls through the opening. When our eyes connect, my breath catches in my throat. Dirk glances around briefly before resting his eyes back on me. "Where's Raffe?" he asks.

I bite my lip, trying to control my emotions. He settles in front of me so that we are facing each other. He waits patiently for me to answer. "He's not coming."

When he doesn't say anything, I chance a look at him. His eyes are on me.

I scratch my head. "Um, he told me he's bowing out."

"What the fuck does that mean?"

"He thinks we should go on our own from here on out." I quickly wipe a tear away before it escapes down my cheek. "Raffe thinks that my love for you is different than it is for him."

"Is it?" he asks.

"It is," I whisper, my bottom lip trembling.

"We should go back to the warehouse." He starts to back away, but I throw myself at him.

He struggles to untangle us so he can get away.

"What are you so scared of?" I cry.

"Jesse, I can't be what you need."

"What the fuck do you think I need?"

He stops fighting. "I can't give you romance." He twirls his finger around the tent that Raffe set up for us. "I can't give you nice." He turns his head to stare at the opening of the tent.

I shove him in the arm and clamber away from him. "If that's what you think I need then fucking go." I rummage through the cooler, grabbing a beer and cracking it open.

"Jesse," he watches me guzzle half of it.

"No. If your spooked go on." I wave my hand at the entrance. "You know, I thought you would be different."

"What the fuck is that supposed to mean?" he says, flippantly.

251

I take another drink and then level my eyes on his. "I thought you would show me what it's supposed to be like." I finish the beer and toss it into the corner of the tent, then flop onto my back, staring at the lights twinkling above me. "It's fine, Dirk. Go. Just fucking go."

He hesitates a moment, then crawls out of the tent.

I lie there, wondering how the day went from perfect to shit in the matter of minutes. It's fine. It's fine. I'll just stay here and drink and drink and drink.

The tent flap flies open and Dirk barrels in. He crawls over the top of me, standing on his knees. His eyes are swirling storms of emotion. He grabs the back of his shirt, pulling it over his head. My eyes trail over his torso as the soft cotton rises. Jesus Christ. I try to scoot up but his thighs clench tighter over my hips holding me captive.

"You want me to show you what it's supposed to be like?" he asks as he unbuckles his belt, tugging it out of the loops.

My heart skitters like an unbridled horse.

I watch as he pops the button on his jeans, sliding the zipper down slowly. My eyes rise to his. He flicks the ring in his lip, and I swear the temperature rises thirty degrees. I can't take my eyes off this goddamn man. He's all fucking sorts of dark gorgeous.

Dirk bends over me, bracing his inked arms on either side of my head. "Last chance to back out, sweetheart."

"Have you ever known me to back out of anything," I whisper.

The swirl in his eyes slows. His thumb brushes over my temple. "You know I'll stop if you tell me to."

"I won't want you to stop." I raise my head and press my lips to his.

252

As quickly as the strike of a match, the tent goes up in flames. His mouth is everywhere, leaving tracks of heat in its wake. His warm hands slide under my shirt. Dirk incinerates every memory of touch that came before him. He pushes my shirt higher. I raise my shoulders so that he can pull it over my head. His eyes roam over my body, even those seem to leave scorching paths behind. "You are so fucking beautiful," he whispers over me, his words warming me from the inside.

His hands are rough and hot and goddammed perfect as they trail over my tanned skin. My eyes fall closed as I focus on them. Jesus, it feels good to have him touch me. I've never felt so... so fucking good.

I thought I would be scared. I was worried my skin might crawl. I was terrified it would feel too much like them.

God was I wrong.

I grab his shoulders and pull him closer so that he is lying on top of me. When I open my eyes, he is there, right there, staring deep into my eyes. He searches my face for signs. His thumb rests over the pulse in my neck.

"How do you feel?" he asks hesitantly.

"Fucking amazing." I draw my leg up, so my foot trails up the back of his calf.

He settles between my legs. Slowly, he shifts and presses his length against me. My stomach flips when he tilts his hips, grinding gently against me. Dirk smiles when I groan and push back against him.

He slides down my body. His fingers glide under the waist band of my shorts, kicking my heart into overdrive. He raises his eyes to mine. I give him a tiny nod before he slides them down my legs and off my toes. He tosses them to the side, not taking his eyes away from me.

Oh my god, this is embarrassing. I throw my arm over my face, hiding from him. When I feel his hot breath on my sensitive skin, I bolt upright. He pushes me back down, grabbing my wrists to keep my arms straight by my side. "I want to taste you, Jesse Miller."

What? Oh god.

This is Dirk. What did I think sex with him would be like? He's not the hop on, hop off sort of guy. He is going to want to... oh god, I don't even know. I'm so fucking naïve.

I flex my fingers as his grip tightens around my wrists. He is waiting for a response.

I inhale and blow out slowly. "Okay," I say uncertainly.

That's all the permission he needed. He releases my wrists and pushes my knees apart. The moment his mouth connects, my back arches off the ground. Holy fuck. Just. Holy fuck.

He chuckles, the vibration taking me places I never knew existed. His tongue flicks over me, making me cry out. Every woodland animal is going to be running for the hills. The more noise I make and the more I thrash in the blankets, the more insistent he becomes.

"It's... it's too much," I pant, fisting the blankets.

"There is no such thing," he stops to tell me. His eyes blaze up my torso. We stare at each other as I try to catch my breath. His scary, motherfucking eyebrow arches high as I feel his finger slide into me.

"Oh, um..." I grip the blankets tighter, my knuckles turning white.

A second finger enters as his eyebrow creeps higher.

"Happy Birthday, Jesse," he smirks.

And then...

"Oh. Oh my god, Dirk."

His fingers curl as his mouth descends on me again, teasing me so... so... good.

"Oh god. Oh god."

White stars burst behind my eyes. The breath caught in my lungs expands. I'm... I'm going to pass out. I just know I am.

"Holy... shitttt," I yell as my legs tremble around his head.

He doesn't stop. He doesn't fucking stop.

A second wave hits me, knocking me clean out of this world. I'm... I'm, holy mother of god, what kind of demon is he?

When Dirk's heat leaves me, I open my eyes. He's kneeling over me, a look of awe in his mood ring eyes. "Fucking beautiful," he says before sucking his fingers into his mouth. The way he's looking at me sends delightful shivers down my spine.

He shoves his jeans down in one swift motion, kicking them the rest of the way down his legs. I've seen him naked once before but good god, I forgot how impressive he is.

His inked hand grips his cock at the base and slides down slowly. A drop of precum falls to my leg. Fuck, I think I can hear it sizzle on my skin. I let my eyes travel leisurely over him. All ink and muscle. I want to get lost in him. I am lost in him.

He moves cautiously closer, his eyes darting between mine. I wet my lips, anxious to feel his body against me.

When he settles between my legs and his skin meets mine, we both groan in unison.

"You feel so good." His hands slide under my head, his fingers tangling in my wild strands. He grips them tightly, holding me still. "Don't close your eyes. Don't look away."

I can't even nod, he has my head pinned so thoroughly. "Okay," I whisper over his face.

His hips tilt. He enters me so gently, with so much care, it brings tears to my eyes. When he is fully seated, he pauses.

"I want to stay like this forever," I say quietly.

He relaxes, a smile forming on his gorgeous face. "Forever is a mighty long time."

"It's not long enough."

My words affect him. He looks away. "I don't deserve you."

"And I don't deserve you. But here we are." I run my hands up his neck, stopping when I reach his dark scruff. He drops his eyes back to me.

His mouth crashes to mine. He unleashes every pent-up emotion he had carefully tucked away under all that ink. Our love making becomes frantic. Suddenly, we cannot get enough of each other, cannot get close enough. I want to crawl inside him and live. I want to be the sugar skull girl trapped behind his tattooed ribs.

We touch, we kiss, we taste, we give, we take… until the predawn birds signal to us that a new day is about to begin.

Together, we are a tangled mess of sweat and limbs.

"Jesus, Jesse," he pants into my ear. I turn so that my back is pressed to his front. His arm wraps around me, keeping me safely tucked close to him.

"I don't want to go back inside," I tell him quietly.

"Me either but everyone will be up soon."

I turn my head to look at him. "What made you come back last night?"

His hand brushes back and forth over my stomach. "Raffe."

My eyes widen. He laughs.

"He was waiting on the dock. Seems he knows me better than I thought." His smile fades, a seriousness falling over him. "He called me a coward."

I turn away from him to stare at the tent, self-conscious that Dirk did not come back on his own.

Dirk leans in so his lips brush the shell of my ear. "He was right. I was being a coward. You had me spooked. I've never felt this way before, Jesse."

His hand roams up between my breasts. It doesn't stop until his fingers are wrapping around my throat. He squeezes gently. His breath hot on my ear. "It scares me because I knew once I had you, I would want more." His grip tightens, my heart picking up a notch. "And then I would want more, and more, and more."

His tongue skates along the shell of my ear, making me shiver in his arms.

"I'll never. Never. Get enough of you." He turns my face towards him. He kisses me with an intensity that scorches my insides and curls my toes.

I will never forget the look on his face when he pulls away. It's scary, frightening, and god if I don't fucking love it.

257

"Raffe was smart to bow out when he did. Because once I had you," he pauses, his eyes boring into mine, "I knew I would kill anyone who touches you."

I swallow hard. He's serious. Profoundly serious.

"You are mine, Jesse Miller. No one will touch you, look at you, even breathe in your direction without going through me first."

We stare at each other. I watch the turmoil swim in his eyes.

"Do you understand?"

I nod slowly. His hand falls away from my neck.

"Does that scare you?" he asks, studying my face.

"No," I whisper, running my hand over my throat. "I feel the same way about you. If any, and I do mean any, woman approaches you... you better send her packing real quick."

His nostrils flare. He rolls me onto my back, smiling wickedly in my face. "Is that right?"

"I'll stick a fork in them, Dirk. I'm not kidding."

He falls onto his back, laughing hard. "Oh, god, Jesse. You are fucking perfect. Perfect," he exclaims between bouts of laughter.

It's music to my ears. I smile smugly to myself. Scary tattoo man is mine. Finally, mine.

When I was a girl, I thought I wanted to be like him. But maybe what I really wanted was simply for him to be mine.

Chapter Thirty-Six

Jesse

My dad looks up when I walk in for breakfast. His eyes follow me as I grab a bowl and sit at the table. Katie slides the box of fruit loops over to me. Raffe comes in to grab a cup of coffee, he plops down across from me. I keep my eyes on my cereal.

"I went to your room this morning to wake you up, you weren't there," dad says.

I shove my spoon in my cereal, my heart beating nervously. "I went for a walk. Couldn't sleep."

"We went for a walk too," Katie chirps in excitedly. "We took Teddy for a walk."

Shifting in my chair, I offer her a smile. "That's good. Teddy seems to really like you."

"I love him," she tells me. She slurps the last drop of milk out of her bowl. Once she puts her bowl in the sink, she bounces over to my dad and gives him a hug. "I better go. Candice is waiting for me."

"Have a good day at school, sweetie," my dad says, bonking her on the nose.

She nods. "Bye Jesse, bye Raffe." She hurries out the door.

The silence that settles over the room is deafening. The only sound the crunch of my fruit loops.

Raffe finally breaks it. "It's amazing, the difference in Katie."

I nod, not looking up. I shovel more food in my mouth so that I don't have to talk.

My dad doesn't say anything to Raffe. Instead, he directs his attention to me. "I didn't see you while we were out walking."

I almost choke on my food. "I didn't see you guys either. Weird." I jump up and scrape my bowl into the trash. "Well, I'm off to my first day at the new shop."

"What, are you too old to give your old man a hug goodbye?"

I rush over and wrap my arms around him. He hugs me tight. "You know you can talk to me about anything, you know that, yeah?"

"Yeah." I give him and Raffe one last look before heading out the door.

Raffe catches up to me outside. "You got anything scheduled today?"

"No," I tell him. "I'll probably be on walk-in duty."

"I'm free today, so I thought I would stop by, and we could work on the rose piece."

"Yeah, sure," I say as I toss my bag in the rod.

He grabs my arm and turns me to face him. "You okay?"

I drop my head and smile shyly.

He chuckles. "Okay, so things went well last night?"

"It... it was amazing."

"That good huh?" He leans against the rod.

"I'm sorry."

He grabs me by the shoulders. "Don't be sorry. I'm not upset. It's...." his cheeks turn pink. "I always wondered what he would be like, you know, in bed."

My eyes go wide. I guess I thought Raffe had only been interested in me but no, he was interested in Dirk too. Now, I really feel bad. The thought of losing Dirk breaks my heart. Is Raffe's heart breaking from the loss?

"Raffe, why didn't you tell me?"

"I thought everyone knew." He laughs sadly. Raffe pulls me into his chest. "I'm happy for him. He was never meant to be mine. I think I let myself get infatuated because he saved me and because of those damn eyes of his. Don't feel bad."

Raffe lets me go when Jeremy one of the guys who works in the shop walks up. "Hey, Jesse, I got the paint for the rod."

I clap excitedly. I'm going to give Sylvia a paint job. "Thank you, thank you."

"When you're ready, come find me and I'll give you a hand. The equipment isn't too hard to use but I can share some tricks and tips with you." He pats me on the back as he walks away, heading to the shop.

My eyes follow him before going back to Raffe but when I turn around, I see Raffe is focused on something up by the warehouse. I follow his gaze. Dirk is standing by the front door, giving Jeremy a death glare. His words from this morning come rushing back. "Oh, fuck," I whisper under my breath.

Raffe stands up straight. "Go on, go to work. I'll deal with Dirk. Don't worry, I won't let him kill Jeremy." He laughs as he walks away. "I'll see you at the shop."

When I get to the shop, Dan is already there. I hop around excitedly.

"You're in a good mood today."

"That's because life is grand," I say dreamily, falling into my chair.

He shakes his head. His first customer of the day comes in and he takes him over to his chair. "Any walk-ins are yours today, Jess," he says from across the room.

I give him the thumbs up. "I'm going to work on Raffe. He should be right behind me."

He nods and gets to work on his client.

Raffe shows up a few minutes later just as I'm getting everything set up. He takes a seat in my new chair. "Nice," he says, running his hands appreciatively over the leather. "Man, this is great not having to drive over to shitsville."

I snap my gloves on, focused on what I want to get accomplished today.

"Dirk says he'll be here shortly."

I glance up at him, snapping my gum. "What? Why?"

He shrugs his shoulders. "Good luck going much of anywhere without him. I think you've created a fucking monster. He's having words with Jeremy as we speak."

"Raffe, I thought you were going to stop him?" I say, thoroughly annoyed.

"Oh yeah, about that. I had to worry about my own ass. Dirk told me all the ways he could break my balls if I so much as touch you."

My gun silences. "But we are friends. He can't do that."

He winks at me. "Don't worry your pretty little head. He isn't going to hurt me."

The door dings. Dan gets up to help the lady at the counter. I mumble to Raffe about how I'm going to give Dirk a good talking to when I notice he isn't paying attention. He's eyeing the pretty dark-haired lady at the counter.

She nervously pushes her hair behind her ear. "I'm looking for Daniel Hoffman."

Who?

"That's me," Dan says.

I glance at the lady again. Her eyes dart around the room. When they pass over Raffe and me, I gasp. Mood ring eyes. The same mood ring eyes I stared into this morning.

She stops on Dan. "Well, this is a little awkward, but I think we may be cousins."

I jolt out of my chair. Raffe grabs my hand to keep me anchored by his side.

LM Terry

"Rachel?" Dan whispers, taking a step back.

The lady clears her throat. "Hm, you remember me?" she asks hesitantly.

Dan nods, dumbfounded.

She smiles and shifts her weight from foot to foot. "I was hoping you…" her bottom lip begins to tremble, but she continues, "might know where to find my brother."

The door to the shop opens as if Gabriel's God orchestrated the whole reunion. Dirk walks in, his eyes immediately seeking mine. His eyebrow cocks up when he sees the look on my face. He rushes towards me. "What's wrong?" he asks, pulling me into his arms.

"Your… your sister," I whisper.

He pulls back to search my eyes, then he slowly drags them away and glances over his shoulder. His arms drop to his side. "Rachel?"

She nods, tears streaming down her face. They stare at each other in a daze. Both lost in the memory of the day they were separated and then it hits Dirk, and he rushes to her, crushing her against his body. "Where have you been?" Dirk asks with pleading eyes. He pushes her back, looking at her from head to toe.

"I'm, I'm fine." She pushes against his chest, uncomfortable with his scrutiny. "It isn't what you think."

He releases her, taking a step back to give her space.

Her eyes wander over his ink before dropping to her feet. "I'm sorry, I don't remember much. I… I remember a few things. The park…" her words trail off.

He runs his hands through his hair. "Do you want to go get a cup of coffee or something so we can talk." He glances over his shoulder. I smile

264

at him encouragingly. His sister is here. Actually here. This is so unbelievable.

She nods. "I'm sorry I didn't mean to intrude on your business," she tells Dan.

Dan's eyes soften. "You're not intruding. We're all family here, you included."

"I'll see you back at the warehouse later today," Dirk says, his eyes glassy with unshed tears.

"Yeah, of course. Maybe your sister could join us tonight for dinner?"

He takes my hands in his and squeezes, a smile forming on his face. He nods. "Things are finally looking up, huh?"

I nod, unable to speak. Things are most definitely looking up.

He holds the door open and follows Rachel out.

The rest of us stand around shell shocked for a minute. Dan heads back to his client and I sit down, pushing my chair close to Raffe. I fire up the gun, bowing my head over his leg.

"Her eyes. Did you see her eyes?" Raffe asks, a hint of awe in his voice.

I glance up quick to catch the look on his face. "Yeah, mood ring eyes."

He smiles and runs his thumb over my ring. "Kind of hard to ignore aren't they."

"They do demand attention." I laugh.

His eyes trail back to the door. "I hope wherever she was, it wasn't too painful. It will kill Dirk if someone hurt her."

We work for a few hours, finally putting the finishing touches on his piece.

"I forgot, Candice caught me on her way to take the girls to school. She told me to let you know she's dropping Katie by after school. She needs you to give her a ride home. She has to run Ally to her dads for the weekend."

"Cool, I'll make sure I wait for her."

He kisses me on the forehead before leaving. Dan leaves shortly after, telling me he will see me later tonight. He's going back to Trap to finish packing. He's moving into the warehouse now that the shop in Trap has sold.

I doodle in my notebook until Katie comes bouncing in the door with Teddy on her heals. He comes over right away, tail wagging, for pets. Katie rattles on about her day as she walks around the shop, taking everything in. "I'm so happy Candice brought Teddy with her when she picked us up from school," she says, sticking her face in a jar of suckers that Dan keeps on the counter.

"Were you worried about him?" I ask, busying myself shutting everything down for the day.

She nods, pushing a pink lollypop in her mouth. "It's a new home and I didn't want him to be scared without me."

"I'm glad that you and Teddy are friends."

She pulls the sucker out of her mouth and is about to pop it in the dog's mouth when I stop her. "You can't give him sugar, sweetie. It will make him sick."

She frowns. "That's sad he can't have candy."

"He doesn't know what he's missing since he's never had it." I tell her, waving my hand for her to follow me out the door.

"I didn't know I missed having a daddy until I got Bill," she says coming to stand by my side.

My heart shatters all around us. I crouch down in front of her. "The adoption is almost final, soon he will be your daddy."

"I don't think he wants me to call him that though." She looks into my eyes sadly.

"Why? Katie you can call him whatever you feel comfortable calling him. He and Candice love you. They want you to be their daughter, just like Ally."

"And you?"

I sigh. "Yeah, me too. We will all be sisters soon."

She smiles brightly at this. "So, you don't think he will get mad?"

"No, he will definitely not be mad." I kiss her on the cheek and stand. "Let's go home and get supper started. What sounds good?"

We step outside. "Pizza!" she squeals.

Teddy growls and pushes in front of us, pinning us to the building. Katie screams at the sudden change in him. I push her behind me and glance around, searching for what has the dog so pissed off. My eyes find the offending person, standing across the street in front of his bike. His black jacket is draped across the seat. The Devil's logo of a large cross embroidered across the back.

Katie whimpers when she sees him.

His eyes take us in. He tips his head, waiting to see what I'll do. I pat Teddy to try and calm him and turn to face Katie. I block her visual of him with my body. "It's okay. Take Teddy and go back inside. He's here to see me. It's just club business. Everything is fine. It will just take me a minute."

She starts to cry. "He's friends with the bad man," she groans.

"I know, sweetie. The bad man is gone. I promise. This one won't hurt you. Just go inside, lock the door, and wait for me."

I unlock the door for her, and she quickly hurries inside. I pull Teddy back. He's still growling at the man across the street. I shove him in and wait to hear the lock click. Once it does, I spin around and storm across the street.

"What the fuck are you doing here?" I demand.

Crow's gaze peruses over me leisurely. He lights up a cigarette, blowing smoke in my face.

I stand there with my arms crossed over my chest, fuming. Fucking fuming that he scared Katie.

"A little bit tougher than the last time I saw you," he says with a smirk.

I take a step back, his words sending me spiraling back to the weekend in the trailer. My eyes go to the silver crow dangling from his neck. He chuckles, happy to have struck a nerve.

"What do you want?" I force my eyes back to his cold, dark, black, soulless ones.

"I'm here to talk about reparations."

I laugh and turn away. I'm not entertaining any ideas of reparations.

"Katie seems real happy with Bill and Candice."

I stop, my foot hovering mid-air.

"You know, I just happen to know her real father. Wouldn't it be sad if he decided to come forward? Especially, now that the adoption is so close to being finalized."

My heart splats on the ground. He could be lying but after the way my life has played out, he's more than likely telling the truth.

"He's not a nice man either. Kinda like the guy from my club you had killed."

Slowly, I spin around.

He blows his smoke towards the sky before tilting his head to look at me. "Not that I give a fuck. I would have killed him myself, had I known."

I stand there. Ready to take the bullet he shoots my way if it means Katie doesn't get caught in the crossfire. "Oh, if you're into killing pedos, then maybe you should start with yourself," I sneer. He's no better than the man that hurt Katie.

He shakes his head and points his cigarette at me. "Boy, do I wish my brother was here to see this." He motions over my body, whistling. "You know your mom used to let us tag team her."

Red. All I fucking see is red. I charge at him. My fist connects with his jaw, sending his cigarette flying out of his filthy mouth.

I grab my hand, pulling it to my chest. Jesus, that fucking hurt. He grabs me by my hair and shoves me over the seat of his bike, my stomach pressing hard into the leather. My head hangs over the other side. I stare at the sidewalk, tears blurring my vision.

He leans over me, pressing himself into my backside. He tugs my hair, pulling me so that his face is next to mine. "If you ever hit me again. You. Will. Regret. It," he spits in my face.

Crow grinds himself against my ass. My anger quickly veers to fear. He won't rape me here, I remind myself. Not in broad daylight.

He pulls me back harshly, tossing me to the ground. My elbows scrape the pavement as I brace myself from the impact. Crow crouches down in front of me. I wrap my arms around myself, hiding my face from him. "This is more like it," he says, happy with the fact he put me in my place.

He grabs my arm, pulling a pen from his pocket. He bites the cap off and scribbles a phone number on my skin. He stands, pushing the cap back on and shoving it in his jeans.

Crow takes hold of my hand and pulls me to my feet. "Call me tonight and I'll give you directions on where to go."

"I'm not going to be able to get away from the warehouse."

He tosses his leg over his bike. "You're a smart girl, Jesse. You'll figure it out." His leg shoots down and his bike roars to life. I don't move until he's completely out of sight. And then I still don't move. I don't move until Katie comes running out with Teddy.

"Jesse, oh Jesse. Did he hurt you?" she cries, hugging me around the waist.

"It's okay, Katie. I'm fine. You ready to go home?"

She nods, wiping tears from her eyes. "I was so scared."

"It's... it's okay. Hey, how bout we pick up that pizza we were talking about?"

On the way home, I glance over at her. She's sharing a piece of pizza with Teddy. I know. I know. But after the day I've had, I need to pick my battles. Her sharing with her new best friend is the least of my problems.

"Hey, we don't need to tell Bill about that guy today. Okay?"

She wipes her mouth on her arm. She nods and turns away from me.

"I mean it, Katie. I handled it. We don't want to worry Bill, do we?"

She shakes her head, still not looking at me.

I sigh and we finish the rest of the short trip in silence. I hope she doesn't tell Bill. I can't risk the adoption not going through.

Once we are home, Katie runs off with Teddy. I set the pizzas in the dining room and head to my room to shower. My elbows hurt like a bitch. I could tell they were bleeding, but I didn't want to draw Katie's attention to them.

When I get to my room, any strength I thought I had, vanishes. I collapse on my bed, shaking. Everything was going so well. I should have known.

Oh god. I told Katie to lie... well, not lie but same thing.

Knowing that I need to make this right as soon as possible, I hop up and head back downstairs. Goddammit, what was I thinking asking her to keep quiet? That's the last thing she should do.

Katie and I bump right into each other as she comes around the corner from my father's office.

She glances up at me nervously.

I drop to my knees in front of her. "Katie, I owe you an apology. I'm so sorry I asked you not to tell Bill about today. That was wrong of me."

She raises her eyes to me while twirling her shirt in her hands.

I brush the hair out of her face, cupping her cute little cheeks in my hands. "I guess I'm used to handling problems on my own, and I didn't think about what I was asking of you. You should never lie or keep scary things to yourself. I'm so sorry, Katie." I drop my head in shame.

Katie's little hands cradle my cheeks just like I had done to her. "It's okay, Jesse. I told Bill about the man who hurt me. It made me feel better. You should tell him about the man who hurt you. You can tell daddy anything."

She called him daddy. Katie, little Katie, giving me her words of wisdom is too much. I break down as she puts her arms around me, hugging me tight.

"I love you, Jesse. I'm so glad you're going to be my big sister."

I sniff back my emotion, returning her hug. "And I'm so glad you're going to be my little sister. We will always look out for one another, won't we?"

She nods her head and uses her hands to wipe away the tears on my cheeks. "I already told him about the bad man that was there today." Katie looks me straight in the eye, not one hint of regret.

"Thank you for having my back, little sis," I give her a kiss on the forehead and then push myself up off the floor. "I better go talk to him."

Chapter Thirty-Seven

Jesse

I talked to my dad. It wasn't as uncomfortable as I thought. He cleaned my elbows, fixed me up a slice of pizza and sent me to bed. Like a child. Part of me doesn't mind, the other part wants to sneak out and call Crow. I'm trying to put all my faith into my dad and the club. I am. I'm trying.

He came in to check on me before he went to bed. I asked what they were going to do about Crow. "He's bluffing, Jesse," was all he had to say.

While that may be true, I don't think Crow is simply going to give up. Me calling his bluff on this is going to anger him. He's wanted to make my dad pay for killing his brother all those years ago and he's determined to do that through me.

My door opens, Dirk's familiar tobacco scent wraps around me. His boots thud to floor one after the other as he takes them off. He slides under the covers, pulling me close to him.

"What are you doing in my room? Dad will kill you if he finds you in here," I whisper.

He kisses the back of my head. "I needed to hold you."

My heart thumps a happy little tune. "How is your sister?" I turn in his arms so I can look into his eyes.

"She's good. I took her back to her hotel." He brushes his thumb over my temple, his eyes bouncing over my face.

"Where has she been all these years?"

"She doesn't remember much of her life before the abduction. She was raised by a couple who couldn't have kids." He pauses to lean in and kiss my lips gently. "She started to realize something wasn't right when she asked why they didn't have any baby pictures of her. The more she dug, the more suspicious she became. So, she did one of those DNA swabs and it connected her to Dan on some ancestry page. He had done a test a few years ago. Anyhow, with the help of a therapist she's gotten some of her memories back, but they are choppy at best."

"Did they hurt her?"

"No, she said they were loving parents. Probably better than our own. My parents gave us lots of things, they had money, but they were never home."

My heart breaks. He looks so sad. "She's here now. It's not too late to have a relationship with her. Look at me and my dad."

His mood ring eyes glow in the moonlit room. "I failed her back then." He rolls onto his back. "And I failed you today."

"What?" I prop myself up on my elbow, wincing. "You did not fail me."

He pushes himself up, grabbing my arm. Gently, he twists it so he can examine my elbow. Starting at my shoulder, he kisses all the way down my arm, pausing over the scrape. His eyes meet mine. "I should have been there today."

"You can't follow me around everywhere."

"Fuck if I can't."

"Dirk," I shove him playfully. "Be serious. I handled it fine on my own."

He pushes me on my back and crawls over me. "From now on, you don't go anywhere without me. I'll drop you off at the shop and pick you up. Period."

"You're fucking crazy," I giggle, trying to roll out from under him.

"I'm serious. I hid your keys to Sylvia. So, the back of my bike is your only option."

My giggles evaporate in thin air. "What?"

He slides my panties off my hips, his mouth trailing behind them as they slip off my toes.

"Dirk." I try to shove him off me, grunting for effect. "For one, you can't take my keys. Two, we can't do this here. Dad will hear us, he's in the next fucking room," I whisper yell, my ire rising with each beat of heart.

His eyebrow pops up over his glowing eyes. Jesus, I can't deny him, so I still beneath him.

"He won't hear me. He'll hear *you*." He pokes me in the chest, a devilish smile spreading over his face.

I watch as he peels his shirt off and unbuttons his jeans. Shit, we are really doing this here.

His kisses make me forget where I'm at. They are everywhere. Where his kisses trail off, his hands take over. Before I know it, I'm panting, fisting the sheets in my hands. He smiles down at me, happy that he has effectively rendered me speechless.

He settles between my legs, nudging me gently. We both moan quietly when he enters me. The rest of the world fades away. There is nothing better than feeling his skin pressed against me.

Dirk doesn't take his eyes off mine as his hand slides up between my breasts. He pauses over my throat before placing his hand over my mouth. He tilts his hips, hitting me in a spot that brings tears to my eyes. *Oh, god. Oh, god. Right there. Don't stop. Don't stop.*

I fall. I fall. I fall.

His hand presses against my mouth almost painfully as he traps my screams of ecstasy behind my closed lips. He holds himself above me, chasing his own pleasure when I combust again. Something about the way he takes control of my body, bending it to his will, turns me on.

When he reaches the peak, his eyes turn a shade I've never seen before. He falls on top of me, his face pressed in the crook of my neck. He removes his hand from my mouth, allowing me to finally catch my breath.

"Now, back to what we were talking about," I whisper in his ear.

He laughs, his whole body shaking on top of mine. His head bops up, a genuine smile on his scary, beautiful face. "Well, that didn't work. I'll have to do better."

He flips me onto my stomach, pressing me down into the soft mattress with a palm to my back. He slides into me from behind in one smooth motion, his legs on either side of mine, effectively pinning me to the bed. *Oh. Oh, that feels fucking good.* He leans down and whispers in my ear. "I'm going to fuck you all night, Jesse."

I moan in response.

"You'll be too worn out to argue with me after that."

The good news is Dirk is a-fucking-mazing in the bedroom.

The bad news is Dirk has figured out a way to effectively shut me up. *If that is indeed bad news.*

Chapter Thirty-Eight

Jesse

Dirk is scowling as Jeremy helps me put the finishing touches on Sylvia's new paint job. I left her with the natural rust color but added the Rebel Skull logo on each of her two doors. She looks bad ass.

I stand back to admire her. Dirk makes his way over to us. Jeremy promptly excuses himself. "What do you think?" I ask him.

"I think Jeremy spent too much time leering over your shoulder."

I bite my lip and back away from him, one tiny step at a time. His predator eyes emerge. I pause. My heart slows as I plan my escape.

This has become our game.

He always wins but I don't mind. It's me that wins in the end. I'm always rewarded for putting up a good chase.

I dart out of the garage, making it all the way to the warehouse before he catches me. He pins me face first against the building. "Jesse, Jesse, Jesse. It does no good to run from me," he growls in my ear.

Pushing my butt out, I rub shamelessly against his crotch. He deepens his growl. His lips lock onto the side of my neck. "We should go in," I whisper, my libido hitting an all-time crescendo. I cannot get enough of this man.

He flips me around, his hands grabbing my ass, hoisting me off the ground. I wrap my arms around his neck, my legs quickly strangling his waist. He groans into my mouth, making me melt against him.

A little squeal pulls our lips apart. Dread seeps into my bones. Shit. Shit!

My feet drop to the ground. Dirk stares into my eyes, a silent apology passes between the two of us. We had been so careful. But the longer we're together, the easier it is to forget we are supposed to be hiding our relationship.

Slowly, he backs away from me. I glance over his shoulder, finding Katie jumping up and down, her hand locked in dad's. His face is red... so red. He tells Katie to run along into the house. She waves to Dirk and I before doing as asked. The minute she disappears inside, my dad is on Dirk.

When his fist connects with Dirk's face, I scream. "Dad, stop." I try to get between the two of them, but he pushes me away, knocking me to the ground.

Dirk takes a few more punches before Dan and Raffe show up, pulling Bill back. "I'm going to kill him," he yells as he tries to fight his way free. Dirk stands up and wipes blood from his face with the bottom of his t-shirt.

I sit on the ground, dumbfounded by the scene playing out before my eyes.

Dan tightens his head lock on my dad. "What the fuck is this about?"

279

My dad glares at Dirk. "He was taking advantage of my baby girl."

Dirk spits a glob of blood on the ground. His eyes sliding to mine.

"He… he wasn't taking advantage of me." I hop to my feet, crossing my arms over my chest.

Dan looks at Dirk. "Is what Bill saying true?"

Dirk raises his hands, shoving them into his hair. "It's… it's complicated."

Raffe bounces between Dirk and the other two, putting his hands out to hold everyone at bay. "Let's just go in and talk about this like fucking adults. Bill, you know Dirk would never hurt Jesse."

"He had her pinned to the fucking wall," my dad growls. His face turning a deeper shade of red.

A black car peels into the driveway behind us.

A round of gunfire shatters the afternoon.

I watch in horror as Raffe falls to the ground. Dan and my dad slide back into the entryway of the warehouse as Dirk reaches for me. I pull away, dropping to the ground, covering Raffe's body with my own.

The gunfire continues around us. As chaos breaks out, men from the club come rushing out, firing at the car that opened fire on us. Dirk crawls to Raffe and I, his gun pointed over the top of our heads. He fires as they peel away.

The quiet that follows makes me wonder if my ear drums are blown. Slowly, I push myself off Raffe. He doesn't move. My eyes drop to the blood on his shirt and then to the blood on my own. Someone screams. Maybe it's me, I don't know. Everything sounds so far away. "Raffe, Raffe," I cry, leaning over his face.

Dan pulls me back as I watch Dirk and my dad cut the shirt off him. Dirk shoves it over an open wound, pressing on it to stop the bleeding.

"Go inside, Jesse." I turn and stare at Dan, not understanding what he's saying.

He pushes me towards the warehouse. I back up towards the door, my eyes stuck on Raffe's face. He looks so peaceful, like he's sleeping. How could he be sleeping through all this? Suddenly, sound comes rushing back. I hear men yelling and a siren blaring in the distance.

When I get inside, the women are crying and hugging on the far side of the room. I keep walking. I walk all the way through the house and out the back door. I circle around the warehouse and make my way to the garage. Sylvia is waiting for me.

I fire her up and pull out of the driveway just as an ambulance pulls in. A glance in the mirror reminds me who I am. I've denied her for far too long. I should have taken a stand long ago. Another peek shows me that Dirk still has his hands on Raffe's wound, his eyes following me out the driveway.

I know they will send someone for me, so I make a turn. It won't take me where I need to go, but that's okay. I've got nothing but time. Miserable, heart-breaking time.

After driving a few hours, I stop in a nearby town to buy a burner phone. My hands shake as I dial. Dirk picks up on the first ring. My throat knots at the sound of his voice.

"Jesse, Jesse is that you?"

I can't talk. Oh my god, I can't even breathe.

"Jesse, baby, tell me where you are."

A sob escapes, releasing a torrent of emotion with it.

"Sweetheart, tell me where you are. I'll come get you." Panic rises in his voice. "Your dad is here. He isn't mad, Jesse. Please come home."

My dad gets on the phone. "Jesse, baby girl. You need to tell us where you're at."

"Is he…" I let my words trail. I can't say it.

"He needs you, Jesse."

I can tell by his tone that Raffe is in grave condition.

"Goddammit, Jesse. Tell me where you are."

When I don't answer, he hands the phone back to Dirk. I hear him mumble something about me being stubborn.

"Jesse, if you want to help Raffe, tell me where the fuck you are."

"Are you at the hospital?"

"Yes, we're all here. Everyone but you."

Good. Perfect.

"Keep everyone there."

"Jesse," he warns.

I tap the steering wheel, trying to rein in my emotions. The desert sun dips behind the mountains. I don't know if Raffe is going to pull through. This might be his last day on this earth. No matter how hard I try to ask about his condition, I can't seem to find the right words.

"I know what you're thinking, Jesse. But this isn't your fight."

"No?"

"No. We do this as a club." His gravelly voice demands I obey but sometimes, you have to be mean.

"Fuck you, Dirk. Just, fuck you."

I hang up.

Chapter Thirty-Nine

Jesse

I always wondered why other kids were afraid of the dark. The dark is nothing to fear. It's what lurks there that you should fear. I tap the cigarettes I bought on the kitchen table. The flick of the lighter briefly illuminates the room. Seems Renee has been able to keep the place somewhat clean since I left.

The sound of a bike pulling up outside, spurs a tingle of excitement in my muscles. The weight of my 380 pulls on the back of my leather pants as I take a long drag, blowing it out slowly. The minute Jimmy opens the door, he sniffs the air, freezing in his tracks.

His head slowly turns towards me. "Well, well, well, if it isn't Sugar. How the hell have you been?" He flips the light on, taking his time molesting me with his eyes.

"Never better." I kick the chair out across from me. He laughs and plops his ass down in it, setting his gun on the table in front of him.

"Care if I bum a smoke?" he asks, his eyes dancing with amusement.

I flick my pack, sending it sliding across the table. "So, what brings you back to Trap?"

"Oh, you know, thought I'd pay my aunt a visit."

He laughs. "Bitch moved out after you left. She didn't like the idea that you both have had a taste of this." He grabs his crotch.

I snort and roll my eyes.

"Come on, you know you've always had a thing for me." He blows smoke in my direction.

I ignore him. He can keep dreaming. "You know what I can't figure out?" I tap my lighter on the table, leveling my eyes on him.

"What's that, Sugar?"

"I pegged you for a top, but I've been thinking about it and I'm pretty sure you're a bottom."

The amusement vanishes as my words prick his faux confidence. "What the fuck does that mean?"

"Crow, now he's definitely a top. I bet he rides your ass like a champ."

His face flames. Jimmy is quickly losing his composure.

"After I had you both, it was obvious."

He picks up his gun and points it straight at my head. "Say that again. Go on, I dare you."

I laugh. "Tell me, how much does it suck being Crow's little bitch?"

Oh, I struck a nerve.

"It was all my idea. I'm the one who found you living with Renee. I orchestrated your undoing. Me. Not Crow."

My laughter echoes through the trailer. "You? You couldn't come up with a plan to save your ass. You had no clue who I was, but Crow did. He's the one who set you up with Renee. He. Used. You."

His hand starts to shake. "I'm calling him. Let's see if you're willing to run your mouth after he gets here. My guess is not at all when his cock is shoved down your scrawny throat."

"Oh, Jimmy. You're too easy. You just admitted who's really in charge. It was never you."

He lays the gun on the table and pulls his phone out of his pocket. He waits, his eyes shooting daggers at me. "Hey, the bitch is here."

Bang.

That was too easy.

I stand, walking calmly around the table. I bend over, staring at Jimmy's glazed eyes, blood dripping down his forehead as I retrieve his phone from the floor.

Putting it to my ear, I light up another cigarette. "Hey, I lost your number."

Crow doesn't say anything for a fat minute. I think I may have surprised the asshole. But the soulless fucker recovers soon enough. "How's your boy?"

"Better than yours."

"I'm surprised your daddy doesn't have you locked away in a gilded cage." I hear girls giggling in the background.

"I'm surprised you found a woman willing to suck your dick."

He laughs. "Well, when you're paying for it, they don't have much choice."

Bingo.

"Anyhow," I draw out. "You going to give me an address or not?"

"I'm a little busy right now, honey." The girls giggle like mindless bimbos in the background.

"Tomorrow then?"

"We'll see." He hangs up as I'm heading out the door.

I park down the street from Bell's House of Tail. I get busy painting. It doesn't take me long. There is only a dozen or so bikes parked in front of the whorehouse. His club has definitely dwindled. When I'm done, I climb the stairs to the abandoned building across the street. I pull Jimmy's rifle out of the bag and wait. I'm a good shot, so we'll see how many I can pick off before they run for cover.

Just as the sun is coming up, the bikers emerge from the building. They are laughing and slapping each other on the back. I let the scope pass over Crow. I'm saving him for something special. I pick out the other six men who raped me. I need to at least get them. They are his most loyal and therefore, the most dangerous.

My scope follows the lone prospect who attended my weekend of hell. He points at his bike. The other guys gather round to see what he's freaking out about. Guess they don't like the giants dicks I sprayed on their bikes. When they disperse to check on the condition of their own bikes. I pop the prospect in the head. I get at least three rounds off before reality sets in and they scatter.

All but Crow. He doesn't move. He stands there, staring straight at the building I'm in as bullets fly around him. I drop the gun and run. I get back to Sylvia, breathing hard. I'm proud of myself. I think I got all of the bastards. I fire her up and head out to regroup for the next scene. Jimmy's phone rings. I pick it up.

"I'm going to cut you from your pretty little cunt all the way up to your smart-ass mouth."

"Sorry, did I miss something? I'm just waking up." I yawn loudly into the phone. "I at least need a cup of coffee before we start any foreplay."

"Ready for that address, sweetheart."

"Oh, hold on, let me find my pen and paper. Let's see, shit, I must have left it back at Jimmy's."

"I'm surprised you're in such a good mood. I hear your boy took a turn for the worst overnight."

My stomach drops. He's fucking with me. He has to be.

Mean, Jesse. You have to be mean.

"It's you who's on the turn for the worst, Crow."

He laughs. "Is that so?" I hear his bike roar to life. He rattles off an address. "I can't wait to see you, Jesse."

I hang up. Immediately, I call Dirk, needing to know if Raffe is hanging on.

"You have two motherfucking minutes to tell me where you are."

I ignore him. "Is he still alive?"

He sighs loudly. "Jesse, please. I'm begging and you know I don't beg for anything. Please, please tell me where you are."

"I'm going to drag him to my hell and set him on fire. I need to protect what's mine. You're mine. Raffe's mine. Katie's mine..."

"Jesse, please tell me you're not in Trap."

"Is. He. Alive?"

"For now," he answers honestly.

Fuck. Fuck!

"I've got to go, Dirk. I'll see you on the flip side."

"Jesse," he yells as I hang up.

Chapter Forty

Jesse

As I drive to the address Crow gave me, which I'm fairly sure is his clubhouse, I try not to think about Raffe. I try not to think about the way he smiled at me when I first met him. I try not to think about how he sacrificed himself for Dirk and me.

Tears streak through my makeup. It's fitting my tears are washing her away. This is the last time I'll have to be her. After today, she won't exist. One more time. The burden will be hers. It has to be.

When I get there, I slide my pistol in the back of pants and stuff my knife in my right boot. I don't know if I'll survive this. If I don't, at least I'll die knowing my family is safe. Crow will have gotten what he wanted, destroying me.

Tiptoeing through the building, I quickly realize that there is no one here. As I'm leaving, I notice a trail of blood leading outside. Maybe I hit him at Bell's or maybe one of his own men got him by accident.

Walking out into the hot desert sun, I pull Jimmy's phone out of my pocket and call Crow. It rings several times before he picks up. "Where the fuck are you at?" I demand.

"You're not the only who protects what's theirs."

I pull the phone away from my ear, staring at Jimmy's phone. How the... oh, oh shit.

"I think you've risked your life enough for one day, Jesse."

"What did you do with him?" I ask Dirk.

"I hauled his ass straight to your hell, just like you planned. See you soon." He hangs up before I have a chance to ask anything else.

My hands shake as I drive to the railyard. How did Dirk know where my hell was? He must have followed me the last time I was there. But my cars are locked. *Like a lock would keep him out.*

The railyard is empty. What the fuck, where are all the squatters? I shut Sylvia's engine off and then pick my way through the railcars until I get a few yards from the ones I've claimed as my own. Dirk is leaning against the one that contains my own personal hell. A cigarette hangs from his lips, his feet crossed at the ankles and a bored expression on his skeleton face.

He painted his face.

"Well, hello, Sugar," he says in his gravelly voice.

I want to run into his arms and make him tell me Raffe is okay. But that doesn't happen.

I point to his face. "So, what's your street name?"

He shrugs his shoulders. "Most people on the street call me asshole."

My gaze drops as I toe an empty can on the ground. He takes a few steps towards me. His cigarette drops in front of me. I watch as he stomps it with his booted foot, then he takes a few more steps and wraps me up in the comfort of his arms.

His breath stirs the hair on top of my head as he speaks. "We need to wrap this up. Raffe is going to need us."

He's still alive!

His next words douse my relief.

"The bullet grazed his spinal cord. They aren't sure he will ever walk again. He got out of surgery right before I left. We need to be there when he wakes up." He squeezes me tighter as if he can hear the grief spilling out of my heart.

Dirk releases me and slides the door open on my railcar of hell. Crow is sitting on the floor, tied up and bloodied. He blinks a few times, one eye almost completely swelled shut. He laughs when he sees me. "There's my girl," he says. Dirk grunts behind me but doesn't say anything, he doesn't even move.

I step inside the car, my eyes roam over my paintings, over my demons. When they land on Crow, he smirks.

"I'm proud of myself. Looks like I accomplished what I set out to do. You've had a tortured life, haven't you?" he asks.

I don't say anything.

"You haven't figured it out, have you?" he taunts.

I squat down in front of him. He shifts, trying to reposition himself more comfortably. "You mean, have I figured out that you've had a part in all of this?" I pull my knife out of my boot and motion over the walls of the car.

He licks his lips, his eyes focused on my knife.

Dirk leans against the door, casually. His presence is a gift from Gabriel's god.

"Thanks to Katie, I've had a lot of memories come back to me."

A creepy smile spreads across his pocked marked face.

"Ah, I'm touched you finally remember me."

"I remember you coming to my grandparent's home. The heating and air technician they never called. But they let you in once you convinced them they should have the heating unit inspected once a year. They were dead the next day."

Dirk straightens, taking a step closer to us. I hold my hand up to stop him. He doesn't retreat but he doesn't advance either.

"I also remember how excited Rick was when he was able to buy himself a bike. I remember the man who stopped by the house to pay him for the odd jobs he had hired him for. You were pretty chummy. I bet you gave him loads of advice."

I tap my knife over his groin. He winces but doesn't miss a beat. "Oh, you know I like it rough, sweetheart," he says as he grinds his hips up towards me.

Dirk clenches his fists beside me. I dig the knife deeper until I hear the rip of his jeans. Crow screams, "Shit, okay, okay."

I ease up but I don't remove it. "And I remember you sitting in the front pew at church when I set Father Gabriel on fire."

He laughs at this. "Oh, I was so proud of you that day."

"And then, there was Jimmy." I stand up and walk around him.

My gaze strays to Dirk. His eyes soften. He didn't know. No one did. Not even me. It wasn't until I felt safe, that I allowed my mind to wander to those dark places I had tried so hard to avoid. Being at the warehouse with my dad, Dirk, Raffe, Dan… the entire club, was the tipping point for me.

This man has wanted to destroy me for so long. It ends today.

"Such great lengths to hurt me. Why? Just to get even with my dad for killing your brother?"

He laughs manically as Dirk grabs a can of gasoline and starts dousing the floor and walls with it. I walk around to face him again.

"I didn't give a shit about my brother. I did it for your mother. I loved her and she loved me. We were going to run away together. I was going to take her away from all this bullshit. But then she got fucked up one night and made a mistake and fucked Bill. She got pregnant with your ass. I forgave her, it wasn't her fault. My brother was always feeding her habit. I knew I needed to get her out of here, away from the drugs."

Crow stretches his legs out in front of him, still unable to find a comfortable position. "We headed out of town. Our first stop an abortion clinic. But your dad had us followed. He took her. I looked for her for months. Only after she gave birth, did he let her go." He narrows his eyes on me, spitting blood at my feet before continuing. "If it wouldn't have been for you, he wouldn't have come for her. He fucking took her away from me because of you."

He glances away from me. "I was taking her away from the drugs. She could have had a good life. You stole that from her."

My mother was going to abort me? Wow. I was not expecting that. When my eyes meet Dirk's, they confirm the horrific truth. He tosses the gas can to the ground and steps out of the car.

I shove my knife back in my boot. The ring on my hand catches my attention, shining black from my anger. I right myself and pull it from my finger. As I toss it back and forth in my palm, I think about how much my dad loves me. How much he sacrificed for me.

I glance over my shoulder. The only mood rings I need are starring back at me, encouraging me to be strong. To protect what is mine.

I turn back to Crow. Carefully, I set the ring on his leg. He stares at it, recognition crossing his face.

"When you see her in hell, let her know I got all my best qualities from Bill. Tell her to be prepared cause when I get there, I'm going to rule that place." I laugh, backing out of the trailer. When I get to Dirk, he hands me his lit cigarette. I take a drag, blowing it out as Dirk steps towards the door of the car.

"Wait. Wait. Let's talk," Crow pleads, rolling his legs under him so he can crawl to the exit. "I'll leave town. I'll leave the state. Hell, I'll even leave the country."

"Sorry, Crow. I learned a long time ago that I have to protect what's mine." I take one final drag before flicking the cigarette inside. Flames immediately erupt, matching the ones I painted on the walls and ceiling of the car. "Till next time." I give him a one finger salute as Dirk slides the door shut, locking it.

We both back away.

Eventually, Crow's screams fade into the night.

"Let's go," Dirk says, pulling me away.

"Wait, I want to burn the other one too."

He stares at me for a moment. When I offer him a small smile, he nods. He dumps the last of the gasoline in my car of dreams. I don't need this one anymore. My dreams have come true. I have a family. I have my dad. I light a smoke and toss it in.

"Ready?" he asks as it goes up in flames.

"No, not really."

He takes my hand in his, pulling me away from the burning cars. When we get to Sylvia, I glance around, looking for his bike. He reads my mind. "My sister dropped us off. She went back to sit with Raffe till we get there."

Once we get going down the road, I roll my head against the seat to stare out the window. My eyes dance over the stars in the inky sky. "I don't think I'm strong enough for what's next."

He doesn't take his eyes off the road. "You killed every one of your rapists in less than 24 hours, Jesse. I think your stronger than you think."

"I didn't want them to hurt anyone else in my family," I whisper.

Dirk reaches for my hand, intertwining our fingers. I turn to face him. A passing car illuminates his skeleton face, making my stomach flip. He did it for me. It's his way of letting me know he understands me… and her.

"This is what we're going to do. When we are with Raffe, we are strong." He squeezes my fingers. "When we are alone," he raises our hands, motioning between the two of us, "that is when we express our fear. Never with him. Okay?"

I nod, choking back my tears.

"And dad?"

He sighs. "He's upset with me, Jesse. I'm not going to lie. But he isn't going to take that out on you. He's worked too hard to get you back to let anything come between the two of you. Don't worry about Bill and me. I'm a big boy, Jesse, I can handle it."

"I can't lose you, Dirk. I can't lose any of you."

"You won't."

Funny thing is, I believe him.

The good news is I put my nightmares to rest. Crow cannot hurt me or my family any longer.

The bad news is I worry the damage he already inflicted will be too great to overcome.

Chapter Forty-One

Jesse

Dirk's sister lets us in a back door of the hospital. They kept everyone here so the police couldn't pin any of the Desert Devil deaths on any Rebel Skull. Not that the police give a shit. I'm sure they'll be happy they won't have to deal with them any longer. Trap will be a better place now that they're gone.

Rachel tells us she is going back to her hotel to shower and get some sleep. When Dirk opens the door to Raffe's room, my breath catches in my throat. My hand flies to my mouth. Oh god. I rush to his side. He's so pale and there are so many tubes coming from everywhere. My eyes run over all the instruments surrounding his bed.

Dirk pulls me away from the bed and pushes me into a chair. My eyes don't leave Raffe's lifeless face. I barely notice the sound of running water before Dirk is kneeling down in front of me. A cool washcloth to my cheek draws my eyes away from Raffe.

"We need to get cleaned up." He offers me a small smile as he wipes paint off of my face. I focus on the calm blue of his eyes.

"Who did you guys kill now?" a faint voice croaks from the bed.

Both Dirk and I turn our heads towards Raffe at the same time. I push Dirk back and quickly move to Raffe's side. I sit down carefully on the side of his bed. He reaches up with a shaky hand and draws his fingers down the paint on my face, brushing my eyes closed as he does.

I keep them closed. Dirk moves to our side and continues his mission to scrub the paint away. None of us say anything. When he finishes, I slowly open my eyes to find the two of them starring at each other.

Raffe drags his eyes back to me as Dirk moves to the sink to wash his own face. "Did you get him?"

I give him a jerky nod, trying to prevent tears from slipping down my cheeks. "How are you feeling?" I whisper.

"Never better." His panty melting smile appears over his beautiful face.

Leaning over, I place a gentle kiss on his lips. When I pull back, Dirk takes a seat on the opposite side of the bed. We give each other a quick look before Dirk delivers the devastating news to his best friend.

Raffe's eyes bounce between the two of us. He swallows hard as he listens. "You mean I might never ride again?"

My eyes drop to the white blanket covering his body.

"No, you dumb ass. I'm telling you what the fucking doctors told me. Now, listen to what I'm telling you." Dirk chucks me under my chin, insisting I look at him too. When I do, he returns his mood ring eyes back to Raffe. "You will walk again. You *will* fucking ride again. Don't listen to these pricks. It will happen because I'm going to make it happen."

Raffe blows out a long breath. "Dirk, I don't know if anyone has ever told you but you're not a fucking god."

Dirk stands up. "I'm as close as you're ever going to get to one." He turns and walks out of the room, leaving Raffe and I alone.

I start to open my mouth, but Raffe raises his hand. "Don't you dare apologize to me, Jesse."

My mouth snaps shut. That is exactly what I was going to do. This is all my fault.

"I'm tired, Jesse. I... I just need to sleep."

I nod, sucking back my emotions. "Yeah, of course. We will be right outside."

He turns his head away and closes his eyes. Before I close the door I take one last look. His eyes are open again, locked on the ceiling. My heart cracks right down the middle for my friend. This is so unfair. Raffe is the best of the best. He didn't deserve this.

I make my way to the waiting room to find Dirk. My dad is sitting in the middle of the room alone. He glances up when I step inside.

"He's walking everyone out. He told them to go home and get some sleep."

My eyes dart around the empty room. "You should get some sleep too," I tell him quietly.

He watches as I pause by a magazine rack, mindlessly running my hand over each copy, not really seeing what I'm looking at.

"Come here, Jesse," he says sternly.

Reluctantly, I plop down in the chair beside him. He lets his eyes roam over me, sighing loudly. "You are so damn stubborn."

"Yeah, well, I hear it's a trait I inherited from my dad." I shrug my shoulders and turn my face away from him to stare at the blank wall across from us.

"Did you get them all?"

"Yeah."

He shifts towards me and leans forward, forcing me to look at him. "Don't pull away from me."

"I'm not."

"How long have you and Dirk…" his words trail off.

I blow out a breath. "I can't do this right now."

"Jesse, I need to know. I need to know." He shakes his head. "It's killing me."

My dad looks so tired. He's as much a victim as I've been.

"Since the day he found me."

His eyes bounce over my face. "Jesse."

I hold up my hand. "I've loved Dirk since I met him. You want the truth; I'm giving it to you."

He leans back in his chair, letting me finish.

"Nothing happened until I turned eighteen, if that makes you feel better."

He winces. "It's not love. It's infatuation and he should have known better."

"You're wrong. It's love. You may not understand it, but I do. He does."

"He was supposed to protect you, not take advantage of you, Jesse."

"Do you know how scared I was when my grandparents died? Do you know how scared I was when I was being molested by a teenage boy with nowhere to run? I had no one."

He runs his hand down his face, shaking his head.

"Dirk materialized out of thin fucking air that day. I remember how relieved I felt that he was there."

I pull my feet up on the chair and hug my legs as my mind conjures up my ten-year-old self.

"He was there when I needed someone and he stayed my someone, dad. Every time I found myself scared, I thought of him. I asked myself, *what would he do? What would he want me to do?*"

He makes a pained sound from somewhere deep in his chest.

"When we met for the second time, it was an instant spark. I'm not going to lie, it spread like a wildfire, but Dirk never let it get out of control. No matter how much I begged, he didn't budge. He didn't take advantage of me." I turn to face him. "I know how it must look."

I drop my head to my knees. Exhaustion of the last eight years finally catching up to me.

His warm hand rests on my head. "Okay, baby girl. Okay."

Tears buried for years burst forth. He wraps his arms around me, holding me tight. He whispers over my head. "I'll never know the girl you could have been. Crow stole that from me... from you. But I want you to know how proud I am of the woman you've become. You are so

302

strong, Jesse. So strong." His voice catches, his grief intermingling with my own.

When I drain myself dry, I lift my head to find Dirk sitting across from us. His fingers steepled in front of his mouth, elbows resting on his knees. My dad gives me a final squeeze. "Get her home, Dirk. I'll stay with Raffe tonight."

Dirk nods and ushers me out of the room.

Instead of driving all the way back to the warehouse, we go to my grandparents. We climb into my old bed, holding each other tight.

I let my fingers trail over the tattoos on his chest. It's nice to be tucked so close to him. I'm afraid to go to sleep. So much has happened, I don't know what I'll find in my dreams tonight.

"I was the one who followed your mom and Crow to the abortion clinic."

I lean my head back, surprised at the sudden break in silence.

"When I called your dad, he told me if I stopped her, he would give me whatever I wanted. I wanted to be vice-president of the Skulls. Something that normally doesn't happen for a sixteen-year-old. He gave me that. When I figured out where you were this last time, he told me he would give me anything my filthy heart wanted. Do you know what I want this time?" He pauses, running the pad of his thumb over my bottom lip.

I shake my head no.

"My filthy heart wants you, Jesse."

I smile and curl back into his chest. "I want you too."

"I'm going to tell you a story, not to hurt you. God, I don't want to hurt you." He pauses, thinking for a second before continuing. "I watched

303

your mom's belly grow for nine months. She used to moan and grumble about being pregnant. I thought what an ungrateful bitch. I was amazed she couldn't appreciate the life that was growing inside her. One day, I asked what she was going to name you. She laughed and said I could name you for all she cared."

Ouch.

"So, I did."

I push away from him. "What? You named me?"

"I wanted you to have a strong name. A name that said, *don't mess with me.*"

Blood pumps in my ears as I stare at the man of my dreams. The man whose strength I have borrowed for the last eight years. "You named me Jesse?"

He laughs. "This is going to sound silly, but I was reading a book on Jesse James. You know, the outlaw. I had to do something to pass the time while babysitting your miserable mother. Anyhow, I thought to myself, hmm, Jesse could be a girl or a boy's name. I liked it. And so, you became Jesse."

"Dirk, I don't know what to say."

He smiles. "How about that you like your name. That would be a good start."

"I love my name. I've always loved it."

"Good." He kisses the end of my nose. "Let's get some sleep."

I tuck myself in close to him, closing my eyes. I fall asleep in the arms of the man I've always belonged to. It may seem weird to some but to me it's perfect. Dirk and I are a perfect match.

When I wake up, I find Dirk in the garage. He's standing there, deep in thought. He startles when I move in the doorway.

Chuckling, I make my way over to him. His scary eyebrow pops up. "Sneaking up on me now?" he asks.

"What are you doing out here?"

"I have an idea on how we can help Raffe."

I hug him around the waist. "Let's hear it."

"Well, it all starts with my sister."

"Your sister?" I ask, confused.

"Did you know she just happens to be a physical therapist?" A wicked grin spreads across his face.

"He isn't going to like this, is he?"

"He isn't going to have a choice."

I shake my head back and forth. When Dirk has an idea, there's no talking him out of it. "Okay, let's get this plan of yours in motion."

He kisses me on the forehead. "This is why you're perfect for me. You're not even going to try to talk me out of it."

Chapter Forty-Two

Jesse

I t's been a busy couple of weeks. My dad and Candice had their wedding. Katie's adoption went through, which we celebrated with a big party. My dad went all out with bouncy houses, clowns, and ponies. Katie was thrilled. I'm so happy for her... for all of us, actually. She's brought so much joy to our lives.

With all that going on, Dirk and I still spent most of our time at the hospital. Raffe has been down, understandably so. He decided he wants to be transferred to a rehabilitation facility in Arizona, not because he thinks they will help him. But because he doesn't want to burden any of us. It's been heartbreaking to watch his spirit fade. He's basically given up.

I run my hands down my jeans nervously. Today's the big day. Dirk spins me around to face him. "You can do this. He will understand." He shrugs his shoulders, then adds, "Well, eventually he will understand."

I blow out a long breath, square my shoulders and then push the door to his room open. He's sitting up in bed starring out the window. His eyes slide to mine, and he offers me a small, fake smile. "Jesse, what are you doing here? I thought we said our goodbyes yesterday."

Ignoring him, I move over to the chair perched beside his bed and sit down. He watches me carefully. "What's going on?" he asks.

"Do you know how much Dirk and I love you?"

He rolls his eyes. "Yes, I know. You two have been smothering me with love for the past several weeks. It's sickening, actually."

I nod my head slowly. "Did you really think we were going to let you go to another state, to a facility full of strangers?"

"Jesse," he warns. "We've been through this a hundred times. I will not be a burden to the club. I'm going to Arizona. My transport will be here in a few hours. It's done." He crosses his arms across his chest.

"You're going to walk again."

"And like I've said, *if* that happens, I'll be back. If not..." his words trail off. He diverts his eyes away from me.

I stand up and move his call light out of his reach. He tries to grab it from me but he's not quick enough. "What the fuck, Jesse?"

"He's going to take you."

He blinks a few times, trying to absorb my statement.

Dirk opens the door, pushing a wheelchair inside the room ahead of him. "So, are we doing this the easy way or the hard way?"

Raffe whips his head towards Dirk, giving me enough time to inject him. He flinches as I pull the needle from his neck. "You two play dirty..." he slurs before his eyes fall closed.

Dirk and I high five each other before loading him up and wheeling him out of this godforsaken hospital. Victory is ours.

The whole club helped us with the remodel on my grandparent's home, my home. Dirk's sister, Rachel, moved in with us. We also have a room for Raffe, with everything he needs to make him feel as independent as possible, with an attached bathroom that also meets his needs.

The garage is filled with state-of-the-art rehabilitation equipment. We got everything Rachel said would help him. She's excited to work with him. She is confident that with her help, he will walk again. One thing I've learned about Rachel, is that she is just as cocky as her brother. Sure, she's quiet but don't let that fool you. She fits right in with the rest of us.

Raffe slowly stirs awake. He blinks as he struggles to focus on his surroundings. "Where are we?" he asks, sleepily.

"Home," I say, crawling up on his bed and snuggling under the covers with him.

He wraps his arm around me as if it's the most natural thing in the world. He kisses the top of my head. "Okay, that doesn't tell me a lot, but I will admit this is nice. You smell good."

I giggle, turning my face to look into his baby blue eyes. "It's my grandparent's home. Well, was, I guess it's mine now."

He lets his gaze roam over the room. "You did all this for me?" he asks quietly.

"I did this for all of us, Raffe. You belong with your family, not a thousand miles away."

"You are fucking stubborn, Jesse Miller."

I push myself up on an elbow, starring down into his beautiful face. "You knew that the day I met you."

He laughs, running a hand over his face. "I did. You were a ball of energy. You rolled in and changed everything." He notices the look on my face and quickly adds. "For the best. You changed our lives for the best."

My gaze travels down his body.

He grabs my chin. "Stop. You didn't shoot me. Crow did."

I chew on my bottom lip. "I know."

"So, do you feed your kidnap victims here? I'm starving," he teases.

He is already acting more like himself. This was a good idea. Dirk always seems to know what everyone needs. His methods might be a bit cave man, but he is usually right.

"Yes, I bought all your favorites." I hop up, rattling off all of his options.

He laughs, shaking his head. "God, I'm going to get spoiled living with you."

I smile so big that my cheeks hurt. "You're going to be spoiled by Dirk, Rachel and myself."

"Rachel?"

"Yep, she's your new twenty-four seven physical therapist." I lean over and whisper in his ear. "She's even tougher than Dirk, so prepare yourself."

He licks his lips, his eyes narrowing on mine.

"I've seen the way you look at her."

"It's those damn eyes," he admits, laughing.

I rub my hand over his chest, my mood turning serious. "Please let her help you."

He pats my hand. "I'll try. Okay?"

I nod, biting back tears. "It's all I ask."

"Okay then." He lets his hands slap down on the bed, coming to terms with his new living arrangement. "Go get me some food, woman."

Chapter Forty-Three

Jesse

As I'm heading out to the shop, I pause in front of the door leading to the garage. I watch as Rachel helps Raffe out of his wheelchair. She walks backwards, keeping her arms circled around his waist for support as he moves one foot in front of the other, slowly, bracing himself on the bars. He's come a long way in only a month.

Dirk comes up behind me, wrapping me up in his arms, his chin resting on top of my head. Raffe must say something funny because Rachel looks up into his eyes, laughing. He stares down at her, his eyes full of mischief. Dirk and I gasp in unison as Raffe dips his head, capturing Rachel's lips with his own.

Her hands leave his waist to slide around his neck, pulling him closer. The simple kiss quickly turns into one we should definitely not be eavesdropping on. Dirk places his hand over my mouth, backing us up until we are out of their line of vision. He pulls me into the other room before spinning me to look at him.

He searches my face. "Are you okay?"

"What? Yeah, why wouldn't I be?"

"I mean you and Raffe..." He runs his fingers through his hair, tugging on the ends making them stand straight.

"Are friends," I finish for him, placing my hands on my hips.

He spins around in a circle. "He kissed my sister."

"Are *you* okay?" I ask.

He stops in front of me. "I... I don't know."

"They've gotten close over the past month. And you know she has your mood ring eyes, so..."

He smirks. "My mood ring eyes?"

I suck my bottom lip between my teeth. Shit. "Yeah, your eyes are like mood rings. I can tell what you are feeling by the color they are at any given moment."

"What am I feeling right now?" his predator gaze emerges.

"Um. Dirk. I have to go to work. You know it's my first day back." I retreat two steps as he advances one.

"What is it that you think I'm feeling?" He takes another step and I jump back quick. "You seem a little jumpy."

"Dirk, I have to go. You're going to have to wait." I grab my bag off the hallway table, slowly edging for the door.

He laughs. "I don't have to wait for anything, Jesse."

He lunges at me as I dart out the door. As I'm pulling out of the driveway, he yells, "You can run but you can't hide."

I laugh in the rearview mirror as I watch his figure disappear. Damn, I'd like to let him catch me but like I said, it's my first day back. I've missed Dan and the shop immensely.

When I open the door, the little bell tinkles my arrival. Dan lifts his head and smiles at me. "Hey, partner, long time no see."

"Oh, you've seen me," I tease.

"Not here I haven't." He finishes cleaning his area, having just finished with a client.

He drops his large frame down in my chair. "You've got a client coming in about thirty," he tells me.

I take a seat on my stool and wheel myself close to him. I rest my elbows on his long legs, batting my eyelashes at him. He bops me on the nose. "I'm glad you're back, doll."

"Me too."

"So, we haven't had a chance to talk."

"About?"

"You and Dirk."

I sigh and push away from him. "I'll tell you the same thing I told Bill. Dirk didn't take advantage of me. I love him."

"He's sixteen years older than you, Jesse."

"Believe it or not, they taught me math in school."

"Give me one good reason why I shouldn't kill him."

"You're worse than my dad. What the fuck, Dan? He's your cousin."

"And you," he sticks a meaty finger in my face, "are like a daughter to me."

I take a deep breath. Dan is just being protective of me. I know this. He loves his cousin, same as he loves me, but the difference is, he feels responsible for my well-being.

"Dan, I love you." He blushes and turns his face away from me. "You're one of the best things to ever happen to me. You gave my art life. You gave a young, scared girl a place to feel safe. Most importantly, you gave me a love I hadn't felt since my grandparents had passed."

He finally faces me, his cheeks-stained bright red over his dark, bushy beard.

"I know what it's like to be taken advantage of." I drop my head to stare at my hands in my lap. "I know what it's like to have a man take what he wants, despite how I felt about it."

"Jesse," Dan groans. "I didn't mean…"

"I know what you meant. I know why you and Bill both have concerns. You're going to have to trust me. I know the difference. I'm not a normal eighteen-year-old girl. I've experienced things I shouldn't have had to, at far too young of age. I get it… I do. I love you for wanting to protect me, but Dirk is not a threat. Dirk showed me what love should look like between a man and woman. He's showed me how intimacy should feel."

Dan's face heats again but this time he doesn't look away. He studies me a long time before speaking. "He may be my cousin, but he's a straight up jerk, Jesse."

"Oh, Dan, you're all jerks but I love you anyway. Guess I have a thing for jerks." I bite my lip, waiting for his response.

"Fine." He crosses his arms over his chest. "You have my blessing."

I stand up and wrap my arms around him. "I love you, big guy."

"I love you too." When I release him, he wipes his eyes on the bottom of his shirt. "If you ever tell anyone you saw me cry, I'll whoop your ass, little girl."

Giggling, I back away from him to get ready for the client coming in.

"I'm taking off for the day. I don't have anything else scheduled. Lock up after you finish."

I give him the thumbs up. He kisses me on the forehead before throwing his leather jacket on and taking off.

My mind wanders as I busy myself. I'm so incredibly happy. Raffe and Rachel may have taken Dirk by surprise, but I saw it coming. When Raffe looks at her, it's like nothing else exists in the world. I've also noticed the heated glances she throws his way. Especially, when they are working in the garage together. It was only a matter of time before one of them acted on their feelings.

The door dings my client's arrival.

"I'll be right with you," I holler over my shoulder.

"It's okay, sweetheart, take your time. I'm going to keep you busy for the rest of the day," a gravelly voice says. The deadbolt clicks, echoing through the shop.

My hands pause mid-air. A bolt of electricity shoots up my spine. Do I run or stand my ground?

The sound of clothes hitting the floor, spurs me into action. I continue setting up my tray. "So, do you have a design in mind?"

"Eh, not really. Something dark, no color."

I giggle. "No pinks or purples?"

A squeak escapes my lips when his hand cracks over my ass.

I rub my butt, slowly turning to face him. My eyes drink in the dark god in front of me. Sweet mother of Jesus. How am I going to tattoo him? He is a walking distraction. His eyebrow is at a lazy angle. He's enjoying this.

I point to my chair as I snap on my gloves. He flicks the piercing in his lip, before giving me a smile that makes my stomach flip.

"I have something in mind. Trust me?"

"The only person I trust one hundred percent, besides myself," he says smoothly.

Good answer, it makes me smile. I trust him too.

"Okay, let's get started."

He looks sexy as fuck in nothing but his black, tight boxers and the ink on his skin. I zone in on the empty spot on his thigh. I've pictured this design for a long time. I'm super stoked to put my mark on him. I turn some music on and get busy.

He's quiet, a perfect client. I glance up at his face every now and then. His eyes are closed, and he has a serene expression on his face, you wouldn't know I was digging into his flesh with a needle. When I'm finished, I wipe the excess ink off his skin. Perfect.

As I'm studying it to make sure it's exactly how I want it, he shifts so he can get his first peek. I keep my eyes on the design, afraid he won't like it.

His fingers slide into my hair, he wraps the strands around his fist, slowly forcing me to face him. His eyes are stormy, a combination of dark swirls and deep blues. "What's this?" he asks, his eyes moving to my lips, waiting for my response.

"Us." I wince as his grip tightens.

He pulls me up onto the chair, forcing me to straddle him.

"Dirk, I'm going to hurt you. Your tattoo is fresh."

"You hurt me every day."

I'm so confused. Does he like it or not? Did I make him angry?

"Loving you hurts so fucking much. But nothing has ever been worth so much pain." His lips crash into mine, his tongue forcing entry. He moans into my mouth as soon as I allow him access.

When he pulls away, my fingers go to my lips, dancing over them. Jesus, I think he may have bruised them. He grinds his hips upward, making me forget... everything.

"I have to have you. Right. Now. Jesse," he growls. He releases my hair so that he can unbuckle my jeans. I push his hands away so I can do it myself. He pushes his boxers down when I rise to shimmy out of my pants.

Soon enough we are

skin to skin,

soul to soul.

Skull to Skull.

Two people who will do anything to protect what is theirs.

I wrap my arms around his neck. His hands grip my ass cheeks, forcing me to go at the pace he sets. It's brutal, it's wild, it's beautiful. Our eyes are caught up in a negotiation neither of us can deny. They are making treaties, forcing unspoken promises, and sealing deals.

The music continues, muffling the crude sounds of the building storm of our bodies. He sits himself up, pulling me close so we are chest to chest. His heart beats wildly against my own. Their rhythms sync to a perfect beat. Our beat.

A warm sensation builds low in belly. "Dirk, oh, oh." I want this to last forever. Not yet. Not yet, I chant in my head.

Then he groans two words in my ear, and I lose the fight. "Come, Jesse."

And I do. Oh lord, how I do.

He follows close behind, the final signatures on our new contract.

Dirk lies back in the chair, pulling me to lie on top of him. A thin layer of sweat glues our bodies together. I turn my head on his chest, listening to his heart struggle to regain a normal rhythm. "So, do you like it?"

He laughs, shaking us both. It's the best music, it etches lyrics into my heart and pounds notes into my soul. "Yes, I like it. It's perfect. How could it not be? It's us."

I smile against his warm skin. It is perfect. It's two skeletons, locked in an embrace. Their skull faces reflecting their love. Scary, yet... beautiful.

"Dan played twenty question with me when I called to lock down your schedule for the day. I thought he was going to deny me an appointment."

Giggling, I sit up. "He interrogated me too."

Dirk tucks my hair behind my ear, his finger trailing over my cheek before dropping to brush lightly over my breasts. "I'm sorry you have to defend us."

"I'll defend us till I die."

"Let's run away and get married," he suggests, sitting up so we are nose to nose.

"W-what?"

"We could go to Vegas."

"Dirk, my dad wants to kill you now. If we get married behind his back, he will gut you." I rest my forehead against his. "But it is tempting."

"I don't give a flying fuck what Bill thinks."

I climb off his lap and gather my clothes, tossing his at him. "Dirk, you're being ridiculous. Are you sure you even want to marry me?"

"Are you spooked?"

Stopping dead in my tracks, I spin around to face him, narrowing my eyes. "Dirk," I warn.

He slides into his jacket, his eyebrow at a frightening angle. "Call him."

"I'm not doing this."

"I will set the fucking world on fire, Jesse."

I grab my phone and dial my dad. I can hear Dan laughing in the background when he picks up.

"What's up, baby girl?"

"Well, I just wanted to let you know that I'm about to be a kidnapped bride."

It gets quiet on the other end.

"Dad?"

"I'm still here. Do you want to marry him?"

My eyes trip a few times before landing on Dirk. He is intently staring at me. "I do," I whisper.

"Give the phone to Dirk."

I hand the phone to him. Dirk doesn't say anything he just listens. He hangs up, handing my phone back to me.

"Well?"

"Well, what?"

"Dirk, I'm going to kill you myself."

He gives me a wicked grin before hoisting me off my feet and tossing me over his shoulder. A puff of air leaves me as my stomach connects with his shoulder. I beat on his back as he carries me out, locking the door behind us. He drops me on the back of his bike, shoves a helmet on my head before hopping on in front of me. I barely have a moment's notice to grab on for dear life before he is pulling away from the curb.

He doesn't drive us to Vegas like he threatened but we do end up at the cabin. I hop off and glare at him. "Anyone ever tell you how much of an asshole you are?" I stomp my foot, sending a poof of dust into the fading light of day.

"Every motherfucking day," he says seriously, hanging his helmet on the handlebars.

"What are we doing here? What did my dad say?"

"He said I couldn't marry you in Vegas."

"And?" I flop my arms out, encouraging him to go on. Good god, this is like pulling teeth.

"I don't know. I just wanted to be alone with you. Okay?"

My heart drops. My dad said no. Is he ever going to be okay with Dirk and I being together? The answer to that is probably no.

Dirk wraps me up in his arms. "Hey, it's all going to work out. Don't worry your pretty little head. I'm not going anywhere."

"I'm going to call Raffe and let him know we are staying here tonight," I mumble into his shirt.

He pulls back, taking my face in his hands. "I've waited a lifetime for you. I'll wait a little longer."

Dirk unlocks the door for me. "I'll fire up the grill," he says, tugging on the back of my hair.

"Sounds good," I say sadly. I didn't realize how disappointed I would be that my father wouldn't give Dirk his blessing to marry me. I mean, I know it was last minute but...

"Hey, girly," Raffe says cheerfully when he answers.

"Hey," I pull the blanket off the bed and wrap myself up in it. "Dirk and I are staying at the cabin tonight."

"Okay. You sound bummed about it. What's going on?"

"Dirk asked Bill if he could marry me."

"And he said no?" Raffe sounds surprised.

"Yeah, I think Dirk brought me up here to cheer me up."

"I think you should enjoy the evening, get a good night's sleep and I'm positive you'll feel better in the morning."

"If you say so. How are things between you and Rachel?"

"Good."

"Just good?"

He laughs. "Okay, more than good. Maybe even better than great." He sighs dreamily before continuing. "Thanks to you."

"What did I do?"

"You helped me realize I'm worth more than cheap one-night stands."

"I love you, Raffe."

"I love you too. Keep your chin up. Bill will come around."

"Yeah, I suppose. I'll let you go. Dirk probably has supper done."

"Sweet dreams, Jesse."

When I head back downstairs, I find Dirk setting the table. He looks up and smiles. "Did you tell him to keep his hands off my sister tonight."

"No." I roll my eyes.

"I guess they are both adults." He turns away from me to grab the ketchup out of the refrigerator.

"So are we but everyone seems to forget that. They want to make it dirty." My voice cracks on the last word. I don't know why this is bothering me all of a sudden. I've always known it was going to be an issue when Dirk and I made our relationship known.

"Hey," Dirk crouches down in front of me. "What's going on?"

I wipe my tears on the back of my hands. "I don't know."

322

"Jesse, your dad doesn't think we're dirty. He thinks I'm too old for you. Period. I think for a brief moment he thought I somehow manipulated you when you were vulnerable, but he's thought about it. Him and I have even talked about it."

"You have?"

"We have. I don't know if anyone will ever fully understand just how powerful this is." He motions between the two of us. "But we will show them. We're going to live our best life… together."

I nod, feeling a bit better. "I just don't want Bill to chase you off."

There's that damn eyebrow.

"Do you really think I'm a guy who gets chased off?"

I shake my head no, giggling.

"I'm the chaser, you'd be wise not to forget that."

My arms wrap around his neck as I drop to my knees in front of him, our supper quickly forgotten.

We spend the rest of the night making love. On the kitchen floor, the couch, the bed, even outside under the light of the moon.

Chapter Forty-Four

Jesse

The smell of bacon wakes me up. My stomach grumbles as I glance at the clock beside the bed. I smile and stretch my aching limbs. I definitely needed a morning of sleeping in, especially after the amazing night I had with Dirk.

I toss on the clothes I wore yesterday and head down the stairs. When I round the corner, my eyes land on my dad. He is leisurely drinking a cup of coffee. He glances up at me. "Good morning, sleepyhead."

He hops up and heads over to the stove. "I made your favorite, pancakes and bacon."

I sit down hesitantly at the table as he sets a plate in front of me. He takes his seat again, picking up his coffee and taking a sip. His eyes meet mine over the cup. "Go on, eat. It's not getting any warmer."

My gaze slides quickly over the room, looking for any sign of a struggle. My dad chuckles. I narrow my eyes at him. "You didn't kill him did you?"

He laughs and smacks the table with the palm of his hand. "Oh, believe me, if I wanted him dead, he would be six feet in the ground already."

"So, you don't want him dead?"

He reaches over and grabs my hand. "No. Because he makes my baby girl happy."

I let out a relieved sigh and pick up my fork. "Oh, good."

Digging in, I forget all about Dirk. My dad is a good cook, and we never did eat our supper last night. I'm starving. My dad watches me chow down, amusement dancing over his handsome face.

When I'm finished, I push my plate to the side and lean back in my chair, rubbing my hand over my belly. "That was amazing. Thanks, dad."

Just then, Katie bursts through the door in a bright blue sundress. "Dad, Dirk says he's ready!" she yells. When she sees us sitting at the table, she bounds towards us, curls bouncing over her eyes.

"Jesse!" She wraps her arms around my neck, squeezing me tight.

"What are you doing here, little miss?" I kiss her on the cheek as she pulls away.

She looks at Bill her face turning pink. "I messed up Jesse's surprise, didn't I?" she asks him sadly.

He picks her up and sets her on his knee. "You didn't mess anything up. This is perfect, now we can tell her together." She claps happily at this.

"Tell me what?" I ask suspiciously.

He nudges Katie in the ribs. "Go on, you can tell her."

"Today is your wedding day!" she exclaims, throwing her arms high in the air. "Ally and I get to be flower girls."

My mouth falls open.

She whispers something in our dad's ear before bouncing back out the way she came.

When I don't say anything, my dad turns to me in concern. "Jesse? This is what you wanted isn't it?"

I nod, dumbfounded. "He… he told me you said no."

My dad flashes me a white, toothy smile. "I said he couldn't marry you in Vegas."

Oh. *Oh.*

That asshole let me believe my dad said no to us getting married.

He chuckles. "My baby girl deserves better than to be carried off by a cave man in the dead of night. She deserves flowers, friends, and family."

My heart melts as I watch my dad's eyes soften as he speaks. "Oh, dad."

"I'll never get tired of hearing you call me that."

"And I'll never get tired of saying it."

He stands and pulls me with him. He hugs me tight. "I bought you a dress and brought your girly makeup and things. Go get yourself prettied up. I'll be right here waiting."

I hurry upstairs, putting on the white sundress he brought for me. It's beautiful and simple. I love it.

When I walk downstairs, my dad stands from the couch. I stop in front of him. He swipes at his eyes. "You're making all of us soft."

"Maybe all of you were already soft."

He guffaws at this. He hands me a bouquet of wildflowers and then tips his elbow out for me to take. I wrap my hand around the soft, worn leather of his Skull's jacket. He looks down at me. "Ready?"

I nod, thinking to myself how I've been dreaming of this day since I was ten years old.

We walk down the path, the little woodland creatures I painted peek out at us. He squeezes my hand when he notices them. Before long, the path opens to a spectacular view of the Sierra mountains. Our friends are all gathered round. My dad walks us up the aisle they have formed.

When we reach the end, I see Raffe standing with crutches beside Dirk. He gives me a dazzling smile and winks. Dirk nudges him in the ribs. Raffe only smiles brighter and then I let my eyes fall on Dirk. Mr. Scary Tattoo Man. The man who stood in front of me and told me it was okay to be mean. It was okay to protect what was mine. The man who saved me by teaching me how to save myself.

His tongue snakes out to flick his lip ring, making me thank Gabriel's god for giving me such a sexy man. My dad takes my hand and gently places it in Dirk's. He leans over and whispers, "Take care of my baby girl, Dirk, or I'll break every bone in your body."

"You know I will."

"I know. I know." My dad pats him on the back before going to stand with Candice and the girls.

I turn towards the minister, noticing Dan standing by my side. He blushes and looks towards the sky.

My eyebrows raise in amusement. "Hey, big guy."

"Shut-up, you needed a maid of honor."

I smile big. "And you make such a pretty one."

He grumbles before leaning over and giving me a peck on the cheek.

I snag his hand before he pulls away. "I wouldn't want anyone else."

His cheeks turn full out crimson. He clears his throat and straightens his jacket.

The minister begins. I couldn't tell you what he says because I'm lost in mood ring eyes. The same ones that made my heart gooey all those years ago. The only difference is that this time we don't have to go our separate ways.

Before I know it, Dirk is kissing me passionately in front of all our friends and family. My dad coughs loudly and Dirk pulls back, giving me his trademark smirk. He enjoys making people uncomfortable, especially Bill. That's okay, I wouldn't trade this asshole for anyone.

The good news is we are now one, forever bound to protect what's ours... together.

The bad news is, well, in life there will always be bad news but now that I've found my family, I will never have to go through it alone.

Epilogue

Dirk ~ 5 Years later

My eyes follow Raffe as he chases his son around the room. Good god, that little fuck has a lot of energy. Yeah, you guessed it, I'm still the same fucking asshole I was five years ago.

Katie and Ally come out from the bedroom where my wife is. "Do you want us to take Jackson for a little while so you can go see Jesse?" Katie asks Raffe.

"Yeah, that would be great. Rachel will be here in about thirty minutes." He pats me on the back as he passes by on the way to see Jess. I watch the girls play with Jackson for a few minutes before heading back into the bedroom.

We have temporarily moved back into the warehouse because of Jesse's condition. She wanted to be near her dad. Understandably so. She's scared. Shit, I'm scared.

When I open the door, I find Raffe sitting in the chair by the window, Jesse kneeling in front of him with her head in his lap. He runs his fingers through her hair, speaking softly over her. Dan is crouched behind Jesse, rubbing her back.

I flex my fists, reminding myself that everyone here loves Jesse. *This is innocent. This is innocent.* Nope, can't do it. "Everyone, get the fuck out." I spin towards the older woman in the room, pointing at her. "You, too."

Jesse chuckles but backs away from Raffe. Dan helps her to her feet. "Why do you have to be such an asshole? That felt good."

I narrow my eyes at her and she narrows hers right back.

Raffe, Dan and the old woman don't even try to argue with me. They all walk out, closing the door behind them.

Jesse makes her way to the window, pushing the curtain back so she can look down at the lake.

I wrap my arms around her. She leans back, groaning. "I don't know if I can do this," she whispers.

"You can do this. You're the strongest woman I know."

She starts to double over in pain, so I brace my hands under her round belly to steady her. "Breathe, baby, breathe through it."

After a few minutes, she relaxes against me.

"I need to sit," she waddles over to the rocking chair. Bill bought an exact replica of the one we have at home. You should see the nursery at our house. One wall is covered in a beautiful sunset. The others are painted with sugar and spice and everything nice. Yes, you guessed it, we're having a girl.

I'm terrified. That's putting it mildly. I mean let's be honest, between my sister and Jesse, my track record on keeping girls safe isn't the best. Jesse tells me it's nonsense, but I know I should have done better. I could have done better. But as it happens, I've been given another chance. A chance to do better. To be better.

Don't think I'm going to change my asshole ways. Not happening. In fact, it will probably get worse. Now that I'm having a daughter myself, I understand completely where Bill was coming from. He probably should have killed me.

I turn when I hear Jesse reading softly to our little girl. She does this every day. She says it will help our baby with early language learning. She's read every baby book she could get her hands on. Jesse's going to be an amazing mother.

I sit down on the bed and watch as she rocks, rubbing one hand over her stomach while holding the book with the other. She's beautiful. Long dark hair falls around her slim shoulders, the ink on her skin reminding me just how tough my wife is.

When she winces in pain, I rush to her side. "Want me to get the mid-wife?" I ask.

She drops the book in the chair beside her and leans forward, pressing her face in the crook of my neck. "No, not yet," she pants.

I reach around and rub her lower back. Man, nobody prepares you to see the woman you love in so much pain. I wanted to have the baby at the hospital but Jesse insisted she wanted a mid-wife so she could give birth with her family close by. She spent so many years alone, how could I deny her?

We decide to go for a walk down the hall to help things along. I walk behind her, my inked hands bracing her gently under the stomach. Bill watches us pace back and forth. When we head into the bedroom, he follows us inside. He closes the door quietly behind him.

I sit against the headboard and pat the spot between my legs for Jesse. She settles herself, leaning back against me. I continue to rub my hands over her hard stomach. Bill perches on the edge of the bed beside us.

"I think I owe you both an apology," he says out of the blue.

"What? What for?" Jesse asks.

"I was wrong about the two of you. You are perfect for each other. I didn't see it then, not even when I gave you my blessing on your wedding day, but I see it now."

"Bill, we get it. You don't have to apologize," I tell him. "Believe me, I really get it now."

He laughs, running his fingers through his beard. "This poor girl isn't going to have a chance with a boy with an asshole for a grandpa and an even bigger one for a father."

Jesse groans in pain as another contraction assaults her. Bill grabs her hand, and she squeezes the life out of it. I whisper words of encouragement over her head until it passes.

"You're doing so good, baby girl," Bill says proudly.

She breathes deeply through her nose. "I don't want to do this, anymore," she cries.

"The baby needs to come out, Jesse. I've got you. We're going to get it done," I tell her softly, rocking her back and forth in my arms.

She pulls her legs up as another contraction comes fast and hard. "Maybe you should go get the mid-wife now," I tell Bill.

"Help me up," Jesse asks him. As soon as he pulls her to her feet, a gush of water soaks her pants.

"Shit," she hollers.

"Hey, look at me." Bill grabs her chin, forcing her face away from the mess now leaking onto the floor. "I know you're scared but Dirk is going to be right by your side the entire time and the rest of us will be on the other side of that door."

She gives him a jerky nod, her body trembling from the shock of labor.

"This is all a part of it. You're going to get through it. You're a Skull, don't forget that."

She chuckles lightly before another contraction grips her.

"Help her out of her pants, Dirk. It's almost time," he orders. He gives her a kiss on the forehead and a quick hug before rushing out of the room.

I get Jesse out of her wet pants and settled back onto the bed. The mid-wife hurries in and tucks a waterproof liner under her. When she checks Jesse's progress she smiles. "You're at ten. Ready to push?"

Jesse shakes her head no. Her terrified eyes search for mine. I calmly slide up beside her on the bed. The midwife pushes Jesse's legs back into her chest. "Okay, Jesse, give me one nice long push."

Jesse grabs my hand and I brace an arm behind her back to help her to a more upright position. She grunts and pushes as hard as she can before collapsing back against the pillow.

"Good job, girl," the mid-wife praises. "All right, here comes another one. Push."

Jesse grunts and screams as she pushes with all her might.

I'm amazed by how strong she is. This is much harder than I had imagined. It's… it's simply fucking amazing.

We go through the process over and over and I watch as my wife grows more exhausted by the minute. I glance at the mid-wife, concern etched over my features. Is it normal to take this long? She gives me an encouraging smile and nods. Okay, she doesn't look as worried as I'm feeling.

She looks between Jesse's legs. "I see a head full of dark hair, Jesse. One more big push."

My heart full out stops as Jesse pushes, pushes, pushes and then...

the most beautiful baby emerges.

The mid-wife laughs as she grabs our daughter. The baby starts to cry loudly. My eyes reluctantly leave the tiny, gooey bundle to stare admiringly at my wife. She blinks up at me with tears in her eyes. "I did it," she whispers.

"You did so good, baby," I tell her, wiping her sweaty hair away from her face. The mid-wife interrupts us by laying our little girl on Jesse's chest.

We both stare down at her. She quiets and blinks at us. "Hey, baby girl, it's mommy and daddy," I coo.

Jesse snickers. "Oh my god, I'm never going to get used to your baby talk."

"Tell your mama she better watch her smart mouth or daddy is going to spank her cute little behind." I tell our daughter cheerfully, in my baby talk. I smile into her cute as fuck, tiny face.

The mid-wife laughs. "Let me get her cleaned up and then you can feed her." She takes the baby from my wife's arms.

Jesse pulls me down and kisses me softly. "Thank you."

When I pull away, I ask her what for.

"For giving me the most precious gift in the world. I promise I will love her fiercely."

"I know you will. That's why I picked you to be mine."

The mid-wife walks over and hands me a wiggly bundle. I blink quickly, trying to avoid any tears from forming. I turn away so Jesse can't see how weak I am over all this. I walk over to the window. The sun is setting, it casts a spectacular pallet of pinks across the sky as if God himself is saying happy birthday to my little girl. "Welcome to the world, Billie Rose."

The baby pulls her hand to her mouth, sucking wildly at her fist. We decided to name her Billie for Bill. It's also a strong name for a girl. The Rose will keep her sweet and balanced.

I walk her over to my wife and set her gently in her arms. She positions the baby to her breast and Billie Rose latches right on. How can she be so hungry already? I brush my hand over her fine baby hair. She has Jesse's blue-black hair and my blue eyes. I have a feeling I'm going to have to beat the boys off her.

Once the mid-wife gets everything cleaned up and the baby weighed, she leaves the room to let our family take turns seeing our new arrival.

The first in the room is Bill, Candice, and the girls. Ally and Katie go on and on about being aunts and how they are going to paint her nails and braid her hair. Bill is quiet as he takes everything in. His eyes shine bright with unshed tears as he watches Jesse hold Billie Rose in her arms.

Before they leave to make room for the next bunch, Bill leans over and whispers something in Jesse's ear. She laughs and sniffles a little.

"What did he say?" I ask after he walks out.

"He said he owes you big time but last time he let you have whatever your filthy heart wanted you chose me. He said this time you would probably want to be president of the club and he's not ready to give that up just yet."

Hmm, not a bad thought. I shift my head from side to side. Jesse narrows her eyes at me before smacking me in the arm. "Okay, okay. I have everything I need right here." I wrap my arm around my girls.

Dan, Raffe and Rachel come in next. They ooh and ahh over our baby. She looks so small when Dan holds her. He takes her over to the rocking chair and cradles her close to his chest. Jesse wipes her eyes and looks away. Dan is special to her. I know my cousin will protect our baby with his life.

After everything settles down, Jesse takes a call from her friend William. They talk for at least an hour as I rock Billie Rose, unable to take my eyes away from her chubby little cheeks. She stares back. I wonder what she thinks of me. I hope I'm good enough for her.

Jesse ends her call, so I take Billie Rose over to the bed for another feeding. She latches right on. She's going to grow like a weed as much as she likes to eat. Jesse snuggles down in the covers, laying her head against my chest. I rest my chin on her shoulder, both of us admiring our little girl.

"I'm so happy," Jesse says tiredly.

"Me too." I run my finger over Billie Rose's soft cheek. "So, when can we do this again?"

She growls at me.

"Too soon?"

"Yes, too soon." She drops her eyes back to our daughter. "I can't wait to take her home."

The baby blinks at us as if she is listening and maybe she is.

Jesse turns to look at me. "She's perfect. She has your mood ring eyes."

I run my thumb over Jesse's bottom lip, leaning in and placing a kiss on her lips. "She has your old soul."

"You think?" Jesse looks back at the baby.

"I don't think. I know."

Billie Rose is going to be one of a kind... just like her mother.

LM Terry

About the Author

LM Terry is an upcoming romance novelist. She has spent her life in the Midwest, growing up near a public library which helped fuel her love of books. With most of her eight children grown and with the support of her husband, she decided to follow her heart and begin her writing journey. In searching for that happily ever after, her characters have been enticing her to share their sinfully dark, delectable tales. She knows the world is filled with shadows and dark truths and is happy to give these characters the platform they have been begging for. This is her fifth novel.

Facebook: https://www.facebook.com/lmterryauthor/

Website: https://www.lmterryauthor

Made in the USA
Columbia, SC
23 December 2024